In memory of Jean Bouch, a beautiful soul and sadly missed.

Also, for her dear husband, Philip. A treasured family friend.

Jane Isaac studied creative writing with the Writers Bureau and the London School of Journalism. Jane's short stories have appeared in several crime fiction anthologies. Her debut novel, *An Unfamiliar Murder*, was published in the US in 2012, and was followed by four novels with Legend Press: *The Truth Will Out* in 2014, *Before It's Too Late* in 2015, *Beneath the Ashes* in 2016, and *The Lies Within* in 2017.

Jane lives in rural Northamptonshire with her husband, daughter and dog, Bollo.

Visit Jane at
janeisaac.co.uk
or on Twitter
@JaneIsaacAuthor

CHAPTER 1

The peaked rooftop of Billings factory reached into an indigo sky, thick with the promise of rain.

Rhys ran across the car park. 'Come on, let's try the door!'

Connor dragged his feet. It had been fun, sneaking around the deserted industrial estate, throwing stones at the windows; climbing through gaps in the hedging; using the old CCTV cameras for target practice. He wasn't sure he wanted to venture inside though. 'What if it's got an alarm?'

'Don't be stupid, these factories were emptied months ago. They won't be alarmed now.' Rhys tried the handle, but it stayed firm.

A glance skyward. The May rain clouds were beckoning an early dusk, tainting the air a murky grey.

'We should get back, I'm supposed to be in by nine.'

Rhys disappeared down the channel between the factory wall and the metal fencing marking its perimeter. The sound of a boot kicking a door followed.

'What're you doing?' Connor said, jogging across the tarmac to join him.

'What does it look like?' He moved around the back, tried another door. The handle was loose. It rattled, pulled back slightly. Rhys glanced at Connor and tugged harder. The door juddered open. 'Here we are.'

The onset of night was thicker inside. They stepped over the threshold, into a small corridor with double doors facing them. Rhys pushed at one of the doors and they slipped into a wide open room. Pools of light streamed in from high windows, highlighting the scuffs and oil stains littering the floor.

Rhys grinned, held out his arms and turned 360 degrees. 'Whoa!'

'It stinks,' Connor said, grabbing his nose.

'That's 'cos it's been shut up.'

Rhys bent down, scooped up an empty glue can and tossed it up towards a window. It landed just beneath the glass, pinging off the ledge, and fell back at their feet.

Connor nudged it with his toe, Rhys kicked it back. As they moved down the factory, passing the can to one another, Connor's shoulders slackened. It wasn't so bad inside. Not really.

Rhys yanked at the door of a metal cupboard on the far wall. The hinges squealed like nails on a chalkboard as it opened. Inside, a couple of well-used brooms were stored beside a stained mop bucket. They exchanged an excited glance and wrestled the handles off the brushes.

One arm held out for balance, they fought with the sticks, moving up and down the factory like musketeers until Connor lost his footing, stumbled and slipped against a row of oil drums, sending one of them crashing to the floor. The noise reverberated around the factory. As Connor pulled himself up, a line of oil trickled out of the drum, encircling a dirty needle on the floor behind. Spots of blood inside the attached syringe made his stomach turn. 'We should go,' he said.

Rhys wasn't listening. He hadn't seen the syringe, was already halfway up the stairs in the corner, his trainers tap-tap-tapping against the metal lip of each step.

A low hum started in Connor's head. 'Rhys!' He checked over his shoulder and followed.

The door at the top of the stairs opened into another

large room. A full moon had parted the rain clouds, its light streaming through the window and casting a milky glow across clumps of desks the former occupier had left behind. Discarded chairs were scattered about haphazardly.

Connor gripped his nose with his free hand. The stench was stronger up there. The hum in his head intensified.

A faint scratching sounded.

'What's that?' Rhys said.

Another scratch. Behind them. They whisked around, spotted a baby rat crouched in the corner. Rhys inched forward, lifting the broom handle. Then drove it to the floor. The creature scuttled under a desk.

He chased after it, thrust the handle beneath the desk. More scratches. He poked it in further, pulled back. Rushed to the other side, Connor on his tail.

The rat ran out, squeaked. Rhys doubled back to follow it, colliding with Connor. The whole building seemed to shake as they tumbled to the floor. The hum in Connor's head cut.

'Idiot,' Connor said. He pushed his friend aside, checked his limbs. The cords of the carpet were rough, unforgiving. When he lifted his hand, it was damp. It looked like blood.

'Urgh!' He wriggled back, turned. And froze.

A pair of legs stuck out the side of a far desk. Denim jeans; the laces of yellow trainers hanging loose.

He elbowed Rhys. Pointed.

Rhys's jaw dropped.

They peered around the corner of the desk together. And came face to face with a woman propped up against the radiator.

Rhys jumped, screamed. Slid back across the carpet.

Connor stilled, his breaths halted, staring at her. She didn't flinch. Slowly he edged towards her, pointing the tip of the broom handle, still in his hand.

'Don't!' Rhys hissed.

Connor ignored him and tapped her foot. It wobbled from side to side. Glassy eyes stared through a mop of dark curls.

For a second, they gawped at the corpse in front of them, paralysed in fear. Then Rhys scrabbled back and jumped to his feet. 'We gotta get out of here.'

***

Fifteen minutes later, Rhys's words rang out in Connor's head as he arrived home. 'We tell no one.'

They'd run from the factory, out of the industrial estate and kept running, until their lungs burned and their chests ached. Only when they reached the park at the back of Weston High Street did they slump to the floor, hidden in the shadows, pressing their backs against the wrought-iron fence.

The conversation they had there whirled in Connor's mind, like a song on permanent repeat. He'd wanted to call the police. Rhys refused. 'Even if we don't tell them who we are, they'll trace our mobiles,' he'd said. Rhys knew a lot about police work. His father was serving a sentence after stabbing a man in the leg during a pub fight; his sister was awaiting trial for supplying drugs.

'We haven't done anything wrong,' Connor had countered.

'We shouldn't have been there. We were trespassing. No, we go home. Clean up. Carry on as if nothing happened. Someone will find her soon enough.'

Connor's throat had thickened as he'd walked home. In many ways, Rhys was right, he couldn't afford a visit from the police either, his mother was still reeling after discovering he'd skipped the last day of school and spent it playing football in the local park. There was nothing they could do to help the woman. But the gruesome sight of her glassy eyes, all that blood, kept popping into his head, making him shiver.

The living room door sat ajar, a line of amber light seeping in from the hallway. The babble of the television filtered through from the front room. A distant chuckle: his mother. She was watching one of those comedy panel shows she liked so much.

He quietly kicked off his trainers, scooped them up. The chill of the quarry tiles seeped through his socks as he tiptoed across the floor. He reached the washer, cast another glance towards the hallway, ears on hyper alert while he peeled off his jeans, shrugged off his hoody and shoved them in the machine, followed by his trainers.

Connor was used to washing; he'd lost count of the number of football kits he'd put through when his mum was working. The powder skittered about on top of the clothes.

He heard music come from the front room. The show was finishing. He put the powder away, turned the dial, pressed the On switch. The machine did nothing. Connor swallowed, turned the dial back. It was chilly standing there in his pants and socks. He needed to go upstairs, before his mother caught him. But he'd wiped his bloody hands on his clothes, couldn't leave them like this.

Frantically, he turned the dial again. It clicked. Thank God. He crept past the front room and up the stairs.

Connor was just closing his bedroom door when he heard the music stop and his mother pad into the kitchen.

CHAPTER 2

The sound of a high-pitched scream pierced the air. A shrill yelp. Another scream, followed by a low growl. The cats were at it again. Third time that evening. Detective Chief Inspector Helen Lavery rested her back against the pillows, willing them to find somewhere else to finish their argument.

She flipped a page of the notebook beside her and glanced blandly at the scrawl. For eight weeks she'd been signed off work following an injury on duty. Eight weeks and she returned to a stream of training courses. Out of the window she could see the rooftops of the College of Policing in Ryton-on-Dunsmore, where, for the past three days, she'd been engaged in an update on Command Skills. Tomorrow, she was due to head back to Hampton, her home force, for computer-based training.

Helen pulled the tie out of her hair and raked her fingers through it. She'd been looking forward to returning to work and her team at the Homicide and Major Incident Squad; a new case to tax her brain cells. Although endless hours of PowerPoint presentations and role play scenarios left her numb.

She finished the final drops of coffee, placed her mug on the side and glanced around the hotel room. Chic black and white decor mixed with chrome and glass furniture. Smart, perfunctory and soulless. She checked her phone. No messages. Bored, she turned on the television and flicked through the channels. The mixture of game shows and sitcoms didn't appeal, and, after the eighth channel, she switched it off.

Rain lashed against the window. It seemed a fitting end to a frustrating few days.

Helen checked her watch. Quarter to ten. Usually, without the ticking clock of a live case pressing, she'd have been home for hours by now. But the advent of the May half-term holiday meant her mother had taken the kids away for an activity week in Wales – not that she could imagine her mother doing much rock climbing and rafting – and the thought of rattling around an empty house alone was not appealing. Instead, she'd decided to pamper herself with a massage and freshly cooked cuisine on the last night of her course and booked into this hotel near the training centre. The cats outside howled again. Although, right now, she was beginning to wonder if it was such a good idea.

Footsteps along the corridor. A knock at the door. The iridescent hallway lighting induced a twinge of pain behind her left eye as she answered. She held up her hand to shade it. The waiter gave a smile that didn't reach his lips, bowed his head slightly and carried a bottle of red on a round silver tray into the room. A single upturned glass rattled against the metal. He glanced down fleetingly at her empty ring finger before he placed it on her bedside table.

Helen tucked the hand behind her. Only last month she'd changed her wedding band to her other hand – it seemed the right thing to do, John had been dead over ten years, after all – though she still felt uncomfortable when people viewed her empty finger.

'Will that be all?' he said.

She looked at the wine, tempted to ask him to take the bottle back, to say she'd only ordered a glass, but changed her mind at the last minute. It wasn't as if she didn't fancy a couple of glasses. There was nothing to travel home for.

The pain in her head subsided as she closed the door and turned back into the dull lamplight of her room. The bottle was in her hand, the velvet liquid drizzling into her glass when her mobile phone trilled.

'Detective Chief Inspector Lavery?'

'Yes.'

'It's Inspector Carrington from the control room. We've an incident for you.'

A rush of excitement immediately pulsed through her. A new case would excuse her from a week of staring at computer screens.

'What do you have?'

'The body of a young woman has been found in a disused factory on Keys Trading Estate.'

She took down the address, checking back to ensure she'd recorded the details correctly.

'What do we know?'

A rustle of paper in the background. 'A dog walker called the control room after he saw some kids running from the former Billings factory unit. When the patrol car arrived, they discovered the body inside.'

'Any other witnesses?'

'Not yet. CID are in attendance and acting DI Pemberton is already at the scene. He'll be able to give you more information.'

Helen balanced the phone between her chin and shoulder and checked her watch. Keys Trading Estate was off Hampton ring road, on the east of the city. If she left now, she could be there in forty minutes. 'Thanks. I'll give him a call.'

'There's something else you need to know.' The inspector hesitated and lowered his voice. 'The response officer recognised a tattoo on the victim's wrist. He's pretty sure she's one of us.'

Helen's blood chilled. 'Who is it?'

'He thinks it's PC Sinead O'Donnell, ma'am, from incident response.' Helen wracked her brains. She couldn't immediately place her, but with over a thousand officers to choose from in the Hampton force alone, it wasn't surprising. 'She'd been tortured.'

Her mouth dried. 'I hope none of that information has been shared.'

'Not as far as I'm aware.'

'Good. Keep it to yourself for now, would you?' Chances are, if he was party to the victim's identity then others would be too. News spread like wildfire in the police. She rang off, cast the wine aside and dialled Pemberton.

He answered on the second ring. 'Good to hear from you, ma'am,' he said.

'You too, Sean.' The broad timbre of his Yorkshire accent was like a warm coffee on a cold winter's evening. Pemberton was a dependable and reliable detective. In many ways, he reminded her of her late father, James Lavery, who'd managed the Homicide and Major Incident Squad for fifteen years before his retirement. At least her crime scene was in good hands, for now. 'I understand you are at the factory unit. Can you give me a quick update?'

'Sure. Uniform responded to a disturbance at Billings factory at 8.50 p.m. on Keys Trading Estate this evening. Billings is one of the factories the developer has earmarked to flatten and turn into housing on the southern edge of the estate and is currently empty. When the patrol officers arrived, they found the body of a woman, looks like she's been badly beaten, in the first-floor offices. She was chained to the radiator with a pair of handcuffs.'

'What do we know about the informant?'

'Graham Kirby of Cheshunt Walk. Isn't known to us.'

'Did he see anything else nearby?'

'He said not. According to him, he'd been walking his dog down the Bracken Way that runs alongside. He spotted two kids running from the factory through the gaps in the metal fencing. Uniform have gone out to take a first account.'

'What about the victim?'

His voice softened. 'Multiple injuries to the head and chest; looks like her throat's been cut. The pathologist should be here soon, hopefully he'll be able to tell us more.' He paused. 'I guess you'll have heard the rumour mill, that she's police?'

'The control room inspector mentioned it might be a PC, Sinead O'Donnell. Do you know her?'

'No. I know her husband, Blane O'Donnell, though. Works in training.'

Helen's stomach dipped. It was difficult enough to protect the confidentiality of a victim's identity before the family were informed, but within the police it was practically impossible. 'How far has this been shared, Sean?'

'One of the uniform guys attending was a rookie, barely out of probation. He mentioned it on the radio.'

'On the radio?'

Pemberton heaved a heavy sigh. 'Poor lad, he was in shock. Didn't think. It was his first dead body.'

The pang of sympathy that nudged Helen was short-lived. First body and it was a colleague, a mutilated one. But bad news was a sad fact in their line of work and confidentiality paramount. The system relied heavily on discretion. Obtain identification, inform next of kin, then confirm before any names are publicised. It was ingrained into officers from the beginning of their basic training. 'Where is he now?'

'The duty sergeant sent him home.'

'Has anyone spoken with Blane yet?'

'Not that I'm aware of.'

'I take it he's her next of kin?'

'I believe so.'

'Get a mobile fingerprint machine down there, will you? We'll need to get her identity confirmed and, if it is her, contact Blane before the gossip spreads further. Has anyone reported her missing?'

'Not yet. According to the duty rota, she's been on annual leave the last couple of days.'

'Okay, see if you can contain it. I'll be there as soon as I can.'

'Will do. The machine's already on its way.' He was quiet a moment. 'There'll only be prints available from her right hand. The fingers have been chopped off at the knuckle on the left.'

CHAPTER 3

Helen signed the scene log and ducked underneath the blue and white police tape. Billings factory was a 1970s prefabricated construction, with a rolling factory door marking the goods-in entrance at one end of the building, and a reception area at the other.

The car park out front was empty. Flashing lights on the police cars parked beside the cordon intermittently lit up the surrounding derelict units, all awaiting destruction. The council had sold the land, part of their plan to renew urban areas, although she recalled reading about the new owner in the local news, a property developer, experiencing financial difficulties. They'd certainly been sitting empty for a while.

Billings was the last unit, at the bottom of the road. Thin shrubbery feathered through the gaps in a two-metre-high industrial metal fence at the bottom, marking the boundary line. The only access point she was aware of was along Carter Road, which fed off Cross Keys roundabout. One way in, one way out. She made a mental note to get the fence checked to make sure there were no breaks or gaps where someone could climb through, or for fibres caught from clothing.

The reception area was lit with temporary police lamps, the door open. Helen nodded to a couple of CSIs crawling around the bottom of a staircase but didn't enter. Instead, she retrieved a torch from her pocket, the wide beam illuminating the ground as she wandered down the side of the building. She wanted to get a feel for the layout of the unit, the entrances and exits. The metal fence that encased the industrial estate ran the perimeter of the building. Her forensic suit crunched as she passed one fire door, then another. The second door was open, exposing a dark corridor beyond; the undergrowth nearby recently flattened and trampled.

The bushes were thinner at the rear and she could see the silhouette of the Bracken Way, fifty yards or so in the distance; the disused railway line the dog walker had been using when he reported seeing the disturbance.

She continued around the building. The factory door was rolled back when she reached it, a chasm of darkness the few police lamps in the area did little to illuminate. A weathered sign hung at an angle above and read, *Billings – for all your fabrication needs*. The first 'i' hung loose, the once green letters faded and patchy. A dank, mustiness seeped out to meet her. The factory itself appeared to be empty, the concrete floor chipped and worn, the walls scuffed from years of heavy loads passing through.

She noticed an officer approach and couldn't resist a chuckle. Acting DI Sean Pemberton resembled a bear in his white coveralls. He paused beside her, pulled back his hood and stared into the factory beyond.

'It's a bloody nightmare with no electricity,' he said, digging hefty hands into his pockets. 'We've had to borrow every police lamp in the county.'

'I bet.' She looked up at the sky. 'At least the rain's held off here. It's been torrential in Coventry.'

'For now.' He snorted. 'How are you, ma'am?' He smiled, his bald head glistening as a strobe of light flashed across it. 'It's been a while.'

'I'm okay, thanks. You've lost weight.'

He'd taken it upon himself to visit her a couple of times while she was off work. Updating her on the office gossip in his usual laconic manner. He'd never been an affectionate man, a trait which often made him the butt of jokes when colleagues tried to embarrass him at social events with hugs and the odd peck on the cheek, and this made the genuine warmth of the gesture more touching.

He patted his paunch. 'Mrs P's diet seems to be working.'

'It does.'

She turned back to the factory, switched off her torch. 'Have we confirmed her identity yet?'

'About ten minutes ago. The first fingerprint machine they sent out was faulty.' He cleared his throat. 'It's definitely Sinead.'

A memory pushed to the forefront of Helen's mind: a dead cop, killed during their last case when they took down a network of organised crime. Colleague deaths were rare, yet only eight weeks later, just as her own injuries healed and she returned to work, she was visiting the cadaver of another officer.

'Has someone been out to see her husband?' she asked.

'The uniform shift sergeant is on his way.'

Her shoulders relaxed slightly. She desperately hoped they'd reach him before the rumours. 'Thanks. Have you had a chance to look around?'

'As much as I could in the poor lighting. Uniform entered through a fire door at the rear, which is possibly the one the offender used because the lock was broken. We checked all the other access points: the factory door here, another fire exit on the side of the building and the reception door, and they were secure. We only managed to get the keys from the owner to open it all up about half an hour ago.'

'So, it was either somebody with a key or they used the broken fire door?'

'That's about the sum of it. We did find a used syringe behind some oil drums on the factory floor. Looks like someone's been shooting up here.' He held an open hand towards the reception entrance, inviting her to walk with him. 'Charles has already made a start.'

Helen fell into step with Pemberton, thanking her lucky stars that out of the two pathologists covering their area, they'd struck gold. Doctor Charles Burlington had a keen eye, a rare enthusiasm for his work which went way past the remit of the job.

Pemberton led her down to the reception entrance. The smell was different there, more potent. Her feet clattered the forensic boarding as she followed him up the stairs. She nodded to a CSI who stood aside at the top for them to pass. It was a vast area to meticulously examine and would take them several days to complete.

They crossed a small landing, down a corridor and into an open-plan office. The metallic stench of blood mixed with faeces was stronger in the confined area, more pungent. Helen had seen her fair share of bodies in her ten-year career: the freshly killed; those that had festered awhile, the flesh grey and rotting; crisp charred remains. Every one had its own unique smell, but this was different. Stronger. Almost as if in death, Sinead O'Donnell's body was conveying the horror of what had happened here, her final scream pervading the air. She resisted the temptation to cover her nose, aware her colleagues would have to work under that lingering aroma for many hours to come.

A police lamp illuminated an area in the middle of the room. They zigzagged through the desks to a man in blue coveralls on his knees, examining a contorted body beside a radiator. The legs of the victim stuck out awkwardly, the laces of her trainers hung loose. Blue painted nails decorated a limp hand fastened to the radiator pipe with a pair of handcuffs. Blood and faeces soaked the surrounding green carpet, turning it motley shades of ruddy brown.

'Hello, Charles,' she said.

The man in the blue suit immediately turned, stood and pulled back his hood. He wasn't a tall man, medium height, and sported an athletic stance that could be mistaken for someone ten years younger, probably due to spending half his day scrabbling around examining bodies. She'd often marvelled at the absurdity of the dead keeping him young.

'Helen! I wondered if it might be you.'

'Sounds like you've missed me, Charles.'

He slipped off a latex glove and pushed a wave of peppery hair out of his face. 'Well, you know how it is. Don't get much company in my line of work.'

She laughed.

'How are your boys?' he asked.

'Off sailing and rafting this week. My mother's taken them to Wales.'

'Ah… A bit of rest for you then.'

Their gaze dropped to the victim. One hand was hooked to the radiator, the other sprawled out to the side; the stubby half fingers, cut above the knuckle joints, reaching away. The woman's head lolled forward, her sleeveless shirt so saturated with blood, it was a job to know what colour it had originally been. Straggles of chestnut curls hung over her face, but her eyes were open wide, her face taut, in one final act of defiance.

'Do we know how long she's been here?' Helen asked.

'No,' Charles said. 'She's pretty much bled out. I don't think she's been dead long, rigor has only just started to set in around the neck and shoulders. Within the last four to eight hours, I'd say.'

'What about cause of death?' The words sounded pitiful, surveying the shattered frame in front of her. There were so many injuries to choose from.

'Ultimately, a cut throat.' He pulled on the glove and lifted the victim's head back to expose a messy wound running from one side of her neck to the other. When he rested her head down, the wound was covered perfectly. 'From the amount of blood and the direction of the spatter across the walls, I'm pretty sure she was killed here.'

Helen bent in closer. 'Any particular sort of knife?'

21

'Something with a smooth edge. A kitchen carving knife would do it.' He parted locks of hair at the side to show splinters of bone, blood and grey matter. 'She was hit on the head too, with a blunt instrument. But the neck wound caught the carotid artery; she'd have bled out pretty quickly after that.'

'Okay, how long before you can do the post-mortem?'

'I'm getting the preliminaries done here, then I'll start on her first thing in the morning.'

Helen's gaze rested on the cuffs. 'Are those police issue?' she asked Pemberton.

He crouched down, examined them closely. 'They're not ours,' he said slowly. 'Different catch. There aren't any markings on them either.'

His words were drowned out by a kerfuffle outside. Raised voices. A man shouting.

Helen exchanged a glance with Pemberton and moved to the window. But the office windows looked out to the side and the voice was coming from the car park out front.

'Excuse me,' she said to the pathologist, and moved out to the window on the landing. The lights of the police cars illuminated a fracas in the road. Officers wrestling to hold back a tall man, over six foot she guessed, who wouldn't look out of place in the front row of a rugby scrum. The three officers restraining him clearly struggling.

Pemberton joined her, staring out across the tarmac. 'Looks like Blane O'Donnell's arrived.'

CHAPTER 4

Blane didn't see the officer cross the car park, didn't notice her stop the other side of the cordon. Lost as he was in the fug of the struggle; pushing and shoving with all his might. Hurling expletives through gritted teeth.

He needed to get inside the factory. To Sinead.

'Blane O'Donnell?'

The crisp words caught him by surprise. He froze, his vision clearing. It was the detective chief inspector he'd read about in the force newsletter, the one who'd recently been commended for arresting a local gang leader. She looked tiny, standing there in white coveralls, beside her oversized sidekick.

Blane swallowed and nodded.

'Detective Chief Inspector...'

As she spoke, the officers around him loosened their grip. And he spotted his chance. A sudden jerk, an explosion of energy as he lunged forward. Under the cordon. Towards the door.

A blurred movement in front. Someone blocking his path. He sidestepped. A hand reached for his forearm. He flailed out. A fist connected. Instantly, he was tugged from behind, his arms clamped in a vice-like grip, holding him back.

Blane blinked. Watched the DCI stumble back. Shit! He'd

hit her. He hadn't meant to hit her. He hadn't meant to hit anyone. He just wanted to get to Sinead.

'Helen Lavery,' she continued, clutching her shoulder.

He'd missed her face by a whisker. 'I'm sorry, ma'am. I didn't mean to...' His words trailed off.

'Of course you didn't.' Her shoulder crunched as she rolled it back.

'I need to see Sinead.'

'You know I can't let you do that.'

Frustration twisted inside him. 'You can't stop me. It's my wife in there.'

'And you will see her. When the time is right.'

A rush of anger. Tearing at his insides. He squeezed his eyes together, shut it out.

'Why don't we go and speak in my car?' the DCI said. 'Just you and me. I'll give you as much information as I can.'

'What about Sinead?'

'I'll arrange for you to see Sinead, as soon as it's practical. I promise.'

He was aware of the grips loosening. A hand at his back, leading him to a Subaru at the edge of the cordon. The cold leather of the back seat as he sat inside. But he barely saw any of it. He was in a tailspin, a swirling vortex of emotions, his heart fighting to burst out of his chest.

He dropped his head into his hands. Concentrated on his breathing. In and out. In and out.

It was a while before he opened his eyes and, when he did, he was surprised to find the DCI beside him. A slip of a woman. How the hell did he manage to hit her? He worked in defensive tactics, for Christ's sake. Trained other officers daily on how to restrain themselves and keep their cool.

'I'm sorry about the shoulder, ma'am.'

'It's okay, really.'

She was lying, the discomfort obvious in her face.

He wound down his window, inviting in the fresh evening air. 'What happened to Sinead?'

'It's too early to say exactly. Does Sinead have any connection to Billings factory or the industrial estate?'

'Not that I know of.'

'What about enemies. Are you aware of anyone who might have wanted to hurt her?'

'No.' He looked across at the factory. The wonky signage, the works entrance door folded back, a wide-open mouth. 'Is it true, what they're saying? Had she been tortured?'

'There are a number of injuries. We're still establishing the extent of them. I'm so sorry.'

Acidic bile rose in his throat. He tore his gaze away, focused on the back of the seat in front of him.

'How has she been recently?'

He took his time to answer, navigating through the mist in his mind. 'I don't know. Things have been... difficult.'

'In what way?'

'Her mother suffers from early-onset Alzheimer's. She's in a home nearby, deteriorating rapidly. And my own mum is downsizing; I've been spending a lot of time there, renovating the house, getting it ready for sale. It's been a strain.' He pressed a hand to the side of his face, the heat providing a short respite from the pain fizzing at his temple. 'Sinead's been under pressure, what with the children, work, family stuff. I organised a holiday, to give her a break. That's where she should be now.'

'How old are your children?'

'Thomas is five. Our daughter, Ava, is three.' His hand slipped down to his chin, thick calluses scraping against his cropped beard. His children. So young. So innocent.

'When did you last see Sinead?' the DCI asked softly.

'Um, this morning.' Was it only this morning? It seemed like days ago. 'She'd taken a few days' leave from work to go on a yoga retreat in Derbyshire. The kids and I saw her off.' Twelve hours ago. He could still see her wide smile as she crouched down and wrapped the children in hugs, smothering their faces with kisses, asking them to behave for their father.

Climbing into her Fiesta with promises of presents on her return. Waving out of the open window as she drove down the road. 'I thought it would do her good,' Blane said, snapping back to the present. 'You know, to get away for a few days.'

'Was she going alone?'

'She was expecting to. I'd planned to go up and join her tomorrow. A surprise. We rarely get any time on our own these days.' He bit back tears, passed on the details of her car and the direction in which she was travelling.

The DCI jotted down the details. 'How did she seem?'

'Fine. Normal. I think she was looking forward to the break, to be honest.'

The police tape crackled as it fluttered in the light breeze.

'Blane, I'm sorry to have to ask you this. Where were you between 10 a.m. and 10 p.m. today?'

He knew this was coming, he'd been in that chair so many times himself, asking the questions. But it still stung all the same. 'After we waved Sinead off, I dropped the kids at my mum's house, then went to work. I booked on at about 10.30 a.m. – you'll be able to check the duty system – and finished at 5 p.m. I went to the gym afterwards, got home in time to put the children to bed around seven.'

'At your mother's house?'

'Yes. The kids often stay there when Sinead is on shift, especially recently while I've been doing the renovating. Mum cooked dinner. She was there with me all evening.' He reeled off the address, watched her scratch it down. 'Sinead phoned me, you know, about twenty minutes after she left. It was her first holiday away from the children. She wanted to check they weren't too upset after she'd driven away.' He looked down. 'It was the last time we spoke.'

'I'm sorry. Do you have the details of her mobile phone? It doesn't seem to be with her.'

'It would have been in her bag. Sinead took a handbag everywhere with her. I used to tease her about not carrying it on duty.' Used to. He flinched, retrieved his phone and passed over her number.

'Do you feel up to giving us a list of her friends, associates? I realise how you must be feeling. The sooner we get started. Well… you know.' She was being kind. Taking it gently.

He nodded. 'I don't want a family liaison officer.' It wasn't a request, it was a statement.

He didn't miss the look that flickered across the DCI's face. He was the closest person to Sinead; it didn't take long for the suspicion to kick in. But he was unmoved. The last thing he wanted was another cop in his home, near his children, observing them in their hours of grief. They needed stability not strangers.

'Okay, we'll respect your wishes for now. We will need to send officers around to ask questions and take a statement though. And there may be a search required, of your family address. We'll be as discreet as we can.'

He retrieved a ring of keys from his pocket. The metal chinked together as he detached one and handed it over. 'That's my front door key. Mum has a spare. I'll keep the children at her house for now.'

'One last question, did Sinead have a particular close friend? Someone she maybe confided in? Or family nearby?'

'Her mum was her closest confidante before she became too ill. The rest of her extended family are back in Dublin. Sinead has lots of other friends though, she's always messaging someone.'

The seat creaked as she thanked him, slid out and crossed the tarmac to her colleague. Whisperings of 'a first account' and 'make sure he's not alone tonight' floated over. Blane's gut clenched. He looked back at the factory where his dead wife lay and rubbed the mole on the side of his temple. Things were never going to be the same again.

CHAPTER 5

A round of applause started as Helen entered the room, gathering momentum as she strode to the front. The warmth of the welcome prompted an inadvertent smile.

Helen faced the detectives sprawled in front of her, some in chairs, others perched on the edge of desks, a few stragglers standing at back. 'Thanks for the welcome, everyone. It's good to be back, I just wish it was in better circumstances.'

She glanced at the empty noticeboard beside her. Photos of the victim had been taken, a map prepared of Billings' layout and its location on Keys Trading Estate, along with anything else of any significance, but for the moment she'd asked for the board to be left empty. Over the years, these officers had dealt with more than their fair share of death in all its shocking configurations, and every body was saddled with its own dose of sadness. But the familiarity of this being a colleague, someone they might have shared room space with, someone they may have known, made the loss more traumatic and she needed to prepare them for the task they were about to undertake.

'At 8.50 p.m., uniform discovered a woman's body at Billings, a disused factory unit on Keys Trading Estate. The body was that of Sinead O'Donnell. Many of you will already know Sinead was one of us.'

The low drone of a passing lorry outside was the only sound to fill the room.

'This is going to be a difficult enquiry,' Helen continued. 'Some of you in here will have known Sinead, perhaps you worked with her at some stage. I must ask you to detach yourselves. I need people who can remain impartial, independent. We won't catch whoever did this, we won't get justice for Sinead, if our emotions get in the way. So, I'm offering you an out. If there's anyone in here who doesn't think they can work the case, either because you knew Sinead or know her husband, Blane, personally or for another reason, then please either leave now or come and see me afterwards. I won't think any less of you.'

A sea of eyes stared back at her, unmoved.

'Okay, if anyone feels uncomfortable or compromised at any time during the investigation, again I need you to come and see me straight away.' She waited until she was sure the request had hit home before she carried on.

'Billings factory unit has been empty for some months, much like the others down that road,' she continued. 'One of those earmarked for the new housing development. Let's find out who has had access to the keys, like property developers, former owners. We'll also need to get a list of all the staff who previously worked there. We know the lock on one of the fire doors was broken. It may have been faulty for a while and the staff knew about it.

'I've had a brief look around the perimeter and it looks to be contained by fencing. CSIs are going to double-check at first light to ensure there were no breaks in the fence and no sign of any other access points. We can't rely on CCTV on the estate for this one, we'll need to check the nearby roundabout for any cameras.'

'Is it true she was tortured?'

Helen followed the voice to Steve Spencer, a spindly officer with salt-and-pepper hair, perched on the side of a desk at the back. One of the longest-serving officers on the homicide squad, Spencer could always be relied upon to ask the awkward questions.

'Sinead suffered multiple injuries. We won't know the full extent of them until the autopsy tomorrow morning, but we do know the tips of her fingers were removed on one hand and she was badly beaten.'

'Could this be linked to Operation Aspen?' Spencer asked.

The atmosphere in the room thickened.

He was referring to their last case, where they'd apprehended Stephen 'Chilli' Franks, a local gang leader. An investigation also sparked by the violent murder of a young woman who'd been tortured before her death.

Flashbacks of a dark cellar crept into Helen's mind. Of lying in a pool of blood beneath her dead colleague.

She shuddered inwardly, forcing the memory aside. 'Chilli Franks is behind bars, on remand,' she said. 'Doubtless, someone will have filled his shoes and be rebuilding the organised crime network we took down and we'll look into that. If there is a link, we will find it. In the meantime, we treat this as a fresh inquiry.' She paused and scanned the room. 'There's nothing wrong with taking precautions though. Let's be extra vigilant when out on inquiries and keep our phones with us at all times, on and off duty.'

'Could be a copycat,' Spencer said.

With similar circumstances, it was natural to jump to conclusions. She'd considered it herself. But she needed to calm things down here, prevent preconceived ideas from an old case colouring their judgement.

'Okay, yes, while there are similarities, there are also marked differences. Both victims were relatively young women, tortured before they were killed. The first was shot dead, the second had her throat cut. The victim in our last case was killed in her own home, Sinead was taken to a deserted factory. Our last victim was involved in criminality, Sinead was a cop. We need to keep an open mind and follow the evidence.'

The ensuing silence was heavy.

30

'Sinead worked on incident response,' Helen continued. 'Let's examine her work record, look at the notes of every call she's attended recently and speak to her family, friends and associates. We need to build up a picture of her life over the days and weeks leading up to the murder.

'She was supposed to be on a yoga retreat in Derbyshire. Blane waved her off from home with their children at 10 a.m. today. Why didn't she get there and where has she been since? Her Fiesta, handbag, keys and mobile phone are missing. Let's check police cameras in the area for sightings of her car and request her phone records. We'll start with the last twenty-four hours, then track back.'

A hand rose from the side of the room, a young woman with spiky raven-coloured hair. Helen smiled at Rosa Dark. In her mid-twenties, she was the youngest detective on her team, a tenacious investigator whose enthusiasm outweighed her experience in abundance. 'Could this be a robbery gone wrong?' Dark asked. 'Maybe they pinched her handbag and wanted her pin numbers?'

Helen thought back to the scene of the crime, Sinead's battered body propped up against a radiator. 'It doesn't explain the factory location, or the level of violence. Most robberies occur on the street, where the offender can make off quickly. We'll check her bank accounts and credit cards for any sudden withdrawals, but I've a feeling there's a lot more to this.'

'What do we know about the informant?' Dark asked.

'Graham Kirby, forty years old,' Pemberton piped up from the back of the room. 'Lives on the housing estate nearby. Claims he was walking his dog down the Bracken Way when he saw two kids run out of the back of the factory and down towards the road. Thought they were up to no good and reported it. I doubt he expected it to turn into a murder inquiry.'

'Has he given a description of the kids?'

'Black jeans and dark hoodies pulled over their heads. One was about 5 ft, the other smaller.'

'That's it?'

'He only saw them from a distance.'

'There was a used syringe and needle found at the factory,' Helen said. 'Forensics are checking it for prints and DNA. We'll do a public appeal for any sightings of the kids or anyone else near there today. The family are staying at Blane's mother's house for the moment, so let's get a team out to search the O'Donnell's family home and start door-to-door nearby, to see if anybody's seen anything suspicious recently.

'Okay, everyone. Thanks for your support. I'm not going to pretend this is going to be easy. It never is. Let's work together and nail this bastard.'

The officers gathered their notes and made off. Helen flipped open a buff file on the table beside her and stared at Sinead's beaten body. Her head was lolling forwards, tangled curls falling over her face. That morning she'd been heading out of Hampton, ready for a holiday. Within twelve hours, her bloody body was abandoned in a derelict factory. What had happened in between?

She felt a presence beside her and looked up to find Pemberton peering over her shoulder at the photo. 'Why that location?' she said to him.

'It's remote, deserted. People wouldn't have heard her screams.'

'Why leave her there?'

'Perhaps they planned to return, clean up and dispose of the body after dark.'

She chewed the side of her mouth. 'Can we trace the source of the handcuffs?'

'We can try. But without markings it'll be like looking for a needle in a haystack. They're readily available and cheap to buy online.'

***

Helen's phone was ringing as she made her way into her makeshift office in the far corner of the incident room. In years gone by, they'd have set up a mobile incident room, close to the murder scene, but, with advances in technology, current policy was to keep staff ensconced in the homicide suite at headquarters, where whiteboards, screens and phone lines were already established. She slid past her window, with the view of the car park below, and felt a twinge of sadness. She missed those days. There was something about a close presence to the crime scene that sharpened the senses.

The ringing stopped.

She fished her phone out of her bag and checked the screen; two missed calls from Superintendent Jenkins. She took a breath and redialled.

'Helen?'

'Hello, sir.'

'I've heard the news. It seems we've got you back early.'

'It seems so.'

'What can you tell me?'

Sharp, perfunctory. Jenkins certainly hadn't improved his social graces in her absence.

She gave him a brief overview of the case. 'Forensics are working on the scene. The pathologist is examining the victim in situ for the moment.'

'I hear she was badly beaten. Do we think she'd been compromised?'

'We don't know yet. It's a line of inquiry we'll have to follow up. I've raised it as a critical incident, locked down Sinead's computer account and requested a change to all entrance access codes force-wide, in case there's a security breach.'

'Okay. Keep me informed. How are the troops dealing with the news?'

'As well as can be expected.'

'I'm told there was an altercation at the scene with Blane O'Donnell.'

'It was nothing. He was just a bit upset. Perfectly under-standable given the circumstances.'

'Hmm. Yes, I heard about the leak. Where's the constable now?'

'He's been sent home.'

The line quietened. They both knew the officer would be questioned, possibly even disciplined. The reputation of the whole force depended on discretion. Jeopardise that and the ability to maintain integrity, do their job and keep the public safe, failed.

'Okay. I'm on my way to see Blane, then I'm coming into the office. Pull the press officer in. The chief constable wants a press conference organised pronto. It won't be long before the media jump on this one.'

'Will do.'

'And Helen?'

'Yes?'

'Make sure you take it easy and use your team. I don't want you taking any risks.'

Helen sank into her seat and changed the subject. 'Any news on the new inspector?'

Her team had been down an inspector for some months. Pemberton was substituting and not interested in applying to the board to become permanent and, with a live enquiry running, she could do with all the staff she could get.

'Ah. Yes, we've got a transferee from Leicester. Ivan Newton. He's joining us on Monday. I'll see if I can get you any extra help in the meantime.'

'Okay, thanks.'

She ended the call, swivelled her chair and stared out of the window. Ivan Newton. For some reason, the name rang a bell. But thoughts of him were drowned out by another of Jenkins' remarks. *Use your team.* Images of a dark cellar tripped into her mind. Grazes stinging her calves, a sharp pain in her head. The last time she'd wanted to use her team, he'd complained about his budget and given the case to another unit to wrap up, refusing to support her. A move that forced her to follow her instinct and go out on a limb. And she'd been right.

She shivered. She'd almost died in that dank cellar. The detached retina behind her left eye, which was just starting to settle down, had taken several weeks to mend. Weeks in which she'd been laid up, off work.

She'd made her reports. He'd made his. The file was prepared, the case awaiting a court hearing. Yet he'd never mentioned her actions, never discussed them with her, instead holding shallow conversations about work-related subjects when he'd visited her to discuss her return to work. But the incident stretched between them.

A single knock at the door. Helen turned as Pemberton entered. 'We've found Sinead's car.'

CHAPTER 6

The wind had picked up, brushing the rain clouds aside. A full moon lit up the surrounding countryside. Sinead's car was in Ashdown Lane, a country road on the fringe of the Hampton border, situated close to the motorway junction. Pemberton turned off the main drag and steered the pool car down the lane, slowing to avoid the potholes. They were nearly a quarter of a mile in when they spotted the police cars, the beam of their headlights fixed on a red Fiesta surrounded by blue and white police tape.

The sound of an owl calling to its mate punctuated the distant thrum of motorway traffic as Helen climbed out of the car. Ashdown Lane was an old road, its usage long since usurped by the nearby A road, and was mainly accessed by the local farmers these days, feeding cattle in the nearby fields. Although a few locals trundled down on occasion to enjoy the views over open countryside or cut the corner towards the motorway junction when the surrounding roads were congested.

'Odd place to leave a car,' Helen said. There were no houses nearby. The nearest dwelling was Ashdown farmhouse, another quarter of a mile up the road. She couldn't see any walkways or bridleways close by either.

'That's what the officer thought when he found it,' Pemberton said.

They greeted the uniformed officers at the vehicles, wandered over to the cordon. Having attended the murder scene, neither Helen nor Pemberton could risk getting close to the car before the CSIs examined it, in case they unwittingly transferred hairs or fibres belonging to the killer. But it was worth the trip to get a feel for the location, the setting where Sinead disappeared, even if they had to stay on the wrong side of the police tape.

The Fiesta was parked at the side of the road. All the doors closed, it looked like somebody had left it there to take a walk.

'Is this exactly how it was left?' Helen asked one of officers.

He nodded. 'The nearside tyre's as flat as a pancake.'

She eyed his body-worn camera. 'You discovered the car, right?'

He nodded.

'Can you play the footage back for me?'

He removed the camera from the holder on his chest, pressed a button to rewind, then clicked another to replay.

The edge of a car door swung open. The lens bobbed up and down as the officer climbed out. A flashlight illuminated the tarmac in a tunnel of light, the beam rising to the Fiesta and drawing closer as it circulated the vehicle. He flicked the light inside the windows to check the interior. A gloved hand reached out and gripped the driver door handle. It flipped up, but the door stayed firm.

'Doesn't look like she was surprised,' Helen said. 'She took time to park up and lock the car before she left.'

The camera moved back around the car, zooming in on the flat tyre while the officer inspected it.

'It appears she was on her way to the motorway, took this road as a shortcut and got caught out,' Pemberton said. The sound of his phone ringing filled the air. He checked the screen. 'It's the office,' he said and moved away to take the call.

'We're missing her bag and phone,' Helen said to the

officer. 'I don't suppose you noticed anything obvious inside the vehicle?'

He shook his head. 'It looked to be empty. Do you want us to break into the boot and check?'

'No, thank you. We'll get forensics to lift it as it is.'

She looked back at the footage. The torchlight was still concentrated on the flat tyre, examining it, inch by inch. She imagined the officer crouching down, flattening himself against the ground to get a closer look. The road was unkempt and littered with potholes, it wouldn't have been difficult to puncture a tyre down there if you didn't drive carefully. She was pondering this when something glinted, catching her eye. The lens zoomed in on the head of a silver screw protruding from the tyre.

'Pause there a minute, will you?' she asked.

Pemberton finished the call and re-joined her. She pointed out the screw.

'Interesting,' he said. 'Can you get the footage emailed to the incident room please?' he asked the officer. The CSIs would take photos at various angles when they arrived, but he was keen to share the film to give them context. 'So, she'd driven over a screw, given herself a flat. Could have been working its way in there for days before it punctured.'

'Or somebody planted it.' Helen gazed at the surrounding fields. The sky was spotted with stars, like tiny torchlights diluting the darkness. 'No sign of a struggle?' she asked the officer.

He shook his head.

'Sinead's call records have come through to the incident room,' Pemberton said. 'Last call she made was to Blane at 10.23 a.m.'

Helen frowned. 'Yes, Blane mentioned her calling him to check on the children. He didn't say she mentioned a flat tyre though. It's odd she didn't phone him back, attempt to change the tyre or call a breakdown service to help.'

She looked back across the surrounding fields. The

pathologist estimated time of death between 2.30 and 6.30 p.m. Sinead was last seen by Blane at 10.00 a.m., which meant they had a four and a half to eight and a half hour gap to fill.

'It has to be a good few hours walk to Hampton centre from here,' she said to Pemberton. 'Even further to Billings. We know she had her mobile. So, either someone was in the car with her and they used their phone to get help, or somebody picked her up here or nearby.' She was mulling this over when her own phone rang. It was DC Dark.

'Sorry to bother you, ma'am. We've arrived at the victim's house to do the search and the next door neighbour's kicking up a real fuss. Asking to speak with a senior officer. Now.'

CHAPTER 7

The O'Donnells lived at number 21 Richardson Close, on Hampton's modern Langlands Estate, in a row of semi-detached houses at the bottom of a cul-de-sac. Driveways divided each set of houses. There was no garage and in the obliging moonlight Helen could see down the driveway and into a back garden contained by a white picket fence, with a park beyond.

The curtains of number twenty-one were open; lights shone from every room and she could see officers milling about inside. The soft hue of lamplight was shrouded by curtains in many of the houses nearby, residents recently disturbed by the house-to-house inquiries. While she hadn't wished to disturb residents in the middle of the night, they needed to establish if anybody had witnessed a disturbance at the O'Donnells' recently, or seen anything unusual in the area that day, and with the clock ticking, these questions couldn't wait until morning. It was still possible the killer could be somewhere nearby.

DC Spencer emerged from the neighbouring front door as they climbed out of the car.

Helen nodded towards the O'Donnells'. 'How's the house search going? Any sign of spare car keys?' It would be easier for the CSIs to access the car rather than risk contamination by breaking in and, since Blane didn't have the keys, she was hoping there was a set at the property.

Spencer shook his head. 'Haven't seen anything obvious yet. They don't have a key rack or cupboard.' Not unusual for cops. Most didn't have key racks, a legacy of dealing with so many burglaries where key dishes and cupboards were on show. 'Dark's with the neighbour,' he said. 'An Yvette Edwards. She's very distressed.'

'Are you sure there's no one else available to see her?' Helen asked. On the car journey over, she'd requested urgent checks on the residents of number nineteen and the Police National Computer and force intelligence records were clear. This was a family not known to them, not accustomed to police presence, and there was no suggestion they were involved in Sinead's murder. But, still, she'd much rather another senior officer, without case contact, responded.

'The shift sergeant's tied up with a disturbance in Hampton centre.' Spencer rolled his eyes. 'Some old boys went heavy on the beer after a darts match and started a brawl. Multiple offenders, apparently.'

'Okay, thanks.' She turned to Pemberton. 'Do you want to get back to the station, see if there's any news on cell-siting Sinead's phone? I'll get a lift back.' Pemberton's face eased as he moved off to the car. He clearly didn't fancy placating a hysterical woman at one o'clock in the morning. Neither did Helen. But she was curious. Neighbours often shared confidences. If she calmed her down, something might slip into the conversation.

Helen avoided the doorbell, instead tapping on the pane of stained glass that ran the length of the front door. Almost immediately, Dark appeared.

'Thanks for coming,' she said.

'No problem. Is she alone?'

'Yes, her husband's a security guard at one of the food factories in Hampton. Works nights. I've called him, explained the situation. He's just waiting for someone to relieve him before he can come home.'

Dark led her through to a sitting room at the front of the house, where a blonde woman, who looked to be in her early thirties, sat in a white flannel dressing gown. She sniffed into a tissue and looked up as they entered.

Rosa introduced them both and excused herself to make tea.

A lamp in the corner cast shadows over the mint-green walls and was reflected in the mirror above the fireplace, giving the room a cosy feel. Two landscape watercolours adorned the far wall, a family portrait of a child and parents was surrounded by enlarged holiday snapshots on the wall behind the sofa.

'May I?' Helen pointed at the sofa beside Yvette.

The woman nodded for her to sit down.

'You asked to speak with a senior officer,' Helen said kindly. 'I'm heading the investigation. How can I help you?'

Red-rimmed eyes looked across at her imploringly. 'I want to know what happened.'

'I'm afraid I can't tell you any more than my officer told you earlier,' she started, although the sheer look of desperation on Yvette's face immediately softened her tone. 'Let me go through things again for you.' Helen explained where Sinead had been found, careful not to detail the injuries or divulge any more than necessary. It was always useful to hold back. You never knew when a snippet of information might drop out in interview, indicating guilt or leading them in a different direction.

'How was she killed?' Yvette asked when she finished up.

'We believe she died from a wound to her neck,' Helen said. 'Do you know whether she knew anyone from Billings or had any connection there?'

Yvette shook her head. 'I don't understand it,' she said absently. 'I saw her this morning, packing up her car. She was excited about her trip.' She pressed the soggy tissue to her cheek.

'Did you speak with her?'

'Only to say have a lovely time. I was on my way back in.'

'On your way from where?'

'Dropping off my daughter, Amy, at Brownie camp. It's her first holiday away from home.'

Helen gave a rueful smile. Perhaps that explained her reaction. The first holiday was a difficult time for any mother. She remembered Matthew, her eldest's, first school trip to Wales in Year Five. He'd cried the night before, said he didn't want to go. She'd put him on the coach the following morning with mixed feelings, bitten her nails to the quick during the week he was away, and when he returned on the Friday, the first thing he'd said was, 'Can I go again next year?'

She glanced at a photo of a girl in school uniform beside the television. The child was petite with blonde hair, a younger version of her mother. 'I'm sure your daughter will have a great time,' Helen said reassuringly.

'I hope so. I'm glad she's not here with all that's happened.'

Scratches and footfalls filtered through the walls as officers searched the rooms next door.

'How long have you known Sinead?' Helen asked.

'We met the O'Donnells when we moved into the close two years ago. Their children were babies then. Blane was often busy, so Sinead and I shared a coffee occasionally when she wasn't working. Last year, I was diagnosed with breast cancer. I had to have a mastectomy, followed by chemotherapy and radiotherapy. She was a rock, helping out with Amy, my daughter. Taking me shopping when Mum wasn't free. Sinead's like that. Drops everything for a friend in need.' She cast her eyes down. 'Or she was.'

'You knew her quite well then?'

'I suppose. We looked after each other's children. She doesn't have any family nearby on her side, not any that are able to help anyway.'

'Oh?' Helen settled back into the sofa. She was already familiar with Sinead's family set-up from Blane, but she needed to cross-reference the details. Differing accounts at this early stage in the investigation often exposed crucial clues.

'Her brother was in the Irish Defence Forces, killed in

action before she moved here. Her mother has early onset Alzheimer's. Sinead moved her across from Ireland, to a nursing home in Hampton about four years ago, after her father died. The disease is aggressive. I don't think there's much left there now, poor soul.'

'What about friends?'

'She mentioned some colleagues at work, I gave the details to the other detective earlier.'

'How has she seemed recently?'

'I haven't seen a lot of her, to be honest. Blane's been away, working on his mum's house. What with the kids and work, she's been too busy.'

'When did you last see her to talk to, apart from this morning?'

'Oh, goodness.' She lifted a trembling hand, touched her chin. 'Must be a couple of weeks since we had a catch-up.'

'Can you remember what she talked about then?'

'The children. Her mother. She was more interested in asking me how I was doing. Sinead didn't like talking about herself. Whenever the conversation moved to her, she made a joke and changed the subject. It took me a year to discover her mum had Alzheimer's and then I only found out by mistake. It's a shame. If anyone needed someone to talk to, it was her.'

Helen eased forward. 'What do you mean?'

'She had so much on her plate.' Yvette reached across, pulled a fresh tissue from the box beside her and blew her nose. 'I did hear her crying in the bathroom the other night. The walls are paper-thin in these houses.'

'When was this?'

'Sunday.'

'Did you go and see her?'

'It was late. I sent her a text and she replied to say she was fine. The following day, I asked her about it when I saw her on the driveway. She claimed it was Ava, throwing a tantrum because she couldn't get her own way. But it was Sinead crying, I'm sure it was.'

CHAPTER 8

Helen stood in front of the small mirror in the ladies' toilets and brushed her hair. They'd stayed with Sinead's neighbour until her husband arrived home, and taken a brief account from him. It was after 4 a.m. when she got home herself, barely time to take a quick shower and don a fresh suit for the early-morning press conference.

The picture Yvette Edwards had painted of Sinead as a busy mother under pressure, struggling to hold down her full-time job while raising her children and caring for her own mother, might explain the tears she'd heard. But the extent of Sinead's injuries, the brutal torture, suggested she was involved in something more sinister.

Both Yvette and her husband claimed they were home all day. He was sleeping off his night shift and rose around 4 p.m.; she was home doing her chores. There was no reason to suspect them. Yvette's request to speak to a senior officer appeared to be a reassurance exercise, but, still, she was a friend who lived close by and her description of Sinead as someone who avoided discussing private matters left Helen uneasy. Why the need for so much secrecy?

Helen tucked the brush in her bag and checked the zip on her trousers. She'd lost weight this past couple of months, even with her mother's attempts at feeding her up, and her size 12s were hanging off her. She cast one last glance in the mirror and then wandered out of the ladies'.

'That's better!' Vicki Gardener, the press officer, said. With her caramel French plait and smart suit, Vicki was one of those women who always looked perfect, no matter what the hour of day or night. She reached across, straightened Helen's jacket and swept a loose hair off her shoulder, then handed her an A4 sheet with two typed paragraphs, double-spaced, and a list beneath: the press brief, along with potential questions.

'We need to reach the early-morning news,' Vicki said, her Australian accent dragging out the words. 'It's all about encouraging witnesses to come forward, while giving the press enough to quash the speculation. Let's keep it short, tight and stick to the brief.' She pointed at the A4 sheet and motioned for Helen to follow her down the corridor.

They turned the corner and immediately the sound of muffled voices and chair legs scraping the floor could be heard from the conference room; the hacks had made an early start to their day, ready to catch the low-down on the night's events. Helen spotted Jenkins in the middle of the corridor in a slick black suit, alongside the chief constable. The gold buttons of the chief's blazer glinted under the fluorescent lighting.

Chief Constable Adams was the first to greet Helen. 'Good to see you back at work,' he said. 'Shame it isn't under better circumstances.'

Jenkins gave her a nod of awkward acknowledgement.

'Okay. Everyone ready?' Adams said.

He opened the door and the noise intensified. A wave of camera flashes followed them as they took to a temporary stage that Vicki had put together for the occasion. Adams stood in the middle, sandwiched between Helen and Jenkins. Out of the corner of her eye, Helen could see Vicki's watchful gaze beside the door.

Adams tapped the microphone twice. 'Thank you.' The room instantly hushed. He went on to announce their sadness at losing one of their own officers in such tragic circumstances and express the force's condolences to the family.

Jenkins shared the address of where Sinead was found. Helen then appealed for information about the kids seen running from the factory and any sightings of Sinead on the day she disappeared. She also asked for witnesses who'd seen the car to contact them and finished by echoing the condolences, passing her thoughts on to the family and asking the press to respect their privacy at this difficult time. The media could be so intrusive; the last thing she wanted was for them to camp outside Blane's mother's house, seeking an exclusive photo of the distressed family for their next news piece.

As soon as she finished, a hand rose from the back of the room. 'Andrew Steiner, *Hampton Herald*,' the man said and stood. 'I understand the officer was tortured. What can you tell us about that?'

Helen felt Jenkins's knee twitch beside her. These details hadn't been released to the press, which meant another leak. That was all they needed. 'The officer suffered extensive injuries,' Helen said. 'I don't know where your information is coming from, but I'm not at liberty to say more until a full autopsy has confirmed the details and the family have been informed.'

'Torture suggests a need for information. How can you be sure your officer wasn't compromised?'

Helen hooked his gaze. 'As I say, until I have a medical opinion, I can't add anything further. And I'd ask you to respect that until the family are updated. The circumstances will be fully investigated.'

Another man in an oversized jacket, with a thatch of grey hair, stood beside her. 'Chris Watts, *The Evening Chronicle*,' he said. 'This is the second police death this year. What steps are the force taking to protect other officers?'

'The safety of our officers is always of paramount importance,' Adams cut in, his deep voice crushing the murmurs gathering in the room. 'From what we've seen so far, this is an isolated incident, but, of course, our officers will be following the usual protocols.'

'What about members of the public? Should they be taking precautions for their own safety?'

'We always suggest that people are extra vigilant after an attack like this,' Adams continued. 'I can assure you we will be allocating every available resource we have to track down the offender, as we do in every serious crime we investigate.'

Vicki gave an abrupt nod.

Adams raised his hands. 'Right, thank you everyone. That's all we have for now.' He ushered Helen and Jenkins out of the room.

As soon as the door closed, Adams rounded on them both. 'Where the bloody hell did that leak come from?' he hissed.

Jenkins looked at Helen. 'The incident response officer who discovered Sinead put it out on open police radio,' Helen said. 'It could have come from anywhere.'

'Anywhere within the force. Christ, as if we haven't enough to deal with, losing one of our own. I'll be trusting you two to smooth this one over,' he said. 'Keep your information close.' Adams checked his watch. It was still only 6.20 a.m. 'Okay, I'm relying on you both here,' he said. 'I want regular updates throughout the day. We need to shut this one down quickly.'

Silence fell upon them as he moved off down the corridor, closely followed by a harried Vicki. Helen pulled her phone out of her pocket. The house search would be complete, her team back at the office. She scrolled down, about to press call to check for an update when she felt a hand on her shoulder.

She looked up at Jenkins's thick grey hair, the contrasting dark eyebrows.

'Coffee,' he said.

'I need to be getting back.'

'A few minutes won't hurt.' He strode off towards the back stairs.

Helen sighed inwardly and followed him.

When they reached the floor below, they were met by a line

of officers streaming out of the canteen and down the corridor to the lifts. She followed Jenkins, nodding acknowledgements as she passed familiar faces, wondering what was going on.

As soon as they entered the canteen, all became clear. Chairs and tables at the front had been cleared, the space now occupied by a wooden lectern in the centre, where a book was laid out: Sinead's book of condolence.

The sight of so many of her colleagues queuing early to pay their respects knotted Helen's chest. 'I'll find us a space to talk nearby,' she said to Jenkins.

Two doors up from the canteen, Helen found an empty meeting room with a round table in the centre surrounded by a few chairs. She settled herself into one of them and, within minutes, Jenkins joined her with two mugs of milky coffee.

He placed the drinks down and closed the door behind him. 'So, how are you doing?' he said, sitting down and crossing one leg over another, a movement that made him appear at an angle. 'I haven't had a chance to speak with you properly since you returned to duty.'

Surely this wasn't a welfare call. Right now, when they had a fresh body in the mortuary. She shifted in her seat. 'I'm fine, thank you.'

He surveyed her a moment. 'You look pale.'

'That's what happens when you miss a night's sleep.'

'I'm checking you're up to the challenge, Helen. This is going to be a high-profile investigation. You heard the chief, he wants it wrapped up quickly. You've just returned from sick leave.'

During the short time they'd worked together, she'd grown accustomed to his reserved nature, although now she was beginning to wonder whether he was genuinely unable to show emotion or being deliberately obtuse. 'As I said, I'm fine.' She took a sip of her coffee. 'When am I getting the extra resources Adams talked about at the press conference?'

'I'll look into it. You know how things are.'

She levelled his gaze. She was familiar with the cuts, she'd lost half her civilian complement in the past twelve months. But this was a serious crime, a murder. In years gone by, they'd have thrown resources at cases like these. Begged, borrowed and stolen detectives from every department on short-term loan so they could work through the wealth of interviews, witnesses and evidence that dogged the days following a homicide. The chief was already talking about regular updates.

'Adams clearly said—'

'I heard him,' Jenkins interrupted. 'Your new inspector will be here next week. We'll get him to look at resourcing for the whole unit.'

'I need people now. We're struggling to cover the phones.'

'I'll see what I can do.' He lifted his mug, swirled the coffee around and lowered it again. 'What I need to know is, do we need to be concerned, for the force?'

Helen was reminded of the burns on Sinead's arms, the missing fingers. 'It's too early to say. We need to look into the victim's background, her former cases.'

'What about Operation Aspen?' There it was again, their last case, hovering in the background like an annoyingly bad smell.

'I've already spoken with my team. We are treating this as a fresh investigation.'

'That might be the case, but,' he leant in closer, his eyes narrowing to tiny holes, 'what's your gut telling you here? Could there be a compromise? A link with organised crime, either Chilli Franks's old unit or whoever has taken over from him?'

Helen held his gaze a minute. 'We have gained access to Sinead's car and it's being forensically examined. We have a list of contacts to be interviewed and an autopsy yet to be completed. I can only be guided by the evidence.'

'You must have an opinion?'

The use of handcuffs troubled her. Like Pemberton said, it was unlikely they'd trace the supplier, they were readily available on the internet. But she couldn't help wondering if it was a message of some sort. 'It's a line of inquiry we have to explore. We've already spoken to her sergeant, who hasn't raised any concerns. We need to examine her personal file for complaints, check intelligence and speak with the organised crime unit.'

'Okay. Leave that to me.' He uncrossed his legs. 'I'll reach out to force intelligence and the organised crime unit about Franks's old operation, see who's filled his shoes and if there's any connection to Sinead. Let's keep this amongst senior officers, away from the team. I want them to focus on Sinead and the evidence before them for now.' He stood and buttoned his jacket. 'Call me as soon as there's a development.'

Steam rose from his untouched coffee as he strode out of the room.

CHAPTER 9

The bleep of a distant alarm woke Connor. He grabbed his phone, checked the time: 7 a.m.

His mother's gentle footfalls sounded from the room next door. Cupboard doors intermittently opened and closed as she dressed and prepared herself for work.

'Connor,' her soft voice called from the landing. 'It's time to get up.' Their usual morning routine.

Connor grunted and pulled his pillow over his head. He wasn't ready to get up. But he didn't want to stay in bed either. Not after spending most of the night desperately trying to erase images of the dead woman, empty eyes peeping through a mop of dark curls, that kept popping into his head. Churning last night's events over and over.

Every time he tried to shut her out, willing sleep to smother his thoughts, she'd find another opening and force her way back in. It was a constant battle, sapping his energy, wearing him down, until he slipped into a middle ground, somewhere between sleep and wakefulness, when she became more gruesome: a wide Joker-like smile fixed on her inert face; strips of peeled skin, hanging off; open wounds populated by wriggling maggots. The ghouls of his mind feeding on the grisly memories, mixing them with the macabre characters on his games console.

Three a.m. had passed. And four and five. It was after six when he'd finally fallen into an exhausted slumber.

His mobile pinged. A message from Rhys: *Free today?*

He nestled back into the pillows, wondering if Rhys had suffered a fitful night's sleep. If he was struggling too.

The sound of clinking crockery seeped up the stairs. His mother was in the kitchen, emptying the dishwasher. It was almost 7.30.

He recalled the dead woman's yellow trainers, all the blood. Had they found her yet? He hoped so.

By the time he'd dressed and gone down the stairs, Fiona, his mother, was standing at the kitchen counter, making sandwiches. Her copper bobbed hair jiggled on her shoulders as she buttered the bread.

'There you are,' she said, holding the knife at an angle. 'Just in time. Marmite or jam?'

Bile filled Connor's mouth. The thought of eating anything made him want to be sick. 'Marmite,' he mumbled, swallowing it back.

'Okay.' She pulled a pot out of the cupboard. 'Your cornflakes are on the table.'

Connor slid into a chair. The glistening sugar sprinkled across the top of the cereal made his stomach flip. He looked away. The head and shoulders of a newsreader filled the television in the corner. He squinted at the screen, tried to listen, but the sound was low and he couldn't make out her words.

'What time did you get home last night?' Fiona asked, her back to him as she bagged up the sandwiches.

'Can't remember.'

'You could have come and said goodnight. I was getting worried, about to ring you when I came into the kitchen, found the washing machine on and realised you were already back.'

He glanced at the machine, breaths hitching. He'd forgotten about the clothes. 'I was tired.'

'Oh, and don't wear your best jeans to play football. You'll ruin them. I've had to put them on a hot wash.'

Connor swallowed.

'Your trainers are on the line, you'll have to wear your old ones today.' She turned and handed him the wrapped sandwiches. 'Are you all right? You don't look well.' She reached out, touched his forehead. Her hand was warm and sticky and smelt of Marmite.

He ducked away.

'Hmm. Maybe you should have a night in tonight. You sure you're okay for holiday club?'

Connor cringed at the term. Holiday clubs were for primary-school kids, not soon-to-be teenagers. He'd argued vehemently against going and Fiona had insisted. 'When you're a teenager, we'll review it,' she'd said. 'There's only me to look after you and I don't want you wandering the streets all day while I'm at the office.' At least he got to play football, the one saving grace, even if it was with children much younger than him.

'I'll be fine.'

'Okay, I must go, I'm running late. I'll pick us up some of those eclairs you like on the way home. Don't forget your key.'

She bent down, pecked his forehead and disappeared into the hallway. Seconds later, the front door slammed shut.

He grabbed the remote control, turned up the volume. The newsreader had been replaced by a woman in a yellow dress, a banner heralding *East Midlands News* in the background. She was talking about an arson last night at a shoe shop in Hampton centre. He lifted a spoon, pushed the cornflakes around the bowl. When he looked back up, the television screen had changed to a police officer in full uniform, his face sombre. 'This is a tragic death of one of our own,' he said. The photo of a woman flashed up on the screen. Long dark curls scattered across her shoulders; dimples grooved into the cheeks of her smiling face.

It was her. The woman from the factory.

'PC Sinead O'Donnell was a decorated officer, a mother of two,' the man on screen was now saying. 'She will be sadly missed. Her death is being treated as murder.' A female officer in plain clothes appealed for anyone who'd seen Sinead yesterday morning. 'We also urgently need to trace two kids seen running from Billings factory.'

Connor jumped, knocking the table, flipping the bowl of cereal. Milk and cornflakes cascaded down as the bowl crashed to the floor. Connor's eyes were fixed on the blurred CCTV still on the screen. Their hoods hung low on their foreheads and, with their heads dipped, it was impossible to see their faces. But he was in no doubt, it was Rhys and him.

CHAPTER 10

Helen stared at the incident-room boards, now covered with photos of Sinead, her Fiesta, Billings's frontage and various shots of the factory. Pemberton's deeply pitted Yorkshire accent rang out as he pointed to photos of Sinead O'Donnell's car and talked the team through how it was found, but she wasn't really listening. She was studying the map.

Keys Trading Estate was on the east of the county, a stone's throw from the ring road and within half a mile of Police Headquarters. Sinead lived on the south-eastern side, on a modern estate, close to the edge of town. She'd left Blane at 10 a.m., heading west in the direction of the motorway junction, which was twenty-five minutes, or so, drive from her home. They knew she hadn't taken the ring road which circled the town because it would have taken her directly to the junction. Instead, she chose to drive through town and take the country route towards the motorway. Was this a personal preference, or did she pick someone up on the way?

She switched her gaze to Ashdown Lane and the car parked neatly at the side of the road and imagined Sinead driving down, the Fiesta rocking as she swerved to avoid the potholes. Excited at the prospect of a break away from work, her family. Perhaps she'd heard the wheel start to clunk, parked up and taken a look. She'd phoned Blane at 10.23 a.m. to check on the children. Blane hadn't mentioned the blowout, it must have occurred soon after their call. Why, then, hadn't she called him back, or even tried a breakdown service?

Sinead was a cop, trained to watch her back and trust her instincts. She'd be careful about who she took lifts from. Perhaps she'd abandoned the car, walked back towards town and flagged down a passing motorist. Or maybe she was followed. But an opportunist would likely act quickly and dispose of the body nearby. Her killer took the trouble to transport her from one side of the town to another, back to Cross Keys. Charles was pretty sure she was killed at the factory. Which meant Sinead was in a vehicle with them for almost half an hour, alive.

The killer was prepared, with a knife and a remote location organised and ready.

Helen's eyes traced the picture of Sinead, taken before the murder. The lens had caught her profile as she looked away from the camera, smiling, unaware she was being photographed. It showed off her round jawline, the thick dimple in her cheek, her dark lashes. She'd clearly been a very attractive woman. A twinge of sadness. And so young.

She'd spent the last hour leafing through Sinead's personnel file. It was littered with commendations: for disarming a man with a gun in a shopping centre; saving the life of a stab victim by holding a credit card over the wound to stem the blood loss. Her shift sergeant described her as 'a capable officer, well known for her ability to diffuse potentially violent situations'. Not somebody easily intimidated then.

Pemberton stepped back. 'The car's been lifted and taken for forensic examination, but there was no sign of her missing handbag or phone inside. We've cell-sited the phone and the last trace was within two hundred yards of Ashdown Lane.'

'Which means it was turned off when she left the car,' Spencer said.

'Appears that way. We're looking at her call records. She

called and messaged her neighbour a lot.' He went on to give details of the last call recorded to Blane on her phone records. 'Blane O'Donnell booked on for work at 10.32 a.m.,' he said. 'They didn't have a course running, so he was doing an inventory of the gym equipment.'

'Was anyone with him?' Helen said. He wouldn't be the first spouse to kill his partner and feign grief.

'Yes, a support officer called Karen White. She's given a statement confirming she was with him at headquarters all day.'

Another gaze at the map. Billings was on Carter Way, a long winding road leading directly off the roundabout at the bottom. It was isolated from the rest of the estate, one of the reasons it had been earmarked for development. 'If we're assuming the offender left in a vehicle of some description, he must have navigated Cross Keys roundabout at the end of Carter Way,' Helen said.

A groan travelled around the room. Cross Keys was one of the largest roundabouts in Hampton, with seven exits leading in a plethora of different directions through town and out towards the ring road.

'I know. I know,' she said. 'But with the units closed you wouldn't expect much traffic turning into or out of that junction. Let's see if the roundabout cameras picked up anything on Wednesday morning.'

'Sadly, there are no cameras near Ashdown Lane,' Pemberton said. 'We've appealed for sightings of Sinead from 10 a.m. yesterday.'

'How are we getting on with friends and family?' Helen asked.

A phone rang in the background and Spencer grabbed it.

'It's slow,' Pemberton said. 'Sinead's family are in Ireland, she doesn't have anyone close by.'

'Okay, the techies have her laptop. Let's see what they can find there,' Helen said. 'We'll interview her team today. Find out who she is closest to and who she spends her time with, both inside and outside of work. Who followed up on the informant?'

Rosa Dark raised a hand. 'His story checks out.'

Another line of inquiry settled. It wouldn't be the first time the killer had posed as an informant, trying to direct the heat elsewhere.

Spencer dropped the phone into the cradle and stood. 'That was the bank. She has a few quid in her savings account and her credit cards are pretty maxed out. But, get this, £250 was withdrawn from her current account at precisely 6.33 p.m. yesterday evening.'

'After she'd died,' Helen said. 'That's interesting. Where from?'

'The ATM on Weston High Street.'

Weston was a run-down, largely residential area on the edge of Hampton centre, bordering with Keys Trading Estate. 'Tell me they have cameras,' she said.

He nodded. 'They're sending over the footage.'

'Excellent. Let's see what it shows.' She turned back to the room. 'Anything back on the kids from the public appeal?'

Heads shook. 'It's early days,' Dark said, 'and the description is sketchy at best. The CCTV footage is coming through now and the property developer's admin team will be starting shortly. We'll get a list of keyholders and former owners then.'

'Right, Pemberton and I will head down to the mortuary for the autopsy,' Helen said. 'I'm sure I don't need to say this, but this is a very sensitive case and likely to attract national media attention. We've already had leaks. In the press conference this morning, a reporter asked about Sinead's injuries and mentioned torture. It's possible they will refer to Operation Aspen and look for links with organised crime. We have no evidence to suggest this, although we can't rule anything out at present.

'The chief constable is taking a personal interest in this case and has asked me to reiterate the need for confidentiality.

So, everything, every piece of paper that passes through this office, every message, everything we discuss, stays in this room, unless either me or the DI says so. Okay?' Heads nodded around her. 'We need an Authorised Personnel Only sign for the door, and let's get the passcode to this office changed, to ensure it's only homicide team access.'

CHAPTER 11

The little people sat on the settee in Blane O'Donnell's mother's front room, their feet bare. Thomas's polo shirt was on back to front, the label sticking out at the side. The corners of Ava's large eyes were littered with sleep dust, her wispy curls tangled. She was fidgeting, wriggling her bottom deeper into the sofa cushions. Blane's mother placed an arm around her. At three years old, Ava struggled to keep still.

He'd considered waking them in the night to deliver the news. Though there was always the chance it would induce nightmares or stop them from wanting to go to sleep in future, afraid of what they might wake to. He'd toyed with taking them into the kitchen, where they would usually be at this time in the morning, sitting at the breakfast table, surrounded by milk cartons and cereal boxes. But then they might associate the table as a bad place to be around, rather than a place to sit, eat and be social with friends and family.

Blane's stomach clenched. Was there ever a suitable place to tell your children their mother was dead?

Last night was a blur, a whirlwind. He remembered an officer he didn't know, driving him home. Giving an account at the kitchen table. A senior officer arriving to check on him. After they left, the disbelief in his mother's face as he woke her and delivered the news. Them sitting, side by side, in the front room, her soothing and consoling him. Eventually she'd dropped into an exhausted sleep, her head on his shoulder. Blane couldn't rest. Couldn't think of anything other than the most appropriate way to deliver the unthinkable to his children.

Finally, night had turned to day, the birds had started their chorus and he'd woken them at their usual hour and brought them into their grandmother's front room, the most used room in the house.

Slats of sunlight seeped through the wooden blinds, forming stripes across the rainbow teddy bear and doll's head hanging out of the wooden toy box in the corner. A crystal vase on the dresser glinted in the sunlight. His gaze moved to the host of family photos surrounding it: memories captured of moments gone by.

Including his wedding photo.

For years it had sat there, nestled amongst baby photos of his children at varying stages of growth, part of the background, the wallflowers of his mother's sitting room. Yet, today, the photograph was like a magnet, drawing back his gaze every time he tried to tear it away. Sinead looked beautiful. So fresh and vibrant, with her hair tied back, her translucent skin, the thick dimples in her cheeks when she smiled. The flowers arranged strategically over the bump that was later to become Thomas. Their glowing faces, blooming with the optimism of a long future together.

Not like the photo he'd supplied to the homicide team, taken at Christmas last year, on a night out with friends. Sinead hadn't changed much over the past seven years. A few creases had gathered around her eyes, laughter lines in her face. The signs of a happy life. She had been happy. They both had. Yes, they'd been hassled by family pressures recently. Work, childcare, elderly relatives. But it was meant to be short-term. After he finished his mother's refurbishment, she would move to a smaller house, be more comfortable. And he'd have more time for his family again.

His stomach clenched tighter. This morning, he would see her one last time at the mortuary. Although, after what he'd been told, he wasn't sure if that was an image he'd want to be left with.

Two pairs of expectant eyes grew to large pools as Blane O'Donnell crouched in front of them. 'I'm afraid I have some very sad news for you,' he said.

CHAPTER 12

Helen's low heels dragged up the stairs. She could hear the same cadence in Pemberton's step behind her, fighting the fatigue now starting to bite. Charles gave them an acknowledging backwards nod through the window as they entered the outer room of Hampton Mortuary, then turned back to the metal gurney to point out areas of interest for his assistant, who was busy hopping around the body, photographing her from various angles.

Iridescent lights bounced off the metal surfaces as they gowned up. An icy shiver skittered down Helen's spine. No matter what time of year it was, the mortuary always felt cold.

'What are we doing about the possible organised crime connection?' Pemberton asked as he pulled on his overshoes.

'Jenkins is dealing with it. He's speaking to force intelligence himself. Doesn't want the team distracted by it.'

'More meetings.' Pemberton nodded. 'Good for him. Give us a chance to do the real police work.'

Helen allowed herself a wry smile. 'Do you know Ivan Newton?' she asked. 'Inspector at Leicester.'

Pemberton shook his head. 'Never heard of him. Why?'

'He's filling our vacancy, joining us next week. You'll be able to stand down.'

'About time. It's not like we couldn't do with the help.'

'Mm. For some reason, the name rings a bell.'

They moved into the main room together, stepping over a drain as they approached the pathologist. Helen was relieved to see Sinead O'Donnell on the gurney. On the wall to the side was today's date and a list of names – the examination schedule for the morning. Charles had been true to his word and pushed Sinead to the front and she was grateful for his efficiency.

But any initial pleasure was immediately swamped by a wave of sadness. Sinead O'Donnell's body was even more pitiful laid out naked on a metal gurney. The strong cheekbones unrecognisable from the swollen bruises and cuts that decorated her once attractive face and neck. Her eyes were open, empty.

Helen looked at the fingernails and toenails, both painted a matching sky blue. She imagined Sinead's excitement as she'd prepared for her holiday. Painting her nails, packing her clothes. The anticipation of her retreat, a few days of relaxation, a short respite from the demands of being a working mother. Her children were young, their family had other commitments; her husband indicated she'd struggled finding time for herself.

It was all strangely familiar. With her own two boys under five when their father was killed in a helicopter crash, almost eleven years earlier, Helen's own life was thrown into disarray. Forced to deal with the grief, find work and spend time with the children, eventually she'd had to rely on her mother to share the childcare. In recent years, the two women had pooled their resources and bought a house together, with a granny flat on the side to give her mother some privacy, but, still, there was always something: football matches, Air Cadet training, school events to attend. Even with her mother's help, family commitments, coupled with the demands of running a homicide team, meant time for herself was virtually non-existent.

She pictured Sinead packing her bag, loading it into the

boot. Detectives back at the station were in the process of interviewing her friends and colleagues, but no one so far could shed any light on what could have happened to her or how she'd ended up in the disused warehouse.

'How's it going?' she asked the pathologist.

'She's taken quite a battering,' Charles said without looking up. 'Her nose and right cheekbone are broken. There's a crack in her jaw.' He pointed out arcs of purple bruising across her abdomen. 'There's more of them on her back. I'd suggest they're consistent with the toe of a boot or trainer.'

'They kicked her when she was down?'

He nodded. 'That's probably why there are more on the back. The body is internally programmed to coil, protect the organs at the front.' He moved down to the side. 'Cigarette burns on her left wrist.'

Helen watched him turn over the arm, exposing a butterfly tattoo on her wrist. Three tiny round burns littered the area above it. 'On the inside?'

'The skin is thinner there. The pain more severe.'

She resisted the temptation to flinch.

'I found fibres on her tongue.'

'She was gagged?' There was no sign of a gag at the factory.

'Looks that way, at least for some of the time. Maybe to muffle her cries. Whoever did this was systematic in their methods of torture. The fingers were probably the final move. When they'd cut off those, they realised she either wasn't going to tell them what they wanted to know or couldn't. They finished her off by the cut to her throat. The wound is deeper on the right side. I'd suggest they probably grabbed her by the hair to hold her head still, swiped from right to left.'

The silence in the room was broken by Pemberton's phone trilling. He excused himself and left to take the call.

'We've done her hands, her fingernails, although there's not much under them. Obviously one set are missing.' Charles gave a short cough as he continued. 'I'd suggest whoever did this was careful, wore gloves.'

It struck her, the finger stubs hadn't been recovered. Nor had the murder weapon, despite extensive searches.

'There are marks around the ankles from the cable ties used to secure them and welts on the right wrist from where she's fought against the handcuffs.'

There it was, the mention of the handcuffs again.

'No defensive bruising, no sign of any sexual interference,' Charles continued. 'It looks like they took her by surprise.' He turned the head and pointed out the wound. 'This one was inflicted from the side. A blow like that would daze her at least, might even have caused temporary loss of consciousness and given them time to restrain her.'

'What about time of death?'

He checked his notes. 'I can't be any more precise than yesterday, between 2.30 and 6.30 p.m.'

Pemberton popped his head around the door. 'We're needed back at the office,' he said to Helen.

'The ATM footage?'

'No, a separate witness has called in with some dashcam film. Looks like they've captured our kids.'

'Okay, thanks. Do you have anything else for us?' Helen asked the pathologist.

He shook his head. 'I'll run the usual tests, put everything in my report. If I find anything else of immediate interest, I'll call you.'

'Thank you. You can reach me on my mobile.'

She'd turned to go when he called after her, 'Helen?'

'Yes?'

'It's good to see you back.'

***

'Play it again,' Helen said. Pemberton and she were back in the incident room, crowded around DC Steve Spencer's desk.

Spencer pressed a button on his laptop and a surprisingly clear image of a road filled his screen. A red Toyota in front was inching forwards in the semi-darkness. In the distance, they could see a roundabout. Pavements either side were empty.

'These dashcams have quite a reach,' Pemberton said.

'The motorist was on Hampton High Street, approaching Cross Keys roundabout on Wednesday evening,' Spencer interjected. 'He heard our appeal this morning and emailed this footage through.' The time in the corner of the screen read 8.47 p.m.

Two figures appeared. They were dressed in dark jeans, hoods pulled over their heads, shielding their faces from the lens. One much taller than the other. The descriptions and timings certainly seemed to fit with the informant's description.

The kids approached the roundabout, crossed in front of the car and were gone.

'Can you rewind,' Helen asked, 'and play it back in slow motion?'

Spencer grinned. 'I can. That's where it gets interesting.'

He moved the cursor back and clicked another couple of buttons. Frame by frame, the kids approached. *Look up*, Helen thought. *Just once*. But they kept their heads down and turned at an angle, away from the lens. They were almost out of sight when Spencer pressed pause.

Helen exchanged a confused glance with Pemberton. Nothing looked obvious.

Spencer clicked again. One of them glanced sideways at the motorist. It was a quick glance from beneath his hood, not enough to show his face.

'Is that it?' Helen asked.

Spencer shook his head, zoomed in. The photo immediately blurred, the rear lights of the car in front dazzling the lens. Helen narrowed her eyes. A few strands of fringe, barely recognisable, protruded the edge of the hood. 'If I'm not mistaken, that kid's got ginger hair.'

'Brilliant!' Helen said. A distinguishing feature would certainly narrow down their search. 'Any news on the ATM footage?'

Spencer grimaced. 'It's a bit grainy. I've isolated the best part.' He clicked a button and a still of a swarthy man wearing an Adidas sweat top graced the screen. A cap was pulled down over his nose.

'That's a grown man,' Pemberton said.

'Yup.'

'They could still be connected,' Helen said. 'Have you checked with intelligence to see if he's known to us?' she asked Spencer.

He nodded. 'They can't tell from this shot.'

She turned to Pemberton. 'See if you can reach Vicki Gardener in the press office. We could do with the photos of the kids and this one going out to the news teams. Have them placed on our social media channels too.' Releasing the ATM image publicly at this early stage was a risk. The offender might see it, go into hiding. But they were up against the clock and she couldn't afford to wait. They'd circulate it internally and check with other forces, but if a member of the public had spotted him in the meantime, they could make a move.

She faced the rest of the room. 'Right, everyone. We're looking for two kids, one of them ginger-haired, and a grown man with dark features. Go through the files, speak to intelligence, see if there are any matches. Oh, and grab any CCTV from the businesses surrounding the ATM machine. Let's see if we can get a better image.' A low murmur of excitement followed as she turned back to the screen and placed a hand on Spencer's shoulder. 'Well done, Steve.'

CHAPTER 13

Connor picked up a stone from the riverbank and tossed it at the water, watching it skim off the surface before it disappeared. The sun had broken through the clouds, making for a pleasant day. The grass was warm beneath him. He held his head back, closed his eyes, allowing the rays to sink into his face.

It hadn't been difficult to arrive at holiday club that morning and leave within an hour, feigning a headache. When they offered to phone his mum, he'd held up his mobile phone, said he'd call her himself. And he would call her, later. Cathy, the team leader, had been struggling with a four-year-old throwing a tantrum and shot him a grateful look as he left, saying she hoped he'd feel better tomorrow. They were used to him arriving alone, making his own way home. This was his second time with them, and he was one of the oldest there, one of the responsible ones.

Would they still consider him responsible if they knew where he'd been, what he'd seen last night?

Laid out beside him, Rhys grunted, placed his hands behind his head and stretched his elbows back. He'd dressed and made his way to the park as soon as he received Connor's text earlier. When Connor arrived, he was sitting on a bench by the entrance, waiting, a football tucked underneath his arm. They'd barely spoken, falling straight into a game, kicking the ball around, taking turns at the goal. Finally, exhausted, they'd moved down to the riverbank to rest in the sunshine.

But the air was still thick between them.

Connor opened his eyes and lifted his head. A swan passed, gliding along the water, closely followed by a line of cygnets. Further along the bank, a mother was picnicking on a blanket with her toddler. He watched her reach down and wipe the child's mouth while it pointed at the swan. As she did so, a lock of hair picked up and blew in the breeze. Dark hair. Curly.

Anxiety bubbled inside him. He looked back at the water.

'They found her,' he said eventually.

Rhys had sat up now and was scrabbling around on the bank beside him, picking out loose stones from the grass and placing them in a pile. He didn't look up. 'Who?'

'The dead woman in the factory. It was on the telly this morning.'

Rhys shrugged a single shoulder and tossed one of the stones at the water. It skimmed off the surface, one, two, three times.

'I keep seeing her in my mind,' Connor continued.

'I don't wanna talk about it.'

'They said on the news she's police.'

Rhys turned to face his friend. 'What?'

'She's a police officer. We need to speak to somebody.'

'Why?'

'Someone saw us leaving Billings. They contacted the police, gave a description. It was on the news.'

'What kind of description?'

'Two kids, dressed in black jeans and hoodies.'

'That's it? Shit,' he scoffed. 'If that's all they've got, then we've nothin' to worry about.'

'There's footage too, from the street cameras nearby.'

'Doesn't matter. Not if they don't see our faces.' He tossed another stone into the water.

'What if someone else saw us running away? *They* might have seen our faces, contact the police.'

'They won't.'

'You can't be sure. They might think we were involved. I mean —'

Rhys's face hardened. He rounded on his friend. 'No! We tell no one. We agreed.'

Connor looked back at the sparkles of light bouncing off the water. His eyes filled. He couldn't cry. He wouldn't. Not in front of Rhys. But the weight of that poor woman's dead body was twisting his stomach, wringing it out, over and over.

'What would your mum say if she knew you'd gone into the factory?' Rhys said.

He had a point there. Connor could still see his mum's face when she found him at the park on the last day at school. The tightness in her voice as she commanded him to collect his belongings; the way she'd marched him home like a child, his cheeks smarting. He cringed inwardly.

'We'll only get in trouble. And it's not like we can help in any way. I didn't see anyone, did you?'

Connor kept his gaze on the water, gave a juddered head shake.

'There we are then. It's none of our business.'

Silence hovered between them. Connor fixed his eyes on the water, refusing to be lured back to the dark-haired woman beside him, the mother. In many ways, Rhys was right. He needed to crush the tiny voice inside him trying to convince him otherwise.

'Come on.' Rhys jumped up and grabbed the ball. 'Race you back. It's your turn in goal.'

CHAPTER 14

The queue at the canteen had reduced to a trickle. Helen nodded to a passing superintendent she recognised from the east of the county and stepped inside. Apart from the staff behind the counter, she was now alone.

She approached the lectern and ran the tips of her fingers across the white book of condolence. *In Memory* was etched on the front in silver italics. She turned the cover and immediately faced a ream of handwritten messages. It was the same on the next page, and the next: penned scrawls, some accompanied by kisses and hearts. A handful were personal, others broad and general, those that didn't know Sinead personally yet felt compelled to support a fellow officer. The police were good at that, pulling together in times of need.

Blane implied Sinead was popular, but he couldn't provide specifics of close relationships, apart from her mother, who suffered from Alzheimer's. Her neighbour, Yvette, said they were close and claimed Sinead didn't like to talk about herself. They'd checked with the hotel and Sinead had booked a single room on the yoga retreat; she appeared to have been planning to go alone. Was she genuinely private or was there someone else in her life, someone she didn't want anyone to know about?

She turned a few more pages, the sadness of the sentiments, one after another, inducing a wave of déjà vu. Barely eight weeks earlier, she'd stood here, in the same spot, scribbling a message for another officer. One that had been very dear to her. A pain seared her chest as she recalled the expression on Dean's face shortly before he died. The sadness, the horror.

Helen pushed the image into the shadows of her mind and turned to a clean page. It was difficult enough to think of a fresh message for a retirement or a get well soon card circulating the office, but near on impossible not to repeat the feelings already expressed here, especially when she didn't know the victim personally. Eventually, she thanked Sinead for her commitment, her service and sent heartfelt wishes to the family, cursing herself for the bland comment. She then simply signed her name. No need for rank. This was a sentiment, a passing of thoughts from one cop to another.

She closed the book and moved out into the corridor. Sinead's seven-year service had been concentrated on the incident response team in the northern area. Most cops moved around the force and tried other departments to develop new skills. Some took their detective exams, sought promotion or specialised in areas like child protection or community policing. Sinead had never left response. Was that because she enjoyed it so much? Or because the hours fitted around Blane and childcare? Perhaps there was another reason?

She reached the stairs and spotted the familiar gait of Dick Osborne, the training sergeant and Blane's boss. She quickened her step to catch him up.

'How are you doing, Dick?' she asked when she reached him.

'A lot better than Blane this morning.' A broad Glaswegian drawl coated his words. 'I hear you're heading the inquiry.'

Helen nodded.

'Dreadful affair. Poor Sinead. Only met her a few times, but she was a great lass.'

Helen recollected the scant details in her personal file. The commendations, the lack of complaints. 'That's what I'm hearing. How is Blane coping?'

'I've just been out to see him. Poor bastard's in shock. Understandably so. He kept asking if there was any news.' He raised an enquiring brow.

'It's early days,' Helen said. 'You know what's it like, Dick. Lots to follow up.'

He'd done a stint in homicide before Helen joined, he knew the score.

'How long's Blane been with you in training?' Helen asked, motioning for him to walk with her.

'Must be... almost six months now. Came to us from the management of serious offenders unit.'

'I understand the family have been through a difficult time recently.'

'Yeah. Ageing parents, bless them. It's coming to us all. Can't fault him at work though, he hasn't taken a single sick day. Even took on some of the admin when we lost our support worker. Bloody good job he does too, he's a whizz on a computer. Used to be a digital media investigator. The guys tease him for being a perfectionist, but that's no bad thing in training, not in my book.'

'The family problems must have put a strain on their relationship,' Helen said, moving the conversation back on track.

'I wouldn't know. I heard them on the phone occasionally. Seemed okay.'

'Is he well enough to receive visitors? I'd like to update him myself later, if you think he's up to it?'

They were at the top of the stairs now. Dick reached out, touched her arm. 'I think he'd really appreciate that.'

***

Helen re-entered the incident room and immediately spotted four extra faces. Jenkins's concession to her request for more staff was to borrow a handful of civilians from the control room. They'd arrived during her absence and it was a relief to see they were already stuck in, headsets on, scribbling notes. Hardly throwing resources but, with the recent cuts, she was grateful for whatever she could get. She made a mental note to welcome them personally later.

Other officers tapped at keys or had their heads buried in paperwork, beavering away, undeterred by the odd empty chair scattered around the room. As soon as the photos of the kids were released to the press, she'd had to make some changes. Her team were called in last night having already completed a day shift. Many of them had worked over twenty-four hours with only a short break. No one could sustain that level of energy. Mistakes would be made and that was the last thing they needed, especially with the investigation under the media microscope. So, with a heavy heart, she'd sent some of them home for a few hours to get some rest. For the next few days her staff would work shifts around the clock.

She found herself beside the coffee machine and was about to help herself to a drink when the door pushed open. A whoosh of air flew into the room as Pemberton entered. He looked distracted.

'Something happened?' Helen asked.

'We've just taken a call from a woman in Weston who claims they found a handbag dumped in her mother's wheelie bin. When they opened it to see who it belonged to, they found severed fingers inside.'

CHAPTER 15

Crabtree Rise was a pretty row of terraced cottages accessed via a paved pathway off Weston High Street.

'These little places were built in the early 1900s to house workers from Denton's, the nearby clothing factory,' Pemberton said as they turned off the main drag. 'Factory's long gone, of course, but they're a throwback to the old days.'

'Thanks for the history lesson,' Helen said. For a man who'd only spent his married life in the county, Pemberton was astonishingly knowledgeable about it. Though she couldn't deny the cottages were very quaint with their white-washed frontage and latticed windows. Most incongruous with the apartment buildings and houses that had shot up around them during the 1970s, when the council extended the suburb to take on London overspill.

Lilian Cooper's cottage was three doors up from the main road and overlooked a small pocket park opposite. Variegated ivy snaked around its windows.

The front door was answered by a woman who looked to be in her early sixties with short dark hair, streaked with grey, and a fair complexion. A paisley scarf was draped over a white T-shirt, which hung loose over a pair of navy trousers.

'Trudy Cooper?' Helen checked, guessing this was the daughter that contacted them and not the owner of the cottage, who'd she been told was in her nineties. When the woman nodded, Helen lifted her badge and introduced them both.

'Thank you so much for coming,' Trudy said. 'It's given us quite a shock. Go on through.' She directed them into a sitting room that ran the length of the property. It was surprisingly bright and airy, the wonky walls were painted a soft cream and, with the exposed ceiling beams and a sofa arranged in front of a wood burner at one end, and a small round table and chairs at the other, it had a cosy feel to it. An elderly woman was resting back on a reclining chair beside the window.

'Lilian Cooper?' Helen said and introduced them again.

The woman's face crumpled. She looked at her daughter.

'You'll have to speak up,' Trudy said. 'I'm afraid Mum's partially deaf.'

She looked at her mother and gave a sharp nod. The woman appeared to fiddle with the top of her ear.

'Can you hear us better now?' Trudy asked.

She nodded.

'She hates turning up her hearing aid,' Trudy said. 'It picks up loads of background noise. Can I get you a tea or a coffee?'

Helen declined the drinks and introduced herself to the old woman again. 'I understand you've found a handbag,' she said to them both.

'Yes,' Trudy said. 'I found it this morning. It's in the kitchen.' She beckoned them to follow her into a tidy box kitchen that overlooked a yard at the rear. The three of them shuffled in together, instantly filling the area. 'I haven't said much to Mum,' she said in a low voice. 'I don't want her upset.' She pointed to a black handbag with gold looped handles on the surface beside the kettle. 'I thought someone had been mugged at first and the handbag discarded afterwards. Until I opened it up.'

Helen retrieved a pair of rubber gloves from her pocket, snapped them over her hands and turned the handbag so the opening faced away from Trudy, who'd stayed at the door, keeping her distance. Although the woman knew what was inside, there was no need to traumatise her further by showing her again.

She nudged it open. A packet of tissues sat next to a lipstick and a hairbrush with a few strands of dark hair woven into the bristles. She gently pushed them aside to reveal a blue fingernail, attached to a greying finger stub. Helen felt her stomach turn. Three further finger stubs were at the bottom of the bag, scabby blood and bone matter protruding from their ends, amongst a handful of discarded parking tickets and receipts. She pulled out a black leather purse.

Loose change jangled about. Inside was a safety pin mixed with various coins. In the side pocket, there was a photo of two young children, sitting on a double swing, their heads tipped back in joyous laughter. She opened the purse out and immediately faced an array of store and loyalty cards. At the top was a credit card. Helen slid it out and ran a finger over the embossed letters: *Mrs Sinead O'Donnell.*

Pemberton had his notebook out now and was scratching down the details. 'Have you removed anything?' he asked Trudy.

'No. Not at all. I looked inside to check who it belonged to. I was thinking of contacting the owner. And that's when I saw—' She paused. 'I didn't even get as far as the purse. What does it mean?'

'I'm not exactly sure,' Helen said. The severing of Sinead's fingers hadn't been released publicly and if the woman was telling the truth, she wouldn't be aware of who it belonged to. 'You did the right thing to call us.' She pulled an evidence bag out of her pocket and carefully dropped the handbag containing all the items inside.

'What time did you find it?' Pemberton asked.

'Um, I'd just got back from the hospital this morning. It must have been around half ten.' She turned to Helen. 'Mum went in to have her cataracts removed on Wednesday. There were some complications and they had to keep her in overnight. The council empty the general waste wheelie bins on a Wednesday. We're required to take them down to the main road, so I put it out before we left yesterday. I didn't bring it in until we arrived back this morning. And the alley at the back was in such a mess – empty crisp packets, chip wrappers – I had a bit of a tidy-up for Mum as I brought it in and that's when I noticed the bag lying in the bottom of the bin.'

Helen looked out of the kitchen window. A blue Audi filled the small back yard. 'Where's the bin stored?' she asked.

Trudy motioned for them to follow her out and down the side of the car. The wheelie bin was stationed in the corner beside the back alley. There was no fence, no garden to mark the yard boundary.

'This is the back entrance to all the houses,' Pemberton checked.

'Yes. We generally use this entrance instead of the front. I can get the car up here and bring Mum to the door. She can't walk far these days.'

'She does well to still be at home in her nineties.'

'I know.' Trudy rolled her eyes. 'I've been trying to get her to move in with us for about the last ten years. She won't have any it.' She looked back at the rear of the cottage. 'She's lived here for over forty years. Can't blame her really.'

'Where was the wheelie bin when you found it this morning?' Helen asked.

'Pardon?'

'Where do you put it out for collection?'

'Oh, down the bottom.' She walked them past the back entrances of the other cottages and onto the main road. A car whizzed past, and then another. A waitress milled about, serving customers sitting outside a café opposite; a suited man exited the newsagents beside it. It was incredible how quiet the cottage was, tucked away in its side passage, away from the hustle and bustle.

Trudy stood next to a pitted stone wall that marked the barrier between the footpath and the last dwelling of Crabtree

Rise. 'We line the wheelie bins up against this wall. They're generally emptied early afternoon and I call around and bring Mum's back up first thing the next morning. As I say, I was a bit later this time.'

Helen could hear Pemberton in the background, explaining they'd have to cordon off the area and remove the bin for forensic examination. Her gaze rested on a cash machine, sandwiched between a launderette and a French delicatessen, fifty yards up the road. The ATM where Sinead's card had been used. Weston was the closest residential area to Keys Trading Estate. She estimated it taking around fifteen minutes to walk here from Billings. She pulled out her phone, took photos of the street and the area where the bin had been. If their suspect was walking in this direction, there were a plethora of side roads nearby for someone to slip into. She made a mental note to get her team to concentrate on camera footage from the shops and cafés along this route to see if they could get a clearer image.

'I need to ask you and your mum to keep this discovery to yourself,' Helen said, re-joining the conversation.

'Of course.' The woman paled. 'You don't think Mum's in any danger, do you?'

'I've no reason to think that,' Helen said gently. 'More than likely this was a random drop.'

Helen was torn. She wanted to get back to the station, book in the bag for urgent examination, but the woman was clearly in shock.

'Why don't we have that cup of tea now?' she said.

***

Twenty minutes later, with an officer in place, guarding the bin and scene until the CSIs arrived, they climbed back into their car. After a cup of tea, some reassurances and light conversation, Trudy Cooper was visibly calmer. Helen was confident the woman would stay with her mother until the bin had been examined and pretty sure she would keep the incident to herself.

She stared out of the window while Pemberton took a phone call. The discovery of the handbag was unsettling, not least because Sinead's credit card was still in there, as well as the card used at the ATM. Which meant the killer had the bag on his person when he withdrew the cash, then carefully replaced the card in the purse and the purse in the bag. It seemed odd behaviour, to carry the bag around with them, especially one that looked fairly unique with the gold handles. They wanted to ensure the bag was correctly identified and connected to Sinead.

They wanted it to be found.

'Get the team to look out for anyone carrying a handbag of this description, man or woman, within an hour either side of 6.33 p.m., when the money was withdrawn,' she said to Pemberton when he ended his call.

He nodded. 'That was the station,' he said, dropping his phone into his pocket and retrieving the car keys.

'Any news on the cameras at Cross Keys roundabout?'

'Looks like it's a no-go. The CCTV's been pointed away from the estate since the factories emptied. I guess they think the other routes are more pressing.'

'What about security firms visiting the empty units? They must have some kind of occupiers' liability.'

'When Spencer contacted the developers, they said the security contract lapsed. They're struggling for cash.'

Helen sighed.

'The CSIs are still at the factory,' Pemberton continued. 'No sign of the murder weapon yet.'

'What about the keyholders?'

'There are only two. Neither had any connection to Sinead, both were at home with their families. Now it's a case of working our way through previous occupiers and their staff.'

'Have our guys finished speaking with Sinead's colleagues?'

'They're still interviewing, everyone is pretty shaken. Sinead was the longest-serving officer on their team.'

'And?'

'She was popular, capable, funny. Rarely saw them outside work though. Too busy with family.'

'What about her recent cases?' Helen asked. 'Any difficult customers?'

'That's the thing,' Pemberton said. 'According to her sergeant, Sinead was one of the few coppers popular with the crims. Known for her fair treatment. Apparently, he talked about a pub brawl they attended last Sunday evening. She managed to sort it all out, placate the complainant, without making an arrest.'

'Could they at least provide her movements this week?'

'Her last shift finished on Monday evening. Nobody's seen or heard from her since.'

Helen rolled her eyes.

'There was one officer missing, on annual leave. A PC Mia Kestrel. They're crewed up a lot.'

'Great, where is she now?'

'A city in northern Iceland. I couldn't make out the name, they're going to send over the details. We've tried her mobile, the signal's iffy. She's on holiday with her mother, flies back in the morning.'

CHAPTER 16

Blane O'Donnell peered around the edge of his front room curtain at the members of the press, assembled at the bottom of the driveway. The first hacks were there at 7 a.m., even before he'd spoken to his children. Then, as the day progressed, he'd watched their numbers multiply.

He'd never done homicide, but he'd worked more than his fair share of cases over the years and delivered numerous death messages, witnessing first-hand families swamped in grief. It was the rough end of the job. Some cases stayed with him, tragic cases like the toddler who accidentally swallowed a balloon and choked to death. Others he managed to push away into the dark corners of his mind. Empathise and support, remain detached. That's what his police training required. A difficult balance to strike.

But nobody prepared you for being on the receiving end, for being the family of the victim. And knowing what was going on in the background, that his wife's life was being pulled to pieces by an investigative team and his family scrutinised by the media, was like someone placing a noose around his neck and slowly tightening it, inch by inch.

Hours earlier, at the mortuary, Sinead had been taut, cold. Her beautiful tresses coiled like limp snakes behind a bruised and battered face. This time last year, they were in Cornwall, the four of them enjoying a family holiday at the seaside. Now they were three.

High-pitched voices shrieked above, followed by sloshes of water. His mother was keeping the children busy, giving them an early bath.

The look on their little faces when he'd delivered the news that morning would be forever branded on his brain. Wide eyes. A ghostly paleness. The disbelief. The questions and confusion. It had been difficult to work out what to say. They were only three and five, after all.

He needed to shield them from the brutality, focus on easing the loss. At least until they were old enough to be told more detail.

The eerie silence when he'd told them their mother had become ill, so poorly that she'd had to go to heaven, still haunted him. He'd tried to backtrack, to assure them she would always love them and one day they'd be reunited. The words tumbling out of him in a futile attempt to temper their pain. Ava asked if her mum would be home for her birthday next week and burst into tears when he said no.

But what really concerned him, what worried him most, was Thomas, who'd sat silently beside his sister on the floor afterwards, amongst pieces of untouched Lego, staring into space. He hadn't spoken, hadn't uttered a word since he'd heard about his mum.

Blane trapped the tears threatening to fall. At least he could safeguard them from the news bulletins, and they didn't have mobile phones or access to social media. Small mercies to be thankful for.

But this was only the beginning. The beginning of days and weeks of disbelief and questions, little minds desperately trying to process the reality of losing such a vital figure in their lives. And he had no idea how to answer their questions; how to fill the void their mother left behind.

Voices raised outside. The hacks were jostling shoulders, shoving each other aside.

A familiar figure emerged from the crowd. She was wearing the same trouser suit and crisp white shirt she'd worn at the press conference that morning, her dark hair tied back loosely into a half ponytail. Blane watched the chief inspector push a microphone aside and stride up the driveway.

***

Helen excused her way through the huddle of press, avoiding the microphones shoved in her face, the questions levelled at her.

She'd expected a crowd to gather outside Blane's mother's house. It wouldn't take the reporters long to suss out where the family were staying and the O'Donnells were top news – the fact that Blane was also a cop only seemed to fuel their morbid fascination. But this was crazy. They clearly hadn't paid any heed to her comments at the press conference.

Blane had opened the front door before she reached the step. Camera flashes momentarily blinded them as he ushered her inside.

'Vultures,' Blane said, before slamming the door closed.

'I'll make some calls, see if we can get that crowd dispersed,' Helen replied. Her powers were limited, the reporters weren't committing a crime; they were on the pavement, a public pathway, and hadn't ventured onto the O'Donnells' property. All she could do was to repeat her appeal to news editors and request dispensation for the family at this difficult time.

He guided her into the kitchen. 'What's the news?'

Helen's heart dipped at the buoyancy in his tone. 'I'm here to give you an update.' *And I need to ask some more questions*, she thought.

She was treading a fine line here, between the welfare requirements of a recently bereaved family and the pressing needs of the investigation, and it didn't feel good. Without a liaison officer in place, she still had to ensure the family were supported and any outstanding questions answered. The lack of information forthcoming on Sinead in the investigation needled her; she wanted to press Blane again, but she'd have to take it easy.

'How are you doing?' Helen asked. He looked as if he hadn't slept in a week.

'As well as can be expected. I saw the appeal on the news. Have you traced the kids?'

'We're working on it.'

He looked downcast.

'How are the children?' she asked.

'Difficult to tell.'

'We can offer counselling.'

'Thank you. My sergeant was here earlier, he filled me in.' He rubbed the back of his neck. 'Are you sure you don't have any news?'

She retrieved the still photos released to the press and passed them across. 'Do you recognise any of these?'

Blane took his time working through the pictures. 'No. Who are they?'

'These are people who were in the vicinity yesterday evening. People we'd like to speak to. Their photos will be appearing in the press.'

His forehead creased. 'These are the two kids seen leaving the factory, aren't they?' he said, holding up one of the stills.

Helen nodded. 'It's possible they might have seen something.'

Blane's jaw dropped as he cast another glance at the photos and shook his head.

'Your wife's handbag has also been recovered from a wheelie bin on Weston High Street. We're working on the basis her killer took that route away from the scene.' She lowered her voice. 'I need you to keep that to yourself, for now.' She watched for any reaction, but Blane's face remained fixed, grief-stricken. 'Did your wife have any connection to Weston?'

'I... I don't think so.'

Distant chatter filtered down the stairs.

'My mother's giving the children a bath,' he said. He indicated for her to sit and slid into the chair opposite with a slight thud.

'One of my officers phoned you this morning, I understand, to let you know we'd found Sinead's car?'

Blane nodded. 'In Ashdown Lane. Looks like she was taking the back route to the motorway.'

'That's what we think.' She went on to describe how the car was found with a flat tyre. 'The last phone call she made was the one to you,' Helen said, 'at 10.23 a.m.'

He looked perplexed. 'That was when she asked about the children.'

'Did she mention any problems with the car, at all?'

'No. She didn't speak for long. The line wasn't good, I think she was on the hands-free.'

'It seemed odd she didn't call a breakdown service or attempt to change the tyre herself.'

Blane closed his eyes. When he opened them again, they were watery. 'We don't have breakdown cover on our insurance. When money's tight, you turn down the optional extras.'

'What do you do for cover?'

'We get by.' He swallowed. 'Or we did. I tended to change the oil, do the servicing. I can't understand why she didn't ring me again. Are there no cameras on the road leading to Ashdown Lane? She must have been heading west on Sevenfields Pass to approach that road.'

'Sadly not. We're working on the assumption someone picked her up, either there or nearby. The car was parked neatly; there were no signs of a scuffle.'

'You think it was somebody she knew?'

'Either she knew them, was content to go with them or—'

'They knocked her out.'

'Yes. Look, I'm sorry. I need to ask you again if you know

of anyone she'd argued with, perhaps someone that had a grudge against her?'

'Everyone liked Sinead.' His answer was heartfelt, throaty, almost as if he was trying to convince himself.

She heard the sound of a woman's voice, chivvying the children along. Blane's mother. The children were out of the bath now, little footfalls running around above them.

'Billings, the factory where she was found, has been bothering me,' he added.

'What about it?'

'It's probably nothing. We were talking about going into business together, Sinead and I. To run self-defence classes. Like what I do at work, only with the public. I'd do the training, she'd do the admin. A sideline to earn some extra cash. The nursing home is expensive, and Sinead's mother's savings are nearly all gone.'

'Won't the council help with funding?'

'They only give a contribution. Bracken Hall's one of the most expensive homes in the area. Sinead chose it because it gets top marks from the inspection agencies. Her mother, Maeve, deteriorated so fast, we didn't think we'd ever be in a position that her savings would run low. And when they did, she was settled. Sinead didn't want to move her. So, we needed to find the additional funding. Billings was one of the premises we looked at.'

'Billings?' Helen pictured the bleak factory, the smell of used oil permeating the air. She couldn't imagine anywhere less suitable.

'Yes. We spent ages looking for premises in Hampton but couldn't find anything with parking nearby. Everyone drives these days. A friend of Sinead's told her the developer was offering space at the empty units on the industrial estate while the project was on hold. It seemed like a good option for us, with easy access, free parking. As soon as I walked into Billings, I knew it wasn't suitable. Some of the other units were better. We nearly took Wilton's shoe factory, three doors down. They had a double conference room that would have worked.'

'Why didn't you?'

'My mother stepped in. Said we worked hard enough and needed to spend more time with the children. Asked me to spruce this place up and help her sell it – she's been looking to downsize for ages – then she'd sign over half of the equity to us.'

'That's very generous of her.'

'I know. Sinead wanted us to get builders in, speed up the process. We don't have the ready cash though and, frankly, it's only cosmetic, I can do it myself.'

'When did you look at Billings?'

'Last December.'

Helen baulked. 'Why didn't you mention it earlier?'

'I'm sorry. My head was all over the place yesterday. I don't see how it would be relevant anyway, we were barely in there a few minutes.'

'Have you been back to the factory since?'

'No.'

'What about Sinead?'

'I don't think so. I can't see why she'd have any reason to.'

***

Helen pressed her foot on the brake. Again. Hampton High Street was busier than usual at that time on a Thursday afternoon. She watched a woman stride past with a toddler in a buggy, the rising wind blasting her hair back into her face. A man in a shop doorway, vaping.

With no sign of a break-in at Billings, they were pretty sure the killer accessed through the broken lock at the back entrance. Sinead could have noticed the lock when she'd looked around. Perhaps she'd visited again afterwards. Helen needed to find out more about the connection between the victim and the factory, and fast.

The line of cars edged forwards to the traffic lights marking the crossroads at the end of the high street. As she arrived, they turned to red. She braked again. The route to her office at headquarters was straight over. She was tapping the steering wheel, waiting for the lights to change, when she noticed a sign to the right for Little Hampstead.

Building up a picture of Sinead's movements was becoming an itch Helen couldn't scratch. The calls and texts made from Sinead's mobile had been matched to colleagues in her team, her neighbour and Blane. Apart from several made to her mother's nursing home, including one on the morning of the murder. Bracken Hall was on the list to be visited, but, having been advised of her mother's lack of recognition, and with the wealth of other inquiries waiting, it was low priority.

She chewed the side of her lip. Bracken Hall was on the road out of town, on the way to Little Hampstead. It would only be a short detour. Yvette, Sinead's neighbour, mentioned Sinead was close with her mother before she became ill and visited daily. She indicated right, turned the corner, then pulled over and dialled the nursing home. It was time to pay them a quick visit.

CHAPTER 17

Fiona Wilson heeled the front door closed behind her and called out, 'Only me!'

The television they left on during the day prattled away in the kitchen. Apart from that, all was quiet.

She peeled off her jacket, kicked off her shoes and called out again, listening for Connor's answer. Where was he? He must have fallen asleep. That's why he hadn't answered her calls. She'd tried several times since the holiday club had phoned and told her he'd gone home sick, and every time it went to voicemail.

She bustled into the lounge, expecting to find him snuggled under a duvet on the sofa, feeling sorry for himself. But he wasn't there. The kitchen was empty too. Where was he? In bed?

Fiona climbed the stairs, calling out intermittent greetings as she ascended. The door to Connor's bedroom was closed.

She pushed open the door and was surprised to find the room empty. The curtains were drawn, creating a dingy grey hue. The pungent aroma of worn socks made her heave. His duvet was on the floor, beside an empty plate littered with breadcrumbs, a glass with remnants of what looked like old milk in the bottom.

Fiona lifted the duvet, shook it out and placed it on the

bed, then scooped up the plate and glass. It wasn't like Connor to fake illness and take a day off. Although… He did bunk off school on the last day of term. The school had called her when he hadn't arrived. When she couldn't reach him on his mobile, she'd been forced to leave work to search for him. She recalled how frantic she'd been, only to find him playing football in the park with that Rhys boy, the one that always stooped, despite being short. He was bad news, that one. A bad influence.

She remembered shouting and hollering at Connor, grounding him for the weekend. He'd been apologetic, remorseful. Emptied the dishwasher, vacuumed his bedroom to make amends. Surely, he wasn't pushing the boundaries again. He'd always been such an easy child. Settled in, wherever they'd landed, never any trouble. Until recently. It was that Rhys, it had to be. Things had changed since they'd become friends.

Back downstairs, Fiona made for the kitchen. She'd go over to the park and find Connor. Give him a piece of her mind. Anger burned within her. Anger mixed with anxiety. What if something bad had happened? But… no. After last week, it was more likely he was playing football. She recalled how he'd come home last night, crept up to bed without even saying goodnight. It wasn't like him. He was getting older, he'd be a teenager this year. Of course, he'd want to become more independent. But not like this. She hadn't worked her fingers to the bone, sometimes holding down two jobs, to raise him on her own, for him to go off the rails now. She'd been too lax since they'd moved here. He'd be grounded for more than a weekend this time. Perhaps she'd keep him in indefinitely.

She was grappling with her keys when the television caught her eye. They were showing footage of two kids crossing a road. She spotted a Sainsbury's Local in the background, flanked by Albert's Bakery. It was nearby, close to the Cross Keys roundabout down the road. The screen switched back to a newsreader with sheets of blonde hair, parted at the middle, and far too much make-up on for that time of day. Her face turned sombre as she talked about the murder of a woman in a derelict factory on Keys Trading Estate.

The women at Fiona's work had talked about the murder earlier. The dead woman was a police officer. Rumour had it, she'd been taken there and tortured before she was killed. And she'd left two little ones behind. Fiona shivered. She'd never felt comfortable passing that industrial estate since those factories had been emptied.

'If anyone saw this man near Weston High Street or these children near Cross Keys roundabout on Wednesday evening, police ask you to call the incident room urgently,' the newsreader continued as photos flashed up on the screen. Her face slackened and she moved on to talk about an accident on the motorway. Fiona wasn't listening. She needed to see the footage again.

She scoured the room for her laptop, eventually finding it sandwiched between a couple of magazines on the edge of the table. Various windows popped up on the screen when she searched for local news. She flicked across until she found a still of the children walking across the road and clicked on it, replaying the footage.

She watched the two kids running, stopping as they reached the main road. Twilight was drawing in. Car headlights flickered, illuminating the entrance to the gloomy road that led into Keys Trading Estate as they passed. For a split second, they paused. Heads darting about, searching for a gap in the traffic. They found it, squeezed through. And were gone.

Fiona rewound and played it again. They were dressed in dark clothing, their faces obscured by hoods. One was several inches taller than the other. The shorter one stooped, his head tilted to the side.

No, it couldn't be.

The footage ended. She clicked on an article below. There was a photograph, zoomed in to the head of the taller child.

Revealing wisps of a fringe sticking out of the side of his hood. A ginger fringe.

Fiona looked past the laptop, towards the fridge. At the photos of Connor and her: in the Great Hall at Harry Potter World; a selfie in the stands at Chelsea football ground. Their ginger hair shone out, beacons in the crowd. And always him with the long fringe he swept to the side.

He was her one constant, the only child of an only child. All she had. Surely her son couldn't have been near the industrial estate when that poor woman was murdered? If so, why was he so keen to get away? And why hadn't he told her? He'd said he was out playing football. Placed his kit in the machine when he came home. Although this wouldn't be the first time he'd lied.

CHAPTER 18

Bracken Hall was an imposing country home with a sandstone frontage, set amid five acres of manicured gardens. Gravel crunched beneath her tyres as Helen swept up the driveway. According to Blane, Maeve McKinney, Sinead's mother, had been living there for four years. Surely that was long enough for the staff to get to know the family.

The nursing home sat majestically on the peak of a hill. Hanging baskets stocked with red begonias beginning to burst their buds hung at intervals along the frontage.

Helen's shoes squeaked on the tiled flooring as she entered the lobby. The original wooden entrance doors had been replaced with electric glass ones, but there were still elements of the traditional features in the carved stonework around the windows, the high ceilings and cornices that circulated the chandelier. Oak panels covered the bottom half of the walls, the top section adorned with a mixture of Constable prints and countryside scenes. It looked more like a high-class hotel than a nursing home.

A suited receptionist looked up as she entered.

Helen introduced herself and held up her badge.

'Ah, yes. You're here to see Maeve,' the receptionist said and smiled. 'It was me you spoke to earlier.' She passed across the visitors' book, asked her to sign in. 'As I said, I'm not sure how much help we will be. Maeve is in stage nine Alzheimer's. She's not aware of her surroundings. Doesn't even recognise her family, let alone staff or visitors.'

'Has she been told of Sinead's passing?'

'Blane's mother phoned Barbara, the owner, first thing this morning. She was told as soon as she woke.' The receptionist pressed a hand to her chest. 'I couldn't believe it when I heard. Sinead was a great girl, always with a big smile on her face and a cheery word.'

'You knew her well?'

'I wouldn't say I knew her well. We passed the time of day, moaned about the weather. She had such a lovely way about her, and gorgeous children too.' Her face fell. 'Poor little mites.'

'When did Sinead last visit?'

'Let me see.' The receptionist retrieved the visitors' book and worked back through the names listed. 'Looks like she came in on Tuesday with the children,' she said eventually.

'And before Tuesday?'

She flicked back a few pages. 'Last Friday.'

'Nothing in between?' That didn't seem to concur with Yvette's account of Sinead visiting daily.

'Not according to the visitors' book, though we do have a problem with our regular families. Sometimes they forget to sign in. And Sinead came and went a lot. Natalia probably knows her best. She's been caring for Maeve for almost a year.'

'Where can I find Natalia?'

'I'm afraid she's on leave. She finished on Tuesday for a week. I'm sure the manager will be able to give you her contact details.'

'Okay, that would be helpful. Sinead made a call here, at 9.45 a.m. yesterday morning. Do you know what it was about? Did she speak to her mother?'

The receptionist hesitated. 'I don't remember it specifically. But she phoned here most mornings, to check on her mother, see if she'd had a good night, that sort of thing. Maeve can't take calls herself any more. Barbara, the owner, might be able to tell you more. I'll give her a call, let her know you're here.'

Helen thanked the receptionist and moved across to an oversized leather sofa, resisting the temptation to spoil the display of magazines fanned out on the coffee table to the side.

She retrieved her phone, tapped out a quick text to Pemberton, telling him where she was, and was pocketing it when a woman in a loose navy shift dress approached. Her attire was smart yet practical, with navy tights and low heels. Greying hair was pulled away from her face and coiffed into a neat bun at the nape of her neck.

'Barbara Williams.' The woman extended a hand covered in liver spots. 'I'm the day manager today. I'm also the owner.' Helen shook her hand. 'We were so sorry to hear about Sinead. Dreadful affair.' She shuddered. 'Why don't you come down to my office?'

'I'd like to see Maeve first, please.'

The manager looked slightly taken aback. 'Of course. You do know the state of Maeve's illness?'

'I do. I'll be brief,' Helen said. 'I don't want to distress her.' She wanted to see Maeve's room, get a feel for the place since Sinead spent so much time there.

'Oh, you won't distress her. I can't guarantee she'll be awake though. I'll take you straight up.'

They continued down the corridor, past a couple of rooms with the similar oak panelling of the reception that looked like they were used as offices. Further down, double doors sat open on a bright room on the right, filled with floral sofas and chairs. Helen spotted an elderly man reading a book in the corner; several wheelchairs arced around the television.

'That's one of our day rooms,' Barbara said proudly. 'We have three.'

At the bottom of the corridor, they waited for the lift doors to open. 'Maeve's on the second floor,' Barbara said, guiding Helen inside.

'How long have you had this place?' Helen asked as the lift jolted and cranked into action.

'Oh, it must be five years now. I was here when Maeve arrived. Of course, she was quite different then. She's deteriorated very quickly.'

'How well do you know the family?'

'Reasonably well. In a professional capacity. We don't encourage personal relationships between families and staff at Bracken Hall.' She closed her eyes, gave a quick head shake. 'It muddies the waters somewhat.'

'What about Sinead? How often did she come in?'

'Most days. She came and went as she pleased.'

'And Blane?'

'Occasionally. We actively encourage family members of our residents to visit. It helps to settle their loved ones. I generally only saw the O'Donnells if they needed to chat about something, or if there was a problem with Maeve. It was usually Sinead I spoke with.'

'Were there many problems?'

'Sinead was… How should I put this? An attentive family member. Read the carers' notes; checked her mother's cupboards to make sure her clothes were folded; wanted to know what she'd eaten for dinner.'

'Was that difficult?'

'Not difficult. No. We pride ourselves in providing the highest level of care here. Let's just say another home might find it tricky with such a hands-on family member.' The lift jolted to a stop. 'Ah, here we are. Maeve is the first door on the left.'

They walked into a large room that was light and homely. Fitted wardrobes lined one wall, with a dressing table in the middle. A bath robe hung on the back of the door. The bed was made up in a pastel floral fabric, which co-ordinated with the curtains and faced a window overlooking a patchwork of rolling countryside at the rear of the building.

'Hello, Maeve.' Barbara crossed to an easy chair at the

side of the bed and crouched beside a petite woman in a pink jumper with a crocheted blanket tucked neatly around her legs. 'I've brought a visitor to see you.' Her hair was dark and cropped short, her complexion shockingly clear and young; she didn't look a day over fifty, even though she was nearly sixty.

Maeve wasn't sleeping, she was staring ahead, entranced. If she was aware of their presence, she certainly didn't let on.

The door to the wardrobe sat ajar, exposing a perfect line of trousers. A pile of jumpers beneath. Helen imagined Sinead coming in to see her mother after a busy day at work. Fastidiously folding her mother's clothes. Checking the carer's notes at the end of the bed. Wiping spittle from her mother's chin. All the while, receiving no reaction, no acknowledgement. Life could be so cruel.

A mosaic of photos filled a frame headed *My Family* on the wall beside Maeve. Pictures of Sinead and her mother in a rose garden in happier times. The children on the beach with buckets and spades. Sinead and Blane's wedding photo. Another of Sinead, Maeve and a young man. Sinead's late brother, she guessed. Children's paintings sat alongside the frame, drawings of stick people above it.

'Hello, Maeve.' Helen sat on the edge of the bed and introduced herself. 'I'm here to ask you some questions about Sinead.' She paused, her eyes focused on the old woman, watching for any hint of a reaction. There was none.

Helen tried a few gentle questions. When she was convinced her words weren't going to be answered, she stood and gave Barbara a nod. It was worth a try.

'Are there any of the carers who've got to know the family?' Helen asked when they were back in the lift.

'Well, Natalia Kowalski is Maeve's regular carer. She works days mostly, was often here when Sinead visited. She'd probably be your best bet. She's away at the moment.'

'Ah, yes. Your receptionist mentioned her. Do you know where I can reach her?'

'No, sorry. She's off until Tuesday. I believe she's gone on holiday. I can give you her mobile number.'

The lift pinged and they climbed out. Helen followed Barbara into an office down the corridor, close to reception. It was a grand affair, with oak panelled walls and a large desk beside the window. She imagined many a family sitting on the leather chairs in front of the desk, discussing their relative's needs.

'When did you last see Sinead?' she asked.

'I asked to see her last Friday.'

'Why?'

Barbara gave a thin smile. 'She was a little behind with her payment.'

'How far?'

'A month.' Barbara squared her hands on the desk in front. 'We've received payment from the local authority, it's the family top-up that's outstanding. We don't usually allow our families credit, but we do try to extend the payment period where we can. Maeve has been with us for several years, I was aware of the family's financial struggles. I believe they've been in the process of arranging additional funding.'

'What did Sinead say when you confronted her about the debt?'

'She told me she was having a few admin problems with the bank, said that she'd get on to them. I'd placed a note in my diary to speak with her again this Friday.'

CHAPTER 19

Later, Helen was awoken by the sound of a mobile buzzing. She blinked her dry eyes open. Vague recollections of driving home nudged her. The cold whoosh of an empty house as she crossed the threshold. Walking into the front room, dropping onto the sofa. She must have fallen asleep instantly. She sat up and flinched at the pain in her shoulder; the bruising from Blane's fist was blooming with a vengeance.

The movement dislodged a pile of papers on her lap. As she reached to grab them, her phone slipped from beside her and fell to the floor. The buzzing cut. The sound of it crashing against the wooden floor reverberated around her head. She cursed the phone, then cursed herself for falling asleep, fully dressed, on the sofa.

The casing was cracked in the corner, but thankfully the phone wasn't damaged. Caller unknown. At least she hadn't missed a call from the incident room.

In the kitchen, Helen poured herself a glass of milk and drank it down in one, relishing the cold liquid cascading through her, awakening her senses. It was almost 6.30 p.m. They were playing the waiting game. Waiting on forensics; for witnesses to contact them in response to the public appeal; for Sinead's colleague to return from holiday. The sheer reality that Sinead had been dead for over twenty-four hours, and she was no closer to finding the killer than when she'd entered the factory the night before jarred her.

Where had Sinead gone when she left her car in Ashdown Lane that morning? And who had she gone with?

What really grated at her, what picked away at the side of her brain, was the systematic torture, the burns on her wrists, the severed fingers. Why?

She replayed the conversation with the manager of Bracken Hall. Sinead was behind with payment for her mother's care. Blane's mother's house wasn't yet ready to put on the market, so no cash would be freed up from there anytime soon. Before Helen left the office, she'd asked her team to double-check the victim's bank accounts.

The sound of the landline ringing interrupted her thoughts.

She padded out to the hallway, her head still thick with sleep.

'Mum?'

Helen smiled. The depth of her youngest son's voice still amused her, even though it dropped several months ago. 'Robert. How are you?'

'Good, thanks. Gran took us abseiling today. It was amazing!'

The idea of her demure sixty-five-year-old mother trussed up in a weatherproof suit with safety equipment and ropes attached to her prompted a chuckle. 'Sounds cool.'

'It was.'

She leant against the hallway table as he talked her through his day of raft building in the morning, abseiling in the afternoon. At fourteen, Robert was young for his age, still keen to chat and spend time with her. Unlike his fifteen-year-old brother, Matthew, a teenager of few words, especially on the phone. She'd barely spoken to Matthew since they'd been away, while her mother and Robert called most evenings.

'What are you up to now?' she asked as he finished up.

'Just been out for pizza. Matt's gone down to the centre to play in a badminton tournament.'

'Ah, well give him my love. Can I speak to Gran?'

There was a rustle in the background and Jane Lavery's smooth tone filled the line. 'How are you, darling?'

'Fine, thanks.' Helen looked at the *caller unknown* message on the handset and frowned. 'Aren't you guys using your mobiles?'

'The signal's hopeless here. We've given up on ours, much to Matthew's dismay. He spends most of his time at the centre, where he can tap into their Wi-Fi.'

'I bet.' A wry smile. She couldn't imagine her eldest son lasting five minutes without the internet. 'I hear you've been abseiling today.'

Her mother snorted. 'I was more of a spectator actually. I'm not sure those poor instructors are ready for the sight of my rear descending down Dinas Rock. The boys had a good time, though.'

Helen laughed. 'I'm glad you're enjoying yourselves.'

'You know your boys. If there's sports and pizza, they're happy.'

Helen felt a pang of regret. Her children were growing up fast, it would have been lovely to join them on this break. Spring bank holiday was her favourite week away: coinciding with school half-term, it marked the beginning of summer in her book. Long balmy days. Sunshine. She gave a wistful sigh. Everything seemed better, clearer, in the sunshine. But with her recent bout of sick leave, she couldn't afford to take any more time away from work.

'Anyway, how are you?' Jane Lavery continued. 'Are you back at the office yet?'

'Yes.'

'And... How are things?'

'Oh, you know, the usual. Nothing changes.'

'I can imagine.'

Helen chewed the side of her mouth. The investigation, the murder and torture of another cop, was high profile. She needed to share it with her family before they heard it elsewhere, reassure them she was safe. But she needed to find the right words.

The phone line crackled. Voices chatted in the background. 'Mum?'

It was a while before Jane replied and, when she did, she was flustered. 'It looks like we got the wrong time for the badminton tournament. Matthew's already started. I need to go.'

'Could I just—'

'I'll speak to you tomorrow, darling. Love you.' And she was gone.

Helen dropped the phone into the cradle and gripped the edge of the table. She meant to tell her about the new case, give her mother a chance to prepare her boys.

If she closed her eyes, she could still see her boys' anxious faces in the hospital room after her last case. Gaping at the split in her lip, the bruises on her forehead. The concern in her mother's face. They'd played down Helen's injuries to the children, but the fear in her mother that day, the awareness her daughter had faced a close call with death, remained raw.

During the long days at home these past weeks, Helen had contemplated a move away from the dangers of front line policing, taking a sideways step into admin or the control room. Since John died, she'd been mother and father to her boys. They needed to feel secure, confident that when they parted in the mornings, they'd be reunited with their mother at the end of the day.

Problem was, she'd been raised by a murder detective and while never party to the specifics, they'd followed James Lavery's cases when she was a kid. Celebrated the successes, mourned the disappointments. And walking back into the incident room yesterday felt like she'd stepped into an old pair of comfortable slippers. It wasn't that she wished serious crime on the good residents of Hampton. Not at all. But when it did occur, she couldn't envisage a scenario when she wasn't involved in the manhunt. That's what she'd joined the force for. To follow in her father's footsteps, rid the streets of serious offenders.

And the attack on her had been a one-off, hadn't it? An incident unlikely to occur again during her career. Surely, she could be a good mum and still manage the murder squad.

Of course, she could. It was merely a matter of reassuring her family, keeping them updated, convincing them of her safety.

They were still in those crucial golden hours. Maybe they'd get a breakthrough and trace the ATM suspect. Things could be so different tomorrow. And her mother, who rarely checked the news channels on holiday, was less likely to hear with restricted Wi-Fi. She resolved to call her family in the morning. In the meantime, they could all enjoy a well-deserved rest.

Her mobile vibrated in the front room, pulling her from her dilemma.

'Evening,' Pemberton said. 'We've checked Sinead's bank records again. She's on overdraft. And Maeve's account, that she has power of attorney for, is down to double figures. She was also turned down by the bank for a loan last month. Unless she has hidden funds we aren't aware of, it doesn't look as though she was in a position to pay those nursing home fees anytime soon.'

Helen took a moment to think about this. Had Sinead involved herself in some scheme, or borrowed the money from a less discerning source in the meantime?

'Did you manage to reach the carer?' she asked.

'Not yet. Her mobile goes to voicemail. I do have some other news. We've had a call from a woman in Weston. Believes her son was one of the kids seen running from the factory on Wednesday. She's bringing him down to the station now.'

CHAPTER 20

Connor gnawed on his thumbnail and watched the detective in front of him look down at her notes. When he'd seen police interviews on television dramas, they'd sat in small windowless rooms with plain white walls, facing each other across a thin-topped table. This was more like a doctor's waiting room, with comfy chairs, a coffee table to the side, a bland painting of a vase of flowers on the wall. He'd been offered a drink when he arrived, his mother given a coffee.

He was still in a police station though, being questioned in connection with a murder inquiry, and the soft surroundings and gentle treatment did nothing to calm his nerves.

'Let's go through this in detail, shall we?' The woman eased forward as she spoke, a biro wobbling between her fingers. She was younger than his mum, with impish features, and in that lilac fitted shirt and tailored trousers, she looked more like a teacher from his school than a police detective. 'I'm Detective Constable Rosa Dark,' she'd said when they arrived and she'd led them into this room, 'you can call me Rosa.' That was forty minutes ago. Before she'd showered him with questions about his presence in the factory on Wednesday evening.

The sofa cushions shifted as his mother wriggled beside him. He'd had the shock of his life when he sneaked in from the park earlier. He was pulling his phone out of his pocket, about to ring his mum to tell her he'd come home sick from holiday club, when he walked through the back door and found her at the kitchen table, a lit cigarette resting in the ashtray beside her.

She never smoked in the house. And when she didn't greet him, instead coldly commanding him to sit down beside her, terror had crept its spidery legs down his back.

She knew.

He'd slipped into the seat, his gaze resting on the smoke swirling into the air from the ashtray. The laptop open in front of her. Freeze-framed on the news footage of two children crossing the road in the semi-darkness. He'd said nothing. Watched as she pressed play. The screen changed to a fresh-faced reporter, repeating the police appeal for two kids seen at a crossing near Cross Keys roundabout. The photo he'd seen that morning flashed up.

For a split second, he wondered if he was wrong. Perhaps she was fishing, checking to make sure it wasn't him. He'd been out on Wednesday evening. Billings factory was only a fifteen-minute walk from their home, only ten minutes from the park. It was only natural she'd confront him when she saw the news and ask him if he'd seen anything. He was about to deny all knowledge, say he knew nothing about it, he was at the park playing football, when another still graced the screen, a close-up of one of the boys, showing the edge of a floppy ginger fringe. And his stomach had plummeted.

For months, his mother had pestered him to cut his hair. 'You're too old to have hair that long,' she'd said. Connor had refused. He liked it touching his shoulders, didn't want to look like the nerdy boys from school. Now he wished he'd taken her advice.

'You say you went into the factory alone,' the detective said, pulling him back to the present.

Connor pushed his fringe aside, cursing it again. He'd played down what he'd seen. Said he'd wandered through the factory, taken a look around. Didn't mention he'd gone upstairs to the offices and saw the woman. How could he? The very image of her made his guts twist. He wasn't about to answer questions about her.

'Yes,' he said.

'We have a witness who spotted two boys leaving the factory together.'

He looked away. Felt his cheeks heat up.

The detective stared at him. 'If that's the case, then who is the other person in the photo?' She passed a still across of them both, standing at the curb, about to cross. Rhys's shoulders were hunched. His hands in his pockets.

'I don't know.'

'What do you mean?'

'I don't know him—'

'Yes, you do!'

His mother's words made him wince.

'It's Rhys Evans,' Fiona said, her voice chipping. 'It's bloody obvious, he always walks with his shoulders hunched like that.'

'Mum!'

'Mrs Wilson, I have to ask you to calm down,' the detective said. 'This is Connor's opportunity to tell us what happened.'

Fiona crossed her arms.

Connor ignored her eyes burning into his temple. She'd started on about Rhys as soon as she'd switched off the footage at home earlier. What a bad influence he was. 'You wouldn't have been there if it wasn't for him,' she'd said. She'd been happy Connor had made a friend when he first took Rhys home. Given him one of the special eclairs she kept for treats, talked to him about the Premier League. But the moment she heard his father was in prison, his sister on bail for a drugs charge, she'd flipped. Didn't want him in the house.

She didn't give him a chance.

Connor's chest tightened. She had no idea how difficult it was to make friends when you joined a school in the middle of the autumn term. As soon as she'd separated from her boyfriend last year, she'd applied for a transfer at work and put their Sheffield home on the market. 'We'll get a nice house in the country,' she'd said. 'Be much better for you to grow up out of the city. There'll be loads of parks and grassy areas for you to play football.'

So, boyfriend number four was left behind and they moved on. It was the same every time, although they usually moved to different areas of Sheffield; this was the first time they'd left the city. Connor had no idea who his own father was. When he'd questioned his mother about it, she'd said, 'You're better off without him,' and 'Don't we have each other? What more could we want?' It was becoming more and more difficult to fit in and, at twelve years old, all Connor faced on his first day at school were hooded glares and cold shoulders. He was the new boy in a new area. There wasn't even space for him on the football team.

They teased him for his floppy ginger hair. Called him carrot-top. Not even original. He'd spent several days hanging around the bike sheds during break, willing the time to pass, until Rhys shouted across from the field one lunchtime and invited him to join their football match. Well, it wasn't really a match, more a makeshift game using bunched-up sweaters as goalposts. They were a man down, needed him to even the teams, and as soon as Connor started, his skills were admired.

They'd walked home together that day, Rhys and him. Discussing their favourite soccer teams. He supported Chelsea, Rhys Manchester City. The next morning, Rhys was waiting for him at the top of his road. It was good to have company on the way to school.

'Is it Rhys Evans?' the detective asked.

Connor shrugged. He recalled Rhys's words: 'We tell no one.' Rhys had been kind to him. Offered friendship when everyone else ignored him. He wasn't about to get him into trouble. 'I told you, I don't know who it is.'

'We will find out,' the detective said.

He shrugged again.

***

From the first-floor window, Helen watched the boy and his mother walk away from the station. He was tall for his age, but skinny. And he looked like a deer caught in headlights. Not at all the cocky youth she'd expect to find creeping around factories on a summer's evening.

She turned to face Pemberton, who'd been standing behind her, watching over her shoulder. 'What do we know about him?' she asked.

'Connor Wilson. Twelve years old. Moved here from Sheffield seven months ago. Lives on the Station Road. No intelligence; he's not known to us.'

'What about his movements earlier on Wednesday?'

'Claims he was at holiday club until 4 p.m. We'll get that checked of course. His mother works at Mitchell Levy insurance brokers in town. She said she got home shortly after 4 p.m., they had dinner together and then Connor went out at seven.'

'Seems late for a youngster to be going out.'

'I suppose with these light evenings.' Pemberton lifted a single shoulder, let it fall. 'He goes over the park most evenings. Has to be in by nine, according to her.'

'And was he home by nine?'

'His mother said he came in and went straight to bed. She checked on him after the ten o'clock news and he was asleep.'

Helen worked through the timings in her mind. No one had contact with Sinead after her phone call to Blane at 10.23 a.m. on Wednesday. 'Charles estimated time of death between 2.30 p.m. and 6.30 p.m.,' she said.

'When he was at home with his mother.'

'Exactly. Look at him, lanky thing. There's no way he

111

could get Sinead to the factory or manoeuvre her around. Not on his own.'

'I agree.'

'What about the clothes he was wearing?'

'Laundered. Trainers too.'

Helen said nothing.

'He was scared. We've reached out to the other kid his mother mentioned, Rhys Evans.'

Helen sat back in her chair. 'I know the Evans family. I was their community officer when Old Man Evans used to go on a bender on payday and spend his month's wages. He'd come home and knock seven bells out of Lynn, his wife. It was my charge that put the father away in the end for ABH. He broke her cheekbone, three ribs, then threw her down the stairs. It's amazing she lived.'

'Her daughter was caught with twenty grams of cocaine a couple of months ago,' Pemberton said. 'Charged with possession with intent to supply. She's currently on bail.'

'Where's Rhys now?'

They were interrupted by a knock at the door. Spencer's head appeared around the door frame. 'We've got Rhys Evans downstairs and his mother's doing her nut. I'm surprised you can't hear her up here.' He nodded at Helen. 'She's asking for you by name, ma'am. Won't speak to anyone else.'

CHAPTER 21

Helen could hear Lynn Evans's thick Welsh accent bellowing expletives as she navigated the stairs towards the front office. She gave the counter staff a knowing look and let herself into the front reception.

'I'm not talking to you and neither is my son. I told you—'

Helen strode into the foyer to find Lynn on her feet, her forefinger in an officer's face.

She broke off mid-sentence. 'Finally,' she said to Helen. 'How long does it take to get anything done around here?'

Helen snorted. She nodded for the officer to go. 'I'll take over here.'

'Are you sure?'

'It's fine. Mrs Evans and I are old acquaintances.'

The Welsh woman straightened her back and shot him a defiant look.

He rolled his eyes and moved away.

'Shall we?' Helen said, manoeuvring Lynn and her son into an adjacent interview room.

'How are you, Lynn?' she asked. 'It's been a while.' She recollected Lynn's bloody body laid out on a stretcher, the night they were called. The scared, sleepy faces of her young children as social services lifted them from their beds. 'He's gone too far this time,' she'd said. Eight months later, it was a very different

Lynn Evans that appeared in court. Pressing charges had given her strength and she looked taller, stronger, although the scars remained for all to see. Helen remembered visiting her after the conviction, a woman desperately trying to rebuild her life after a history of abuse. She'd signed up to do a healthcare course, was planning a better future for her and the children.

'Fine,' Lynn said. 'Well, I was until your lot came knocking at my door.'

'How's Eddie?'

'Out in nine months. I've told him, he needn't come knocking at our door. We don't want him.'

Her staunchness was impressive. Few domestic violence victims ever reached this level of confidence. She'd listened to the advice, taken on board the counselling and pulled her life back together. It was heartening to see.

'How's Bronwen doing?' Helen asked. There was no point in pretending she didn't know about Lynn's daughter's charge.

'Keeping her nose clean. If she doesn't get off, best we can hope for is a suspended sentence. She needs to keep her job at the supermarket. You do know she's expecting?'

'I didn't.'

'Yup. Little one due in October. Prison's the last thing she needs.' She looked away, her face bleak. 'Prison's the last thing any of us need.'

Helen gave an empathetic smile. Whereas Rhys had been of nursery age, Bronwen was ten when her father was convicted. As much as Lynn tried to do her best and carve out a better life for them, she wondered what effect watching her father beating her mother, living on the scraps of a dysfunctional family, must have on a youngster growing up.

Her gaze wandered to the young boy with her. Rhys Evans looked even smaller than he did on the footage, almost as if he'd shrunk over the past twenty-four hours.

'Why don't we sit down?' she said to Lynn, pointing at the chairs. She'd taken no papers in with her, no notebook. Like Connor, Rhys had refused a formal witness interview. But

Helen still needed an account of what he'd seen and didn't want to put them off by looking official.

Helen surveyed Rhys. 'Do you know why we've asked you to speak to us today?' she said in her gentlest of voices.

A muscle flexed in Rhys's cheek.

Lynn dug an elbow in her son's side. 'I've told him he's to talk to you,' she said. 'Tell you what he knows.'

Rhys raised his head, exposing a waxy, taut face. 'I don't know nothin'.'

If he corroborated Connor's account, the likelihood of his involvement in the murder was thin. It was always possible he'd spotted someone nearby though, and the pressing need for information weighed heavily. She wasn't prepared to give up without a fight.

'Rhys, you're not in any trouble,' she assured. 'We're talking to anyone that was close to Keys Trading Estate on Wednesday.'

A hint of suspicion flickered across his face. 'I wasn't there.'

'Where were you?'

'Oakwall Park.'

'Was anyone with you?'

He looked away.

Rhys hadn't been arrested. He'd been invited in as a witness, she had no right to take his prints. But... he didn't know that. 'Of course, we are examining Billings factory for fingerprints and forensic evidence,' Helen said. 'So, we will know who was present.'

His eyes widened.

'I'm not interested in the fact that you were in the factory,' she said. 'But I'd like to understand why, and what you saw there.'

***

Back in her office, Helen rested back into her chair and looked out of the window at the car park below. The sun was sinking, the sky still a beautiful cornflower blue. Rhys's account, when she finally prised it out of him, was short and curt. He'd clearly thought Connor had mentioned his involvement and, when she neither confirmed nor denied it, he'd admitted being there. He said they'd been messing about on the industrial estate, tried the doors to Billings, found the faulty lock and accessed the factory. He also claimed he hadn't seen or heard anyone else nearby.

What troubled her was their accounts differed: Rhys admitted they'd wandered upstairs to the offices and stumbled across Sinead's body. He described the scene, said they didn't know what to do and scarpered. Connor claimed they hadn't ventured upstairs. Hadn't seen Sinead. Why?

And they'd both laundered their clothes.

Rhys was small for his age and self-assured. He made up for any shortfall in his height with attitude. According to Dark, Connor was more reserved. Just over a year younger than Robert, in many ways her recollection of him reminded Helen of her youngest son. How would Robert react to seeing something like that? Would he deny all knowledge? Blank it out? Sinead's broken body at Billings was certainly a sight no child should ever see. He'd be scared witless, no doubt, and fear made you do and say things you wouldn't normally.

The door clicked open behind her. She turned to find Jenkins entering.

'Helen, I hear you've got suspects in custody?'

'I'm sorry?'

'You've traced the boys.'

'Ah. They're witnesses, not suspects, and reluctant ones at that. I've released them. They were two kids messing about on the industrial estate when they happened upon a body.'

'Why didn't they call it in?'

'I don't know. Maybe they were traumatised at the time.'

'How do you know they weren't involved in some way, or lookouts?'

'If they were lookouts, or had gone to check on the body, why did they suddenly leave the factory? As far as we are aware, there was no one else around. They were both accounted for during the day. Connor was at holiday club and then home with his mother. Rhys's mother took him to a dentist appointment in the morning and confirmed he was at home with her for the rest of the day. Sinead disappeared in the morning, we believe she was killed between 2.30 and 6.30 p.m. It couldn't have been them.'

Jenkin's face hardened. 'Did they see anything at the factory?'

'They're saying not.'

'Oh, for the love of God.'

'We've advised them to see their GP if they feel any adverse effects from what they saw, sent them home to rest. I'll get Rosa to visit them, try again tomorrow. They're twelve-year-old boys. There's no way they could have lured Sinead there alone or inflicted those injuries themselves.'

'So, where does that leave us?'

'Sinead's best friend is due back from Iceland tomorrow. We're hoping she can give us a better insight into the victim.'

'And that's it?'

'No. We're still working through the results of the public appeal, waiting on forensic reports and checking CCTV.'

'Right. I've spoken to intelligence, got them to reach out to their contacts in the field and they've come back with nothing, so we're meeting with organised crime at 8.30 a.m. tomorrow in the conference room. Let's see what they can tell us. Senior officers only.'

She watched him march across the incident room and let himself out. Although Jenkins had never been the sort for small talk, he was certainly more intense than usual. She had hoped a fresh case would help them resolve their differences and restore his faith in her. Now she was beginning to wonder.

The investigation snuck back into her mind: two boys and a factory. The set-up didn't ring true. Every part of her body ached with fatigue. But before she could go home and get some much-needed rest she needed to go back to the beginning. To the scene of the crime.

CHAPTER 22

Night was drawing in, veiling the surroundings in a khaki dusk. Helen parked up outside Billings and cut the engine. Sinead's abandoned car was found on the other side of town in Ashdown Lane and Helen was struck by the distance. Once again, she questioned, what brought the victim and the location of her death together?

The only connection to Billings they'd found so far was a visit Sinead and Blane made to the factory end of last year. Stranger attacks were rare, most people were killed by someone close to them, someone they knew. Blane had visited Billings, he knew the layout. Though he was at work from 10.30 a.m. on the day of the murder, his movements accounted for. Friends and family described them as a close family, there was nothing to suggest his involvement. And the nature of the attack didn't follow the pattern of a domestic, which was usually spontaneous and carried out at home.

So, who brought Sinead here and why?

She climbed out of the car, lifted a takeaway coffee from the drinks holder and smiled at the burly uniformed officer guarding the property.

'Evening, Gerard,' she said as she approached. She'd been paired up with PC Gerard Board on a couple of night shifts during her early days in the force. Ten years later, his hair was greying, his girth widening, but the same toothy grin remained. Gerard was a career policeman, dependable. Nothing untoward would get past him. 'How are you doing?'

'Been better,' he said.

She remembered guarding a crime scene herself as a rookie: a tedious task, the hours ticking by slowly. By the time relief arrived, she'd been gasping for a drink. She passed over the coffee. 'You can't have long to go until you retire.'

'Two months, three weeks and five days.'

'Not that you're counting.'

He laughed.

'How are the family?'

'All good, thanks. My youngest graduates in the summer. She's going to be a teacher.'

'Just when you are about to retire. Nice timing.'

Another laugh. He thanked her for the coffee and peeled back the lid.

'Any visitors?' she asked, looking at the cobwebbed windows of the empty building beside him.

He shook his head. 'The CSIs left shortly after seven. It's been quiet since.'

The clouds were drawing in. With no electricity in the factory, visibility was already poor. She needed to get in there quickly if she wanted to take advantage of the ailing daylight. 'I'm going to pop inside, take another look,' she said.

He nodded and took a sip of coffee. 'I'll sign you in on the log.'

She took a moment to pull on a forensic suit and retrieve her torch, then made her way to reception. It was empty, apart from the forensic boards and a few yellow CSI markers. Her team had traced the keyholders, checked any visitors and were still tracking down all the ex-workers, but there was nothing so far to suggest the keys had been compromised.

Helen walked down the side of the building, past the fir trees and the metal fencing, marking the boundary to the unit next door, and around to the rear. Through the high picket fencing, she could see the Bracken Way down the hill, where the informant had been walking his dog on Wednesday night when he spotted the boys, running out of the unit.

She nudged open the door and climbed through the tape. The inside corridor was darker and she had to rely on her torchlight to guide her. On the main factory floor, the area brightened, courtesy of twilight streaming in from the high windows. Her nose twitched at that same musty smell. Coloured markers decorated the old oil drums at the far end, where the syringe had been found.

The lab found traces of heroin in the syringe, and although both boys denied it belonged to them, Connor's mother had gasped when it was mentioned. Rhys's mother had immediately pulled back his sleeves, checked his arms, much to the boy's irritation. They seemed too young, and too lucid for that matter, to be dabbling with such a heavy drug at their age, but if the job had taught Helen anything, it was not to make assumptions. There was no intelligence on either of them, nothing to suggest they were linked with any of the drugs gangs, but it was still possible they'd obtained the heroin and picked the factory as somewhere quiet to experiment. Now their mothers were aware, she hoped they'd talk to their children, keep an eye on them.

Helen tried to imagine Sinead entering the factory with her killer. Did she walk through with a weapon at her back, or was she knocked out and carried? The blow to the side of her head indicated surprise. It would have taken a degree of strength for one person to carry Sinead unconscious. Unless, of course, they weren't operating alone.

They'd had no leads back on the photo of the man withdrawing cash on Sinead's card at the ATM. Not surprising really, given the scant description. Robberies were not uncommon in Hampton, especially in the less salubrious area of Weston, although she found it hard to believe anyone would risk transporting a victim to a derelict factory to beat and torture them for a measly two hundred and fifty pounds. No, there was more to this.

The question mark over an organised crime killing tormented her. She couldn't deny there was family history between her and Chilli Franks. She could still remember her father arresting Franks for throwing acid in the face of one of his adversaries in the 1990s and Chilli's threats to the Lavery family at the time. James called them 'the shallow threats of a condemned man'. But when Helen faced him, twenty years later, it was obvious Chilli still harboured the same grudge.

Since his release from prison in 2004, Chilli outwardly appeared to clean up his act. He'd taken over the Black Cats nightclub, appeared to run a legitimate business and operate within the bounds of the law. Reams of intelligence suggested he was involved in horrific activities – maiming, killing, drugs deals, people trafficking – but ostensibly they seemed empty claims. They could never find enough evidence or witnesses to support the allegations and he'd managed to evade arrest. Until recently. She shuddered. He was undoubtedly one of the most dangerous criminals she'd ever put away and even though he was now in a police cell, under lock and key, he still managed to worm his way underneath her skin.

They'd had no luck tracing the handcuffs and the use of them continued to bother her. Was it some kind of sign? The idea that Sinead might have been killed as a result of her actions against gangland crime, however honourable, sickened her.

She wrestled with the notion, considering other organised killings she'd investigated: Kieran Harvey was sixteen when he was shot dead last year, his young body left beside the curb. Leon Stratton was seventeen when he was shot and left in similar circumstances. They were both connected to the East Side Boys, a local drugs gang, their bodies left in the road as a message.

Sinead's body wasn't left out, it was hidden away. Even her handbag and missing fingers were dumped unobtrusively.

It didn't make sense. In fact, there was a lot about Sinead's murder that didn't ring true, and it was risky to leave her corpse there. Even if they were planning to return and move her later, it didn't explain why they'd chosen that particular location.

She climbed the stairs to the offices. From the volume of blood, Charles was pretty sure Sinead was killed where her body was found. The light was fading in the office area. Helen switched on her torch and weaved through the forensic markers.

The pungent smell of blood and faeces continued to clog the air. It would be a while before the trauma-scene cleaners could move in and eradicate the final remnants of Sinead O'Donnell.

She stared at the radiator.

The station techies found nothing of interest on her laptop. The CSIs recovered her overnight bag from her car boot. They knew Sinead had money worries, yet her lifestyle appeared to be clean-living and ordinary and, so far, they'd found nothing, not even an inkling of intelligence, to suggest she was involved in something untoward.

The single syringe found in the factory troubled her. They'd had no luck tracing the owner; the fingerprint bureau only managed to retrieve smudged prints, nothing distinct enough to analyse. But, if it didn't belong to the boys, she couldn't help wondering who it did belong to. The nature of the crime indicated a degree of planning: the murderer would have taken steps to visit the factory beforehand, check its layout. The user may have seen someone nearby, either on the day of the murder or earlier. The labs were yet to report back with the DNA search on the blood found in the syringe. She'd make it a priority to chase them again in the morning. Witness or suspect, she needed to speak to the user of that needle urgently.

CHAPTER 23

Early-morning sunlight streamed in through PC Mia Kestrel's kitchen window, bouncing off the table's thick veneer.

Helen eyed the unopened suitcase beside the washing machine. 'What time did you get back?' she asked.

'About twenty minutes ago.'

Helen blew across the top of her coffee. 'Thanks for seeing me so early.' Mia lived on Helen's way to work and she'd called by on the off-chance, relieved to see her car outside. A statement could be taken later.

'It's the least I can do.' Mia cradled her mug with an empty stare. She looked younger than Sinead, closer to her early twenties, and there was a delicate prettiness to her features. 'I couldn't believe it when Sarge phoned me.'

'He phoned you on holiday?' Helen's team had tried to contact Mia several times, to no avail.

'Tried to. Left numerous messages. I picked up his voicemail with all the other messages on the way home. It was such a shock.'

'It was. The force is offering counselling. I'm sure he'll discuss that with you.'

'It's odd. You know, we see this all the time, people killed in road accidents, injured in fights; dead bodies. But when it's someone you know… Well, it's just so tragic. And sad.' She met Helen's gaze. 'She was a great girl.'

'Everyone's said the same,' Helen said. 'I'm so sorry.'

The drone of a car engine outside broke the silence in the room.

'Do you know if Sinead was connected to Billings factory, or Keys Trading Estate where she was found?'

Mia shook her head. Her eyes welled with tears.

Softly, does it, Helen thought. According to colleagues, Mia was the closest officer on the team to Sinead and therefore their best chance of finding out more about her. She didn't want her to clam up.

'How did you meet Sinead?' she asked.

'I joined her shift from training. She was my mentor. I couldn't have asked for anyone better.' A faraway look crept across her face. 'Got my first body on day one, of all the days! Poor old dear had been dead a couple of weeks. Sinead was brilliant. Checked her over, called everyone out, contacted the relatives. She was so calm and capable. I remember thinking at the time, I want to be like her.'

Helen smiled kindly. Mia's eagerness was exactly the kind of enthusiasm the job needed. 'How long have you been in the force?'

'A little over two years. Passed my probation in March.'

'Congratulations.'

'Thanks. I had a few wobbles along the way, wasn't sure if I was up for the job, but Sinead was great. She always found the funny side of every situation.'

Helen took a sip of her coffee. There were times when she hankered for the old days of walking the beat, responding to calls, the one-to-one contact with the public. Colleagues pulled together on the streets, and senior officers with their budgets, planning and strategy talk seemed a million miles away. 'You must have spent a lot of time together.'

'We were crewed up all of the time to begin with. Became quite close, I guess.'

'Did you see her outside of work?'

'Not a lot. She was busy with her family.'

'Do you know her husband, Blane?'

'He ran my officer safety training course earlier this year. I've only met him once outside work, in passing at the supermarket. Poor guy. He must be going through hell. And those little kids…' Her shoulders drooped.

'We're trying to build up a picture of Sinead's last week. Did she talk much about what she did in her spare time?'

'I don't think Sinead had a lot of spare time. I don't know how she did it all, to be honest, a working mum, holding down a full-time job and supporting her own mother, especially with the hours we work on shift. She was always running around after the children: Ava went to dance, Thomas played football. I used to call her Wonder Woman.' She swiped a tear from her cheek.

'What did she talk about?'

'Apart from work? The kids mostly. Sinead was never one for talking about herself, even during those long hours crewed up on night-shift.'

Helen paused. What was it about this woman that made her so private? 'What about friends outside the force, mums from the school? Someone she might confide in?'

'She didn't mention anyone particularly. I know she wasn't keen on the school gates, said it was too gossipy. She used to share a glass of wine with her neighbour. Yvette, I think her name was.'

'Are you sure there's no one else?'

Mia was quiet a moment. 'Well…'

Helen angled her head. 'What is it?'

'I did babysit for her a couple of times when Blane was working. She said she was going to the nursing home, to see her mum. I know she wasn't there because they called the landline one time.'

'Did you confront her?'

'I told her the home had phoned. She shrugged it off, said she was there. Called them incompetent, but…'

'You think she was seeing somebody else.'

'I don't know. I do know she had another phone, a separate mobile. She kept it with her, in the side pocket of her handbag.'

'We've recovered her handbag. There was no phone inside.'

'Oh.'

'Are you sure you didn't ask her?'

'It was none of my business. I might be wrong anyway. Like I said, she barely had time to breathe.'

Helen wracked her brains. Sinead's call records had been checked. There weren't any numbers they couldn't account for. Another phone opened up a whole new lead.

Mia guessed her thoughts. 'I do have her spare mobile number. She gave it to me once, when I was babysitting, and her usual phone was playing up. Was very particular about me keeping the details to myself.' Mia scrolled through her phone and passed over the number.

Helen felt a frisson of excitement. 'Thanks. That should really help.'

CHAPTER 24

A line of cars stretched out in front of Helen as she continued on to the station that morning. Before she'd left Mia's, she'd called the number through to the incident room and requested an urgent trace on the numbers it had been used to call.

The car in front moved. She inched forwards. It was almost 7.30 a.m. At this rate, she'd be lucky if she made Jenkins's meeting with organised crime at 8.30. She tapped the steering wheel, then placed her phone piece on her ear and called Pemberton to check how things were going at the office.

Pemberton answered just before the voicemail clicked in and sounded harried. 'Hello again,' he said. 'I was about to ring you. We've retrieved the call records off that phone. It's only been used to call one number.'

'And?'

'We've managed to identify the owner of the number.'

'That was quick.'

'The phone's registered, it was a simple trace.' There was a ring of excitement in his voice.

'Who is it?'

'Number's registered to a Marek Kowalski. Lives in town.'

Wasn't that the surname of Sinead's mum's carer at Bracken Hall? 'Any relation to Natalia Kowalski?' she asked.

'Not sure. I still can't reach Natalia. I've left her a voicemail to contact us. I have Marek's address now, so I'm on my way out to see him.'

'Are they known to us?'

'No. No police record, no intelligence.'

Helen thanked Pemberton and ended the call, perplexed. Usually, if somebody had been trying to cover their tracks, they'd use a burner phone that was untraceable, not a registered phone where the owner's details were recorded. Marek Kowalski hadn't contacted them, regardless of the public appeals. Why?

Frustrated, she turned on the radio. The journalist was talking about how different councils approached household recycling. A man in a suit beside her climbed out of his car, approached the vehicle in front and bent down to talk to the driver.

She was in the middle of Roxten now, a run-down residential area of Hampton known locally as the Rabbit Warren, due to the number of alleys and back entrances that snaked through the estate. Many a time she'd ran up and down those alleys when she'd worked on incident response, hot on the tail of a shoplifter or burglar.

Black Cats, Chilli Franks' nightclub, loomed on the next corner, a dark building with a pair of green cat's eyes painted above the entrance. The metal Sytex screens covering the windows did nothing to lift its sinister appearance. Helen forced herself to look away. Wherever she went, there were hints of Franks's legacy, little reminders of his presence.

While she struggled to believe Chilli would risk ordering the killing of a cop while he was on remand, she couldn't quell the niggling doubts within. After he was charged, there were rumours that people in Chilli's organisation thought he'd passed his best. Others flexing their muscles to take over. Chilli had lost his position, everything he'd worked for. What if he'd lost his grip on reality too?

She tore her gaze away, rested her head back and listened to the radio. The newsreader had moved on to talk about the troubles in Syria. The suit tapped the top of the car in front of him twice, turned on his heels, walked towards her and motioned for her to lower her window.

'There's a jackknifed lorry at Cross Keys roundabout,' he said, bending down. 'Best to turn off at the next junction.

Helen thanked him and was winding up the window when a familiar voice filled the car. 'The safety of our officers is always of paramount importance.' She hiked up the dial and listened to Chief Constable Adams passing his condolences to Sinead's family. The media channels had recorded his statement at the press conference yesterday and were sharing a rearranged edited version. When he finished, the journalist repeated the incident room telephone number and moved on to talk about the upcoming budget.

Helen switched off the radio. National media attention was expected. It would raise the profile of the investigation and encourage more witnesses to get in touch. It would also ratchet up the pressure; the whole of Britain would be watching and waiting, drumming their fingers until they found the killer. But something else bothered her: her family. She still needed to make them aware.

She dialled her mother's mobile. The phone rang out twice before the voicemail kicked in. She tried one of her boys' numbers, to no avail.

The traffic moved quicker once she'd pulled off the main drag and she steered into the office car park well before 8 a.m. Rain clouds were gathering, intermittently blocking out the sun. She was retrieving her briefcase from the boot when a monotone voice popped up behind her.

'Morning,' Jenkins said as he crossed the tarmac to join her. He was in extra early. To prepare for their organised crime meeting, no doubt. 'Any news?'

'As it happens, yes.' They fell into step as they walked up the back stairs together while she updated him on their new findings.

'Where is Mr Kowalski now?' Jenkins asked when she finished up.

'Pemberton's gone straight out to question him.'

'Great, I'll let the chief constable know. He wants to put out another press statement this morning, show some progress. Let's hope this is the break we've been waiting for.'

'I'm not sure about a statement. We don't yet know—'

'Leave that to me,' Jenkins said. 'It's all about keeping the media on side in a case like this.' They'd reached the landing now. He bade farewell and continued up the stairs to his office with renewed vigour. They hadn't even interviewed Kowalski, yet he'd become a sound bite, a snippet of information to appease the media, even if it was only to say, 'a man's helping police with their inquiries'.

CHAPTER 25

A low wail filtered through from the hallway, followed by a rip. It sounded like paper.

'They're mine!' Ava's voice insisted.

'No, they're not.'

Thomas had found his voice that morning and the children were arguing again.

Blane sighed. They'd been crotchety since they woke, before 6 a.m., and, after a night of virtually non-existent sleep, his patience was beginning to wane. He dropped the dishcloth in the bowl, wiped his hands and wandered out to find Ava sat on the doormat, surrounded by scattered envelopes in pastel shades of yellow, pink and cream. Some of them were torn, picked at the edges, others ripped open. Blane's gaze rested on a card poking out of an envelope, a picture of a white orchid with the words *In Sympathy* etched above.

His chest tightened. 'What's going on?'

Thomas immediately let go of the card he was still tugging from his sister. 'Tell her, Dad,' he muttered. 'She thinks they're her birthday cards.'

Blane's heart was in a vice. Thomas had seen bereavement cards before, they'd bought one together when the wife of his schoolteacher was tragically killed in a car accident last year. He rested a comforting hand on his son's shoulder, then dropped to his knees in front of Ava. She was still holding the card with both hands, her knuckles white. 'Sweetheart,' he said. 'I think these might be for all of us.'

'It's my birthday!' Ava said indignantly, jutting her jaw. She tucked the card behind her back.

The vice tightened a notch. 'It is. Next week,' Blane said gently. Out of the corner of his eye, he could see other cards with gentle landscapes, flowers and birds discarded on the mat. He fought back tears. 'But these aren't birthday cards.'

'Yes. They. Are.'

'They're not, darling.' There was no simple way to say this. 'These are cards people have sent us to say they are sorry because we've lost Mummy. Your cards will come separately next week.'

Thomas turned and stalked up the stairs.

Ava let out another wail. 'No, they're not.'

'I'm sorry, sweetheart, they are.'

Her face crumpled. 'I don't want them,' she said, casting the card aside and crawling onto her father's lap. 'Take them away. I want Mummy.' She buried her head in his chest.

The tears came hard and fast, bleeding into the cotton of his top, dampening the skin beneath. He hugged her close, kissed her soft curls, rested his chin on her head. 'I'm so sorry, pumpkin,' he said.

Time stood still. The television in the front room chattered away while Blane rocked his daughter, uttering soothing sentiments. Assuring her everything was going to be all right when, really, he had no idea if anything would ever be right again.

Eventually Ava's sobs subsided, and her body grew heavy as she slipped into an exhausted slumber. How could he pick up the pieces after this? Especially when he was struggling himself. Blane mustered all his energy and stood. Ignoring the cards, he carried Ava to the kitchen and levered them both into a chair, adjusting her limp body into a more comfortable position.

It was a grey day, the sky heavy with the promise of rain. He needed to check on Thomas. But he didn't want to disturb Ava. Another check outside, down the garden. Where was his mother? Over an hour had passed since she'd said she was popping out for some essentials. He could really do with her help now.

The door to the hallway sat ajar, the cards still scattered across the doormat where he'd left them. Sadness bubbled inside him. He imagined their friends and neighbours squeezing through the journalists outside, keeping their heads down until they reached the drive. There'd been notably less reporters that morning, the DCI had obviously spoken to the editors, pulled some strings. Still, there were plenty enough to make a nuisance of themselves. It would be worse on the way out. Once the hacks clocked on and realised the visitors were acquainted with the victim's family, they'd surround them as soon as they left the driveway. How do you know the O'Donnells? When did you last meet? How did they seem? The questions rung out in his ears. They'd nag them for a quote, a photograph for their next news piece.

He adjusted Ava into a more comfortable position on his lap as his mobile bleeped on the table. Another message from a friend or colleague. It had been constant. Messages he'd ignored because he couldn't bear to read them. He grabbed the phone, switched it to silent.

Blane glanced at a photo stuck to the fridge with a couple of magnets: a selfie of Sinead and her brother, Aidan, who'd been killed in action shortly after they'd got together. With her brother passed away and her mother sick, Sinead didn't have any close relatives, but Blane had still spent a good chunk of yesterday calling up her extended family in Ireland to deliver the news. Every phone call on a knife-edge, as shocked relatives wanted all the details. Details he couldn't give because he didn't have the answers. Each call draining him of another ounce of energy. It was exhausting. One auntie made noises about coming over to help. It took all his powers of persuasion to deter her. 'The children are upset. They need stability, time to grieve. I'll let you know when the funeral is, we can get together then.' Despite the kind gesture, he preferred to carry on alone. He had his own mother there to help with the children. Where was she?

As if on cue, a knock at the door. Fist on glass. Surely his mother hadn't forgotten her key. He lifted Ava over his shoulder and made his way out into the hallway.

Blane stepped over the cards on the mat and pulled the door open, surprised to find his sergeant on the doorstep with an orange carrier bag in his hand.

'Dick,' Blane said. 'I wasn't expecting you.' He stood aside for him to enter.

Dick glanced at the sleeping toddler. 'I'm sorry to interrupt,' he said. A card scrunched beneath him. He looked down, stepped off the pile at the door. 'If this isn't a good time…'

Blane followed his eyeline. 'Oh, sorry. Ava found them before the rest of us,' Blane said. 'Thought they were birthday cards.'

'It's her birthday?'

'Next week.'

'Poor lass. Let me get them.'

'No, please—'

Before Blane could protest any more his sergeant was on his knees. Within seconds, the cards were gathered together in a neat pile on the hallway table.

Blane's chin quivered. The kindness was touching. 'Thanks.'

'No problem. Listen, I won't stay long,' Dick said. He followed him to the kitchen. 'I just wanted to bring you this.' He handed over the carrier bag.

'What is it?'

'It's the contents of Sinead's locker. I'm so sorry.' His face contorted. 'The investigation team have finished with them. I thought you'd like them back.'

Blane swallowed, moved Ava to his other shoulder and rested the bag on the table. Through the open top, he could see a striped shower bag, some pink jogging bottoms. A pair of epaulettes, the silver numbers 236 attached to them glinted in the light. Sinead's collar number.

He made to open the bag further when Dick placed a hand over the top of it, blocking his view. 'You might want to open it later, laddie,' he said, glancing at the toddler. 'When you're on your own. There's some personal stuff in there.'

CHAPTER 26

Marek Kowalski lived on Birch Road, on the edge of Hampton, in the middle of a line of 1970s pebble-dashed semi-detached houses that overlooked the nearby Oakwall Park.

Rain had started to fall when Pemberton and Dark arrived, peppering their shoulders as they climbed out of the car. Relieved to find a parking space outside, Pemberton turned up his collar, climbed the few stone steps leading to the front door of number 46 and pressed the doorbell.

A small walled garden was laid to concrete, which had cracked and become uneven over the years.

Pemberton pressed the doorbell again and turned back to the road. Maybe Mr Kowalski had already left for work. He was about to look through the letter box for a sign of life when he heard the thud of feet on stairs. A chain rattled from the inside and the door juddered open to reveal a shirtless man. His toned chest was bare; a pair of washed-out denims hugged his thighs. Dark hair, razored at the sides, was swept back from a tanned face that held the ruggedness of someone who worked outside.

'Marek Kowalski?' Pemberton asked.

The man said nothing, his gaze switching from one detective to another. A gold chain around his neck slipped as he tilted his head.

'Are you Marek Kowalski?' Dark asked.

'Yes.'

They raised their badges.

'Can we come inside?' Pemberton asked.

A cloud flickered across his face. 'What's going on?'

'If we could come inside,' Pemberton said, stepping forward. He wasn't about to have this conversation on the doorstep.

Kowalski reluctantly stepped back and allowed them to pass. He closed the front door and guided them into a sitting room that overlooked the road out front, the park beyond through a grubby sash window. Tired sun-bleached curtains draped its sides. A sofa sat in the middle of the room, facing an oversized flat screen television over the fireplace.

'What's all this about?' he said, indicating for them to sit.

'Would you like to put some clothes on?' Pemberton said. 'We can wait.'

The man huffed and withdrew. Pemberton raised a brow at Dark. Ash from an overfilled ashtray on an adjoining coffee table skipped up as he undid his jacket and sat on the edge of the sofa.

A layer of dust greyed the sideboard in the corner. The original floorboards had been polished, although they'd dulled over the years and were pitted and grooved.

Apart from a clock on the far wall, there were no paintings, photos or pictures hung in the room. Dark peered in closer at a single frame on the sideboard. She picked it up, blew on it, as Marek Kowalski re-entered, a checked shirt now covering his torso. He shot her a hard stare, pulled a stool from the corner and sat down.

'What can I do for you?' he said.

Pemberton paused before he spoke. He could really have done with a tea or coffee, but if the front room was anything to go by, he wasn't sure he fancied drinking out of a mug there. 'Do you know a woman called Sinead O'Donnell?'

He sniffed. 'No.'

'Are you sure?'

'Yes, I'm sure.'

'Where were you during the hours of 10 a.m. and 10 p.m. on Wednesday?' Pemberton asked.

'In Ibiza. I flew back yesterday evening. What is all this about?'

'Sinead O'Donnell,' Pemberton said, repeating the name.

Kowalski's eyes widened. 'Wait, isn't that the woman that was killed? The cop? I saw it on the news yesterday.'

Pemberton stayed silent.

'It's got nothing to do with me. I was out of the country.'

'Have you ever met her?'

'No.'

'Are you sure? Please think carefully before you answer.'

Kowalski flicked a glance at Dark, who'd leant back in to examine the photo on the dresser. 'I don't need to think. I've never met her. What's going on?'

'Can you tell me your mobile number?' Pemberton said, ignoring his question.

He reeled off a number. Dark took out her notebook, scribbled it down and showed it to Pemberton.

'Do you have another number?'

'No. Why?'

Pemberton retrieved an envelope from the inside pocket of his jacket. He pulled out a sheet of A4 paper with a single mobile phone number printed in bold print across the middle and passed it over.

The paper crackled in Kowalski's hand.

'Have you seen this number before?'

He took a moment to scrutinise it. 'Yes, it's my old number.'

'It's still registered to you.'

He shook his head. 'I gave the phone away about four months ago. It's pay-as-you-go. Didn't think the registration mattered.'

'Who did you give it to?'

'My sister.'

'Most people prefer to keep their number when they pass phones along.'

He shrugged. 'I had a few exes bothering me. You know what's it like.'

'No,' Pemberton said.

'They kept calling, getting on my nerves. So, I changed. Natalia didn't care. She was pleased to get a new phone.'

'Natalia?'

'Natalia Kowalski. My sister.'

Pemberton blinked at the mention of Sinead's mother's carer at Bracken Hall. Why did Sinead feel the need to have a secret phone on which to contact her? He kept his face deadpan.

'Do you know if Natalia was a friend of Sinead O'Donnell's?' Dark asked. 'A personal friend.'

'I doubt it. She wouldn't have been Natalia's type.'

'Why do you say that?'

'She wouldn't be. I know.'

'Where does your sister live?'

'On Brooke Street, in the town centre.'

They already knew the answer, the nursing home had given them the details, but it was always possible she'd given a false address. Pemberton glanced at his watch. Brooke Street was barely ten minutes away.

'You won't find her there.'

'Why. Where is she?'

'Somewhere in Derbyshire. She left on Wednesday, I believe, while I was in Ibiza. Went off to a yoga retreat.'

CHAPTER 27

Helen watched beads of rain multiply on the windowpane until they conjoined and snail-trailed down the glass. She tugged at her shirt collar. The conference room was stuffy that morning, even though there were only four of them sat around the end of the table.

Detective Inspector Terry Burns sat forward in his charcoal suit and purple tie, periodically clicking keys on his laptop. He was flanked by his sergeant, an enthusiastic twenty-something in a slick Hugo Boss suit whose name Helen couldn't remember. Burns and she joined the force and completed their basic training together. They both signed up for the accelerated promotion scheme, racing through the ranks at breakneck speed. But that's where the similarities ended. Whereas Helen had reached her goal of heading the murder squad, Burns had always made it quite clear he didn't like to get his hands dirty, convinced his spreadsheets and organisational charts, along with a good measure of the gift of the gab, would take him to the top. He was a career manager of the worst kind and if he said, 'singing from the same hymn sheet' one more time, she was sure she'd throttle him herself.

He clicked another key and a photofit filled the screen. 'Paul Gladstone, head of the other Rabbit Warren gang, or the "East Side Boys" as they prefer to be known. He's been the biggest rival to Chilli Franks's operation for years. Never really had the muscle until now.' A broth of a man with a balding head and goatee beard filled the screen. Dark sunglasses were balanced precariously on top of his head. He looked like he was crossing a road, unaware of the lens tracking him.

Helen sighed inwardly. She'd arrested Gladstone in her younger days for affray. A beefcake of a guy that relied on brawn more than brain. If he was Hampton's answer to replacing Chilli, the residents were safe in their beds for now.

She poured herself a glass of water. Jenkins shifted in his seat beside her.

Burns clicked a button on his laptop and another photo of Gladstone appeared, this time the lens had zoomed in and caught him front-on as he climbed into a BMW. 'Gladstone grew up in the business, his father served eight years for kidnapping and possession of a firearm in the early noughties and passed away soon after he was released. That's when Paul took over.

'Many of Franks's troop jumped ship and joined Gladstone's clan. We've little intelligence on who is left or who's in charge; the arrest in March has made everyone nervous. Even the registered informants aren't talking. Our focus is on Gladstone at the moment.'

Helen passed over the still of their ATM suspect. Despite her officers retrieving CCTV footage from businesses and shops near the ATM, they hadn't been able to retrieve any clearer images.

'Do you recognise this man?' she asked. 'He used the victim's bank card on the night of her murder.'

'Doesn't look familiar.'

She pulled the sheet back, resisting the temptation to roll her eyes – this was going nowhere – and wondered whether her team had traced Natalia Kowalski yet. The secrecy surrounding her association with the victim intrigued her; she was connected to Sinead, yet she hadn't contacted them. Why?

Jenkins turned away from her, towards the screen. Burns was talking about the locations of the Gladstone gang, running through more photos of their members, his young sidekick glued to the screen enthusiastically. She slid her phone out of her pocket, glanced at the empty screen, then switched it to vibrate and placed it beneath her thigh.

'We picked up a couple of boys last night,' Jenkins said, passing the photos over the table. 'They were seen leaving the factory on the night of the murder. Are any of them familiar to you?'

They scanned the photos, shook their heads.

'What about their names, Rhys Evans and Connor Wilson? Do they mean anything?'

'The Wilson boy isn't known to us,' Burns said. 'Is Rhys any relation to Bronwen Evans?'

'Bronwen's his sister,' Helen said.

'She was running around with Stevie Baird, one of Gladstone's minor operatives, earlier this year. I think she's having his kid. A tenuous link really. He was using her to push his supply, dropped her like a stone when she was charged with possession with intent to supply.'

Jenkins straightened his back. 'So, there is a connection between the Evanses and Bairds?'

'A weak one. She was small-time. Wouldn't give up her supplier in interview, but we had enough intelligence to know where it came from. Nothing to suggest her or her family are involved with the wider gang.'

'What if she's trying to get back into Stevie Baird's good books, especially if she's having his kid?' Jenkins asked. 'We interviewed Rhys Evans last night.'

'You think he was involved in the murder?'

'It's likely whoever killed Sinead left her there and planned to move her later. We can't dismiss the possibility that Rhys was a lookout. An old needle was found on the factory floor, we already know someone used the placed to shoot up. If Sinead was involved with—'

'Sorry, sir,' Burns cut in. 'Are you implying that Sinead was bent?'

'I'm not implying anything. She worked on response, was close to the streets. Her area covered the Rabbit Warren. She'd have been aware of the gang's current set-up. If she was involved in something untoward, it might explain the torture.'

Burns looked wary. 'Isn't this a job for Professional Standards?' The notion of a corrupt police officer clearly left an acidic taste in his mouth.

'It's a line of inquiry we need to bottom out,' Helen said reassuringly. 'If anything comes to light, then obviously we'll take that route.'

'So, it's speculation?'

'At the moment, yes.'

'I see where you're coming from. Her name hasn't been mentioned anywhere though.'

'Try again,' Jenkins said. 'Ask you source handlers to check with their contacts in the field. Make sure they're discreet, we don't want to sully the reputation of a good officer. But if Sinead was involved with one of the gangs, we need to know. It could put other officers at risk, especially if someone thinks she's been talking.'

'You think this could happen again?'

'At the moment, we're treating this as an isolated incident,' Jenkins said. 'But if she was connected, we can't rule out the possibility.'

He pushed out his chair and stood, indicating an end to the meeting.

'I must stress this theory is confidential, to be kept amongst us four until we know more,' Jenkins added.

Helen passed grateful thanks to the others before she followed him out of the room.

A stony silence accompanied them along the corridor.

'I don't like this,' Jenkins said in a low voice when they reached the stairs.

Helen chose her words carefully. 'You heard them, the links are flimsy. We do have other leads to follow up.'

'We're under a lot of pressure here. I have to make some decisions and, I'll be honest, I'm not thrilled about you leading this inquiry, Helen, especially with your background and the family rivalry with Chilli Franks.'

Helen's stomach pitted. She'd been expecting this. Although they hadn't found any direct connection between Chilli Franks and Sinead's murder and the meeting failed to bring them any closer in this regard. 'With respect, I think you're overreacting, sir.'

Jenkins frowned. 'You were SIO on the investigation that put Franks away. You were off sick for eight weeks and, as soon as you return, another officer is dead. We can't ignore the timing.'

She couldn't deny the suggestion haunted her own thoughts. The very idea of Chilli Franks on a killing spree, wielding a personal vendetta against either her or the force didn't bear thinking about. She shook the notion away. No. She wouldn't give in and let the embers of an old case, let alone Chilli Franks, force her off a new investigation. She fought to keep her face impassive. 'It could also be a tragic coincidence. Give me time to explore the evidence.'

When she tried to continue, he lifted a flat hand to silence her. 'I'm sure you know I have a shortage of Senior Investigative Officers. And with DCI· Shoebridge already engaged on a review team, I'm out of alternatives. So, I'm going to let you carry on for now. Though if anything comes to light to prove Franks's involvement, then you'll be removed from the case for the safety of the other officers, immediately.'

CHAPTER 28

Connor stood at the side of the makeshift pitch and placed his hands in his pockets. The little kids were playing football. Again. Running up and down, using their jumpers for goalposts. Four aside. Usually he'd be running with them, dribbling the ball in and out of their legs to show off, or acting as referee if the numbers were odd. But today he didn't feel much like playing football with a bunch of primary-school kids.

He glanced back at the bench where one of the play leaders sat reading a book. Play leaders. Even the title was an insult. Hopefully, if anyone from school passed by, they'd assume he was working there or helping with football skills training. Anything was better than them thinking he was part of the club. His cheeks flushed at the very idea.

He stared up at the iron-grey sky. It was going to rain again soon.

His mother had barely spoken after they left the station last night, apart from to confiscate his phone, tell him he was grounded and to keep away from 'that Evans boy'. She had no idea. She moved him from one area to another, at her whim, and he was supposed to slot in, make new friends, pick up his studies at a new school. Now she wanted to vet his friends.

And if that wasn't enough punishment, she'd frogmarched him to the holiday club that morning, given the play leaders a full account of the events the evening before and asked them to keep an eye on him, much to his shame. 'If you act like a child, you'll be treated like a child,' she'd said. No change there then. He noticed she hadn't mentioned the syringe found at the factory. Thank God. It was bad enough his mother checking his arms, giving him lectures. Maybe he should actually try drugs. That'd give her something to talk about.

The ball came hurtling towards him. Connor jumped, chested it to the floor and kicked it back. Usually a ball took his mind off things. Not now. Today he felt as though he was carrying a boulder across his shoulders. When he tried to relax and clear his head, the grisly figure of the dead woman unwittingly sprang into his mind. He couldn't escape.

He glanced around the park. A woman pushed a pram along the path. A dog walker wandered down to the river, an excited spaniel bounding beside him. A movement behind the trees lining the riverbank caught his attention. A man in a baseball cap, a dark T-shirt. He appeared to be watching the game from afar. It seemed odd to watch from such a distance.

'Okay, last five minutes, guys,' the play leader said. 'Then we head back for lunch.'

A chorus of groans followed from the pitch. Connor looked back at the trees. The man had disappeared.

One of the girls kicked at goal and missed. The ball shot across the park, towards the river.

'I'll get it,' Connor said and jogged across the grass.

The ball rolled in between the trees lining the river. When he reached the bank, it had disappeared out of sight. The dog walker was a spot in the distance now, striding along the bank, watching his dog swimming along beside him.

A movement in his peripheral vision made Connor turn. The man in the baseball cap was back, only twenty metres away. Leaning against the trunk of an old oak, staring at his phone. Although he kept looking up, making sweeping glances at Connor. Too many glances. The hairs on the back of Connor's neck stood on end. He looked away, searched for the ball, all the time keeping half an eye on the man. There was something sinister about him. Something he couldn't put his finger on.

The ball was nestled in the weeds at the edge of the river. He moved sideways down the bank, digging in his heels to keep his balance, and retrieved it. For a split second he lost sight of the man. When he turned back, he'd gone. Connor scooped up the ball and cursed his frayed nerves. Why was he so jumpy? He climbed the bank and started. There he was again. The same black T-shirt, dark jeans. Staring at him from beneath the cap, barely ten metres away. A menthol aroma filled the air. Connor quickened his step. As he did so, the man moved towards him. Connor's heart pounded his chest. He could see the kids in the distance now, gathering up their jumpers in readiness to return to the centre for lunch. He moved faster, checked behind. A gust of wind blew, knocking off the man's baseball cap in its wake. It stopped him in his tracks, just long enough for Connor to break into a run. Never had he been so pleased to see Cathy, the play leader, as he was now.

'You okay?' Cathy said. 'You look like you've seen a ghost.'

'I'm fine,' he muttered and pushed past her, back towards the safe compound of the community centre.

CHAPTER 29

Back in her office, Helen took her time updating her policy log, diarising the day's events and recording the basis for her decisions, a mandatory requirement for all Senior Investigating Officers leading a murder investigation.

According to Bracken Hall, Natalia Kowalski had taken a week's leave and finished work on Tuesday. When Pemberton contacted the retreat Sinead was booked into, they'd confirmed an N Kowalski had also booked a room for the same dates. She arrived on Wednesday morning, a few minutes after 11 a.m., they remembered it because the rooms weren't normally available until after 2 p.m. and she'd requested an early check-in. He'd spoken with the manager, taken time to track her movements. Another member of staff served her in the restaurant at 1.10 p.m. when she billed her order to her room. At 3 p.m. she'd received a massage in the spa and paid by credit card. Derbyshire was a couple of hours' drive north from Hampton. Which meant she was out of the way and accounted for on Wednesday, when Sinead was killed.

Natalia checked out of the hotel today at 9.35 a.m. and that's where the trail dried up.

What was she doing booking into the same hotel as Sinead and, if she was innocent, why had she ignored their messages? Sinead's death was reported nationwide. Even at the outside chance her phone wasn't working, she'd likely have heard the news.

The secret phone they used to keep in touch continued to niggle Helen. She'd instigated a search, but Natalia's phone was switched off, untraceable. Police ANPR cameras were looking out for her car on the motorways. She wasn't due back at work until Tuesday and her colleagues had no idea where she was. Once again, they were playing the waiting game.

Sinead appeared to adore her family and loved her job. If she was involved in illicit dealings, she'd be risking everything dear to her. Often, people coping with such a dilemma became anxious, but none of her colleagues had mentioned this when interviewed. Moreover, Sinead was painted as a strong officer, who appeared to put aside her home life when she was at work.

Had she approached a loan shark and something gone wrong? And what role, if any, did Natalia Kowalski play in all of this?

Sinead's phone records suggested she exchanged a lot of messages with her neighbour. Perhaps Yvette Edwards could shed light on Sinead's connection with Natalia Kowalski.

The trill of her mobile broke her thought process. She checked the screen, surprised to see Matthew's name flash up.

'Matt, Hi! Is everything okay?'

'Hi, Mum. Yeah, it's fine. You?'

Confusion riddled her. Her eldest son never phoned. It was a job to get him to send a text message when he was at a mate's house and going to be late home.

'I'm fine, thanks, darling,' she said, fighting to keep her voice even. 'Are you having a good time?'

'Yeah, I was… err…'

'What is it?'

'I connected to the Wi-Fi at the centre and a news bulletin came up on my phone. About a cop that died in Hampton on Wednesday.'

Shit, shit, shit. She'd tried to reach her mother that

morning. Meant to call again and, with everything going on, it slipped her mind. 'Oh, it's a new case we've got on,' she said, lightly. 'I meant to mention it to your gran last night. Nothing to worry about.'

'Is it the same people?' He cleared his throat awkwardly. 'As last time?'

'No, darling, this is a separate case. Not at all linked to the last one.' The lie slipped out too easily. She wrestled with her conscience. She was telling it for the right reasons, to reassure her son, but, still, it was a lie. While she was pretty sure Sinead's murder wasn't linked to Operation Aspen, she couldn't be positive. Not until the murderer was apprehended. 'It was a female officer, killed off duty,' she added hastily.

The line went quiet.

'Are you enjoying the holiday?' Helen said to change the subject. She wanted to keep him chatting, check his tone to be sure his mind was put to rest and the only way to do that was to talk off-piste.

'Yeah. We're building another raft this afternoon.'

'Wow! That'll give you plenty of experience before your cadet field trip next weekend.'

'I know. Can't wait for that!'

The excitement in his voice at the mention of the Air Cadets jarred her. Only last year, Matthew, who'd always wanted to build aeroplanes, declared he no longer wanted to build them, he wanted to fly them. She'd never forget the day he told her: sitting at the top of the stairs outside his bedroom, barely able to move, winded by the shock. And, unbeknown to him, a part of her was still reeling. Losing John, so young, in a freak flying accident set her against anything air-bound. And now her eldest son's ambition was to follow in his father's footsteps. How could she be sure history wouldn't repeat itself? But his passion was strong, and he was stubborn, just like his dad. She soon realised it was either a case of supporting or losing him. So, she'd enrolled him into the Air Cadets, rather hoping it would put him off, and, much to her dismay, he'd thrived. Even his grades at school were improving.

'Good for you,' she said with as much enthusiasm as she could muster. 'Where's Gran, and Robert?'

'At the lodge. I'm on my way back there.'

'Ah. Do me a favour, would you? Have Gran ring me? I'd like to tell them about the case I'm working on myself. No point in worrying anyone unnecessarily.'

'Sure.' He sounded distant. She'd lost him already.

'Okay, have a great afternoon. I'll see you when you get back tomorrow.'

'Bye, Mum.'

Helen ended the call. Perhaps she could still catch her mother before she noticed the case on the news or heard about it from elsewhere.

CHAPTER 30

An hour later, Helen was finishing up her notes when Pemberton entered, carrying a steaming coffee. 'Thought you could do with this,' he said.

'You know me so well.' She smiled, took a sip. 'I was thinking about Sinead's neighbour,' she said, glancing down at her notes. 'Let's make another appointment to see her, check the facts.'

He nodded.

'Any news on Miss Kowalski?'

'Not yet. We can't cell-site her phone, it's still off.'

'What about her brother?'

'He hasn't heard from her since before his holiday.'

He closed the door. 'Just wondered how you got on with the organised crime bods?'

Helen cast her mind back to the stuffy meeting room, Jenkins's warning afterwards. 'Well, if I was a gambler, I wouldn't put money on a connection,' she said, and recapped the meeting.

'So, the Chilli theory is officially dead?' His eyes shone as he laughed. 'Excuse the pun.'

'Looks that way.'

'You don't sound convinced.'

'Oh, I don't know. I can't see what he would gain by killing another cop, but Chilli's unpredictable. If he is responsible, he's hiring his own people, going it alone.'

A movement in the incident room caught her attention. Dark had dropped a phone into its cradle and jumped up. They both rushed out.

'Has something happened?' Helen said.

'Two minutes ago, Miss Kowalski's Volkswagen Polo pinged a camera outside Worthington,' Dark said. 'Looks like she's taken the country route home.'

The entrance door clicked open. Everyone's eyes turned to Spencer, who squeezed in through a tiny crack, closing the door firmly behind him.

'Everything okay?' Pemberton asked.

Spencer lowered his voice. 'Blane O'Donnell's outside,' he said, looking past him to Helen.

'What, here?' She glanced at their murder wall: the plethora of photos of Sinead, the detailed injury shots taken at the autopsy. Blane would have undoubtedly seen worse during his career, but this was his wife, the mother of his children. No partner should ever see a loved one in that state.

She thanked her lucky stars for the lock on the door. 'How did he access the main entrance? All the external passcodes have been changed.'

'Someone must have let him in. He's asking to see you.'

She looked back at Pemberton and Dark. 'Okay, I want you both to get out to Natalia Kowalski's home. Bring her in for questioning if you can,' she said. 'I'll go and speak with Blane.'

Helen could feel her team watch her as she approached the door to the corridor. She cast a brief glance back at their murder wall. It was at the front of the room, flanked by a map of the industrial estate and another of the housing estate where Sinead lived. If she opened the door fully, as she usually would, the edge of the boards would be visible.

She pulled the door ajar and slid through the gap, mirroring Spencer's movement minutes before.

'What are you doing here, Blane?' she said, relieved to find the corridor behind him empty.

'I had some paperwork to drop off for a new course next week.' He glanced down the hallway towards the training department.

'You should be with your children.'

'That's what my sarge said. I thought, since I was here, I'd check to see if there was any news.' He looked past her at the closed door and eyed the keypad. 'Didn't know you guys worked in a secure unit nowadays.'

'Why don't we find somewhere to talk?' She guided him away from the incident room. Pemberton and Dark would be hurrying out any minute. Plus, she didn't want him to catch a snippet of information through the thinly plastered walls. If Helen had learnt anything in a major inquiry, it was to control the flow of information to the press and the family.

She led him into a small room that had originally been planned as the DCI's office when this new station had been built. The idea of being stuck down here, away from her team, during the midst of a major case left Helen cold and when she took the job, she'd asked for some changes so she could have an office in the corner of the incident room, on hand.

Musty air gushed out as she opened the door. Boxes were stacked on the unused desk in the middle, a couple of chairs were pushed to the side. She indicated for Blane to sit. He declined, folding his arms uncomfortably across his chest.

'What's the latest?' he asked.

'We have several leads to follow up.' The discovery of the remains of Sinead's fingers in her recovered handbag hadn't been released publicly and she saw no benefit to passing on this information.

'I heard you were interviewing someone.'

Helen baulked. 'Pardon?'

'On the news, it said a man was helping with inquiries. We all know what that really means.'

She cursed Jenkins's hasty move to put out a statement,

to reassure the public, at whatever cost. 'I can't talk about it, I'm sorry.'

He closed his eyes and when he opened them, his face folded. 'Let me help, please?'

'You know I can't let you do that.'

'So, I get my next update on the local news channel, is that it?'

'You didn't want a liaison officer, Blane. We'll update you as soon as we can.'

'What about the kids you were trying to trace? They weren't mentioned on the news bulletin this morning. Does that mean you've spoken with them?'

'Blane—'

'Please!' His face crumpled again, desperate. 'I need to know. I'm going insane.'

It was always tricky to liaise with families after the loss of a loved one in traumatic circumstances. A fine balance, to release enough information to reassure, keep them on side, without causing alarm. It was even more difficult when they had the inside track and knew what was going on behind the scenes. 'I understand your frustrations. Really, I do.' Helen stared at him squarely when a thought nudged her. 'Were you aware that last month's payment to Bracken Hall wasn't made?'

'What?' He looked astounded. 'No. I'll speak with them. Sinead had power of attorney and controlled her mother's account. I'm sure it's just a problem with the bank.'

'That's what Sinead told them.'

He shot her a quizzical look. 'I knew it was running down, but there should be enough in there to tick along. Sinead would have told me otherwise.' He seemed convinced. Perhaps he didn't realise how bad her mother's finances were.

'Okay. I can't tell you any more right now.'

'We're both cops. Doesn't that mean anything?'

'I'll pretend you didn't say that.'

He took a breath, his face contrite. 'I'm sorry. I want to help.'

'Have you given us every contact you can think of?'

'Yes.'

'And you don't have anything else to add?'

'No.'

'Then go home, Blane. Leave us to it. I'll be in touch as soon as I have some news.'

***

It was a humid afternoon, sticky and uncomfortable in the car. They needed another rainstorm to clear the air.

Pemberton wound down the window. 'I thought she would have been here by now.'

'Maybe she stopped off somewhere on the way,' Dark said.

He stretched out his back. Ivy crept up the front of the terraced house converted to flats beside him, snaking around the sash windows. The curtains of the ground-floor flat Natalia Kowalski rented were closed. They'd tried knocking when they arrived. When there was no answer, they'd scoured the streets for her Volkswagen, which was also missing.

Dark looked down the road, one way and another. 'You don't think she's gone to her brother's first, do you?'

'Don't know.' He got out of the car and wandered up and down the road, double-checking each of the parked cars, then tried the side roads nearby. He was about to give up, to call the office, when a black Volkswagen Polo rounded the corner.

The driver cruised past him, seemingly oblivious to his presence, and reversed into a parking space further down the road. Pemberton gave Dark a nod and they moved down to the car. The driver had climbed out and was fiddling with the lock on the boot when she noticed them.

'Natalia Kowalski?' Pemberton asked.

The boot door opened to reveal a small suitcase.

The woman looked at them both. When she didn't speak, he showed his badge again and she nodded.

'Miss Kowalski, I wonder if you'd accompany us to the station?' Pemberton asked. 'We have some questions we'd like to ask you about Sinead O'Donnell.'

CHAPTER 31

Blane placed a key into the lock of 21 Richardson Close and clicked the door open. A familiar blue carpeted hallway stretched out before him. Children's shoes were scattered to the side. A lump filled his throat. The last time he crossed this threshold he'd been met with the chatter of his children, the babble of the television, Sinead's music in the background. Today the house was screamingly quiet.

Sinead's pink fleece hung on the coat rack, sandwiched between Ava's summer raincoat and Thomas's denim jacket. He pulled the fleece off the hook, touched it to his nose and inhaled a bouquet of fruity perfume. Sinead's smell. Clean, fresh. How could her scent be so strong when her body was no longer there? Tears blurred his vision, tipping down his face, soaking into the soft material. He slid to the floor, buried his face into the fleece and sobbed.

He wasn't sure how long he sat there. For two days he'd fought back the tears. For his mother. For the children. Now his strength was waning, trickling away, water disappearing down a plughole, and the wrench of death grew stronger by the day. He'd lost his wife. His children their mother. And he couldn't even begin to fill the void she'd left behind.

Eventually, his breaths evened. He lifted his head and looked down the hallway, through the open door into the kitchen. He could still see the sparkle in Sinead's eyes when they'd first viewed this house. She'd fallen in love with the kitchen as soon as she'd seen it, with its granite work surfaces, double cooker, central workstation, and enough room for their pine family table in the corner to boot. Many a time he'd arrived home from a long shift to find her trying out a new dish, singing along to Ed Sheeran as she stirred a pan. It was her happy place, her relaxation.

Two days had passed. Two days in which he'd been treated like a member of the public and told the police were following up leads, dealing with inquiries, interviewing witnesses. Where was the camaraderie? Cops looked after cops. Or they always had when he'd joined.

Even his colleagues in training seemed sketchy when he'd visited the office earlier. And the homicide suite was placed under lock and key.

He'd trained as a detective and he knew Sinead better than anyone, yet they wouldn't even let him assist, off the record. His chest hardened. Well, if they weren't prepared to share with him what they knew, he'd find out for himself.

He opened his rucksack, shoved the fleece inside and wandered into the front room. The lump in his throat expanded. This was their family home, with the portrait of the four of them above the fireplace, the bookshelf stocked with children's books on the far wall, the pine chest that doubled up as a toy box in the corner. His eyes rested on the oversized sofa, a wedding present from his mum. They were so excited when it arrived, bouncing up and down on it, standing back, commenting on how nice it looked, how soft the leather felt. Later, they'd christened it, their lovemaking deeper, blooming with the opportunity their future together presented. That was in the early days, when they could enjoy sex with wild abandon, before they had to hush each other, conscious of waking the children. But even in recent years, they'd cuddled up on it to watch television, Sinead resting her head on his shoulder.

A lilac My Little Pony poked its nose out of the top of

the chest in the corner; a soft Peppa Pig toy was propped up against the side. He pulled open his rucksack, placed the soft toy inside. It would be a while before he could bring the kids home. Maybe they would feel calmer having more of their toys with them. He opened the chest, collected a couple of trucks, then crossed to the bookcase and lifted out a few *Horrid Henry* books.

Upstairs, he picked up changes of clothes for his children.

When he'd reached his own bedroom, the bag was brimming. He dropped it to the floor, his heart contracting as he looked around at the pale blue walls, the Laura Ashley bedcovers, the Jack Vettriano print he'd bought Sinead for her last birthday on the far wall. The dressing table was still littered with her hairdryer, straighteners and perfume bottles.

Somehow, he expected the room to look different now Sinead was gone. But apart from the odd ornament out of place, or photo askew, a legacy of the police search, it was unchanged. In the en suite, he spotted a black elastic hair tie on the side of the sink, beside her toothbrush. There was a time when they'd been transparent, told each other everything. Not anymore. There was something Sinead hadn't told him. Something crucial. Something that had cost Sinead her life.

A secret.

The search team would have seized her laptop, outstanding post, address books, anything they felt might provide some clue to her associations and movements in the days leading up to her murder. But they didn't know Sinead. Not like he did.

He opened her wardrobe, ran his fingers across dresses, skirts, shirts, trousers, all arranged haphazardly. She'd never been one for order. She tidied the living space relentlessly, shoving everything into cupboards, wardrobes, drawers and boxes. Open a cupboard and invariably items fell out. He dug a hand in each of the pockets of her coats. Tried the pockets of her trousers and pulled out a used tissue and a stray hair tie.

He turned his attention to her bedside cabinet, moving aside her clock, a tube of hand cream, a half-used blister pack of paracetamol. At her dressing table, he worked through each drawer in turn. He wasn't sure what he was looking for. Some clue about her recent life. He pulled out the bottom drawer, pressed his face to the floor and peered into the gap behind. Apart from a layer of dust and a few stray hairs, it was empty.

He grabbed her jewellery box, moving aside the gold chain he'd bought her for their first wedding anniversary: her father's wedding ring. A nest of bracelets and necklaces. Where would Sinead hide things?

A tap at the front door stopped him in his tracks. The jewellery box snapped shut. He peered around the curtain edge to the empty road outside.

Another knock, harder this time. A distant voice he didn't recognise shouted out. It sounded like they were calling through the letter box.

Blane lifted the rucksack and made for the stairs.

A man in a striped shirt and navy slacks was standing on the front step when he opened the door, a bag hanging over one shoulder.

'Sorry to bother you,' he said. 'I was leaving next door and saw the car.'

'And you are?'

'Andrew Burton, *Hampton Herald*. I wondered if we could—'

'Get off my property,' Blane said, squeezing the words through his teeth.

'If we could just—'

'Now!' He slammed the door and leant up against it, gobsmacked at the sheer temerity of the journalist.

Another knock. 'I think you misunderstand me. I'm here—'

The journalist prattled on. Anger coursed through Blane's veins. He turned back to the door, ready to give the reporter a piece of his mind, when a single thought stopped him. The media. If the DCI wasn't going to let him assist, he was pretty sure the press would. But not here, not now. He wasn't interested in one lone reporter. What he needed, was an audience.

CHAPTER 32

Helen stood beside Pemberton, transfixed at the screen in front of her, watching the interview play out.

Natalia Kowalski was a short woman with cropped dark hair and brown eyes. In her plaid shirt with the sleeves rolled back, she looked more like an A-level student wandering out of school than a twenty-eight-year-old carer at a prestigious nursing home. Pemberton had said she'd barely uttered a word when she'd arrived home earlier to find them waiting and willingly agreed to accompany them to the police station.

Now, sat at the Formica table, with a faraway, almost trance-like, look on her face, it was difficult to decipher whether she was genuinely in a state of shock or carefully hiding something.

'How long have you known Sinead?' Dark asked.

'I met her when I started at the nursing home, nine months ago. Her mum, Maeve, is one of the residents I look after.'

'Were you close friends?'

Natalia bit her lip. A white ring surrounded the tooth sinking into the skin. 'It's awkward.'

'Take your time.'

Her gaze darted about the room, as if she wasn't sure what to say. 'I'm guessing since you've found me, you've seen the messages on her phone. So, you'll know.' Her eyes filled. 'We were very close.'

Helen stilled.

'I'm not sure I follow,' Dark said. 'Can you explain your relationship with Sinead?'

A tear streamed down Natalia's face. 'We started meeting up outside of work about four months ago,' Natalia said with a sniff. 'I liked Sinead a lot. I think she liked me too. She knew I wanted more, but it was complicated. She had children, a husband, and her mum to think of.' She swallowed. 'I was taking it slow, giving us time to get to know one another. I had hoped that—' Her voice cut. She looked away, dried her cheeks with the back of her cuff.

'Did you meet regularly outside of work?'

'Once or twice a week. Sinead couldn't always get away. We spoke on the phone most days though.' Another tear meandered down the side of her nose. 'I'm sorry.'

'It's okay,' Dark said with a gentle smile. She offered her a tissue and they spent some time going through dates and locations where they met.

'Barbara, the owner at Bracken Hall, is very strict about personal friendships with clients,' Natalia said. 'Sinead was concerned about her finding out about us. She didn't want me to lose my job. I'm one of the few people she trusted with her mother, you hear so many horror stories. So, we always met outside of town.'

'When did you last see each other?'

'On Friday. We went for a drive, out into the country. It was my lunch hour.' Another tear plopped onto the table in front on her.

'How did Sinead seem on Friday?'

'Okay. The usual. She liked a joke, wanted to have fun.' A longing glance to the side. 'Our meet-ups gave her the opportunity to forget her worries and be herself for a while. It was good to see her relax.'

Dark opened a buff file and laid out photos of the boys and

the man at the ATM and asked if she knew or had seen any of them before. Natalia studied them for some time before she shook her head. When she asked about Sinead's debt to the nursing home, the young woman's eyes bulged. She clearly had no idea. 'Did Sinead ever mention a factory called Billings?' Dark asked.

'No.' Another tear spilled out. 'Is it true they tortured her?' Her voice was barely a whisper. She pressed the tissue to her face.

'Where did you hear that?'

'On the news. I don't understand. I mean, who would do that?'

'That's what we mean to find out. Did she ever mention an argument, perhaps someone she'd fallen out with? Or maybe someone that held a grudge against her?'

'No, everyone liked Sinead. When she walked into a room, she brightened it up, even though she was struggling inside.' Her face pained. 'I was floored when I saw it on the news yesterday evening. Couldn't believe it. Had to double-check online. Then I didn't know what to do. We were supposed to be meeting for lunch at the hotel. When I couldn't get hold of her, I thought she'd been caught up. By the evening, I started to worry. Then when I turned on the television...' She shook her head, face tight, reliving the moment. 'I switched off my phone, stayed at the hotel. Sat up all night wondering what to do.'

'Why didn't you contact us? We left several messages for you.'

'I don't know.' She sniffed. 'What good would it do? Sinead wanted to keep our close friendship secret from everyone when she was alive. Blane knew I was gay. She worried he might suspect something, didn't want to upset him or the children. She wouldn't appreciate me turning up now after she'd died and talking about how close we were.'

A stray fly buzzed around the light bulb.

'Did Sinead ever talk about her family life?' Dark asked.

'Not much. She didn't like to. There were a few odd comments. I knew she'd fallen out of love with Blane.'

'She told you that?'

'Well, not those exact words. She was always hinting though. She said he was a good father, worked hard for his family. But she felt suffocated.'

'In what way?'

'He liked them to do things together. Everything was "about the family". Sinead had a strong sense of loyalty, to the point of guilt. She hated discussing her personal life, it was a job to get her to talk. I was hoping the retreat would give us some time away from it all, you know, give her a chance to find time for herself, maybe think about the future. She couldn't carry on the way she was going, she'd have a breakdown.'

Helen stepped away from the screen and wondered how Natalia would feel if she knew Blane had booked the trip, as a break for Sinead. How he'd planned to join her. She imagined him making his way to the hotel to surprise his wife, only to find them both there together.

A glance back. Natalia was detailing her movements on Wednesday so they could corroborate them with those on file. It was understandable the two women might meet discreetly, to keep their friendship away from Bracken Hall. The nursing home made it clear they disproved of personal friendships between clients and staff; Sinead cherished her mother, and wouldn't want to lose Natalia as her mother's carer. But Sinead had kept a separate phone and taken exceptional steps to keep their relationship away from friends and family.

Once again, Natalia described Sinead as a private person. Blane didn't know about her relationship with Natalia and neither did Mia, her colleague at work. Nor Yvette, her neighbour. Helen was beginning to wonder if Sinead was ever truly open and honest with anyone.

CHAPTER 33

Helen's mobile phone was ringing when she arrived back in her office, the familiar *Dad's Army* theme tune signalling it was her mother. She clicked to answer.

A warm, smooth voice greeted her: the relaxed tone of someone on holiday. 'Hello, darling. How are you?'

She clearly doesn't know about the case, Helen thought, relieved that Matthew had kept his word. 'Good, thanks. I hear you're building rafts this afternoon.'

A brief chuckle. 'Well, the boys are. I'm going to catch up with some reading. How are things there? Matt said you wanted to talk to me.'

'Oh, it's nothing really. We have a new case on, a murder. The victim was a cop. I wanted to let you know I was all right.' Helen squirmed in her chair.

'Oh, I see.' The line crackled. It was a moment before her mother spoke again and when she did, she sounded agitated. 'Anyone we know?' Having been a police wife for most of her life, Jane Lavery had many friends in the force.

'Her name was Sinead O'Donnell, a young PC. I doubt you'd know her. She was off duty at the time.'

'And you're heading the inquiry?'

'Yes. You might see or hear something on the national news. I didn't want you to worry.'

'Is that wise? Putting you in charge… after what happened in March.'

Here we go. 'Mum, this has got nothing to do with the last case,' Helen said. 'It's a separate inquiry.'

'But… so soon.'

Helen rubbed her forehead. 'This is what I do, Mum. You know that.' This wasn't the time for an in-depth discussion about career choices. 'I don't want the boys to fret. Is Robert there?'

'He's popped out to get another bottle of cola.'

Pemberton tapped her office door. She beckoned him in.

'Okay, well, will you tell him for me? Make sure he knows there's nothing to worry about. It's a case I'm working, same as any other.'

'All right.'

'Thanks. I have to go, I'll see you when you get home tomorrow.' She placed her phone on the desk. Hopefully, her mother would have time to process the information and calm down before she returned home.

'You need to see this,' Pemberton said.

He moved across to her laptop and worked the keys. A freeze-frame of the side of Blane O'Donnell filled a box in the middle of the screen. He was sitting in the driver seat of his car. A hanging basket in the background filled with purple petunias told her he was on his mother's drive.

Pemberton pressed play.

Blane climbed out of the car, turned and approached the cameras. A Peppa Pig soft toy poked out of the top of the rucksack he placed at his feet. He held up his hands, hushed the crowd in front. Waited until they quietened before he spoke. 'My beautiful wife, Sinead O'Donnell, was brutally murdered on Wednesday evening.' He paused. A camera flashed in the background. 'This is a very difficult time for my family, not least because we know whoever did this is still out there. That's why I'd like to personally request the help of both the public and the press in the search for my wife's killer.'

He faced the camera, front on. 'Somebody out there knows something. Maybe they're shielding the offender. Maybe they saw something they're not sure about. Anything at all, however small or insignificant you may think it is, please get in touch. We need your help.'

He spoke eloquently, without hesitation, like a politician delivering a prepared speech.

'That's it.' He picked up the rucksack, held up his free hand and said, 'Thank you.'

A stream of questions followed him up the driveway. Blane ignored all of them and disappeared into his mother's house.

The footage ended.

'He's good,' Helen said.

'Hmm. Can't help wondering what he's playing at though.'

The footage returned to the beginning. Helen looked back at Blane's freeze-framed profile in the car. 'He's been careful. Hasn't criticised the police investigation. It might encourage other witnesses to come out of the woodwork.'

'Vicki Gardener is doing her nut. Wants to speak with you urgently.'

It wasn't surprising the press office were up in arms. Usually, they'd consider asking a victim's family to face the cameras a week or so into an investigation, a planned event, possibly as part of a reconstruction, when they'd exhausted all other inquiries. Blane would know that. 'The timing's interesting,' she said.

'He wants to play a part, root the murderer out.'

She pressed play, ran through the footage again. They'd released Natalia Kowalski earlier, the hotel confirmed her movements, she had an alibi for the day of Sinead's murder and appeared to co-operate fully, even handing over her phone for examination. But the clandestine nature of their relationship and the apparent need for secrecy still puzzled Helen. Natalia referred to Sinead as falling out of love with Blane, a description at odds with others. Was that how she justified her intentions towards Sinead, or was there more in the background they were yet to uncover? Did Blane have an affair in the dim and distant past? Was he trying to root out anyone in particular?

'I take it we've exhausted our inquiries into Blane's background?' she asked Pemberton.

'He was at work, carrying out an inventory of the gym equipment. A colleague was with him.'

'I'm aware of that.'

'There's nothing to suggest he was involved.'

'Take a look anyway, will you? In fact, dig into both of their pasts. Old flames, that sort of thing. Let's check they haven't got any jilted ex-lovers or any other secrets we should be aware of.'

CHAPTER 34

Connor lay back on his bed and stared at the ceiling. Did the detectives question Rhys last night too? He desperately hoped not. Because Rhys would blame him for bringing the police to their door. He'd told him to tell no one about what they'd seen, and Connor hadn't intended to. His hand had been forced and now the whole episode was distorted and knotted and he didn't know what to do. Rhys would be angry. Great, his only friend...

He turned it over and over in his head, the speculation chewing away at him. He had no way of knowing, no way of finding out because, as soon as they got back from the station last night, his mother had confiscated his phone. She'd taken his laptop too. 'I'm not having you messaging that Evans boy,' his mother said when she demanded he hand them over. 'I'll keep them until you go back to school on Monday. The break will do you good.' No laptop. No gaming. No YouTubing. Nothing to distract him. It was like purgatory.

As if on cue, his mother called up the stairs. 'Connor, put the bins out please.'

Another job. She'd been like this since they arrived home yesterday. 'You can do the washing-up, make up for what you've put me through today. Tomorrow, you can cut the grass.' Where was the sympathy? Where was the care? It didn't seem to matter he'd been in a factory where a woman had been brutally murdered. She'd brushed that aside, focused on him lying about where he was. As far as she was concerned, he'd got himself mixed up in something he shouldn't have and needed to accept his punishment. When the detectives mentioned counselling, she'd scoffed. He wondered how she would feel if she knew he'd seen the dead body. If she was aware the grisly sight of that woman haunted his dreams.

'Connor!' Her voice rose a decibel.

He sighed, climbed off the bed and descended the stairs. His mother was watching yet another soap.

'It's recycling week. Blue and red bins,' she called as he passed the front room.

It was already dark, the low clouds signalling an early night. He pulled on his trainers, stepped outside and waited for the security light to illuminate the garden. Rolled his eyes when it failed. Damn light worked when it felt like it. He collected the bins and dragged them along the back of the house, through the aperture between their terrace and the next and out to the front. The road was empty, curtains on the houses opposite pulled tightly shut. It was nearly 9.30 p.m., after all.

He parked the bins under a street light, turned to go, when he heard a low mewl. Then another. It came from the tree in the front garden next door and, when he looked up, he saw a black and white cat balanced precariously on one of the lower branches. He'd seen the cat before, it even tried to come into their house a week ago and his mother had shooed it away. 'Don't encourage it,' she'd said. 'We'll never get rid of it.' Connor liked animals, he'd have loved a dog or a cat for company, but his mother always refused. 'You need to be at home to look after a pet,' she'd say. 'We're not there enough.' The cat mewled again as he stepped closer. It took a step and wobbled, anxiously looking down.

'Here,' Connor said. 'Let me help you.'

It shrunk back as he reached up.

'It's okay,' he said, tentatively reaching out and stroking its head. The animal rubbed its chin against his fingers.

He reached up another hand, took a grip and lifted it out of the tree, stroking its soft back in his arms.

'It's all right. You're safe now.' He stroked it again, placed it down and watched it scamper across the road towards a house opposite.

Connor retraced his steps. He was closing the gate when a hand shot out of the darkness and pressed against his mouth. Dragging him back. Muffling his screams to tiny squeals. The menthol aroma of throat sweets. It was him, the man from the park earlier.

Connor wrestled to free himself. His heart pounded his chest.

Warm breath on his ear. 'You're the kid from the factory.'

A scream rose from the pit of Connor's gut. He tried to release his arms, but the man's hold was firm.

'I won't hurt you.' The voice was gruff. Desperate. 'As long as you tell me what you saw.'

He'd already caused Rhys's family enough grief by talking to the police. He sure as hell wasn't about to speak to anyone else.

The man's grip tightened.

Connor gulped, mustering every ounce of energy. Then lifted a leg to kick out. The man was too quick. He twisted, dodging the heel of Connor's trainer. Stumbled slightly. Set his foot down, just in time for Connor to drive his heel into it. He jolted back, loosening his grip for a split second as he tried to regain balance. Long enough for Connor to wriggle out and run to the back door.

As soon as he was inside, Connor fumbled with the lock and pulled across the bolt. Choking on his breaths, he rushed to the front and checked the door was secure, then doubled over.

'All done?' his mother's voice called out.

She'd thought their trip to the police station yesterday was an end to the episode. As did he. Until now. He should tell her, alert the police. But how was he to explain what happened outside, especially when he couldn't make sense of it himself? Who was that man and why was he here? His stomach twisted, the dilemma wringing it over and over.

Rhys would know what to do. He needed to find a way to contact him.

'Yeah. I'm going up to bed,' he said, battling to keep his voice even. And with that he clambered up the stairs.

CHAPTER 35

The bedsprings creaked as Blane turned onto his side. The street light outside seeped through the old swathes of curtain material, casting spooky shadows across the peeling wallpaper. This was one of only a few rooms left to be decorated and no matter what he did he couldn't seem to eradicate the smell of old wallpaper paste.

He pictured the throng of press earlier. They'd been enthusiastic, keen to listen to his speech. He imagined it going out on the major news channels later that evening, lighting up online sites. Hopefully, someone would come forward, respond to his plea and contact the incident room, although he couldn't be sure the DCI would let him know. He needed to find another way to delve into Sinead's secret.

He climbed out of bed, toes curling on the bare boards, tugged his robe off the back of the door and pulled it over his shoulders. It was 3.53 a.m. The soft rumble of his mother's intermittent snores became louder as he navigated the landing. Blane shuffled past her room and entered the next one along, where his children were sleeping.

Thomas was on his back, his face turned away, a bare arm hanging out of the side of his bed. Ava was coiled into a tight ball, her curls sprawled across the pillow. She'd wriggled onto her side to expose Peppa Pig's tail on the back of her pyjama top. He crept into the room, folded Thomas's arm back under the duvet. Pulled the covers over Ava. They usually had their own rooms at his mother's, they stayed over so often, but with the other rooms partially decorated, space was at a premium. He should take them home soon.

He tiptoed down the stairs, carefully avoiding the creaky steps at the bottom.

Moonlight streamed into the kitchen. He flicked a switch, illuminating the soft under-cupboard lighting, and set the kettle to boil. The room still needed a refit and, while the kettle coughed and sputtered into action, he glanced at the wooden cupboards, the laminate work surface, the deep country-style sink. They'd had a similar sink at home when he was young. He could remember his mother pulling up a chair to it after they'd made a cake together, letting him wash up after he'd licked out the cake bowl.

Sinead had baked with their children. Only last week, he'd arrived home to find Ava sitting on the work surface, swinging her legs, licking a spatula covered in mixture and Thomas at the sink, his hands immersed in mounds of bubbles. The image brought a fresh wave of tears to his eyes.

Would his children remember cooking with their mother? Her walking them to school and taking time off work to watch their assemblies? Or would those special moments be forgotten, their brains too young to solidify them?

Steam rose into the air. Blane didn't notice, didn't hear the kettle switching itself off, his gaze now resting on the broom cupboard in the corner. The cupboard where he'd stored the bag Dick brought earlier: the contents of Sinead's work locker.

Dick's words rang out in his ears. 'You might want to do that later, laddie. There's some personal stuff in there.'

He opened the kitchen door, glanced down the hallway, listened a second.

The plastic crackled as he retrieved the bag from the cupboard. He lifted it onto the table. The first thing he spotted inside was the single epaulette, the silver numbers of Sinead's badge that were pinned onto it glinting in the low lighting: 236. For seven years, that had been her collar number. She'd inherited it from a detective called Noel Rogers, who retired the year before she joined. That's how it worked in the police, the numbers passed along. Blane had known Noel well and they'd joked many a time about the contrast between his love for the gym and hers for all things culinary; the station gym was somewhere Sinead only frequented when the annual fitness tests were due.

He placed the epaulette on the table and pulled out Sinead's shower bag, her pink jogging bottoms, and then lifted out a clean white shirt, the creases crisp from the iron. Police officers always carried a spare shirt in their locker, you never knew when one might get torn in an altercation or sprayed with blood or other bodily fluids at an accident. A grey towel, one from their own bathroom, was beneath, followed by a shoe buffer. A red make-up bag contained a single lipstick, a palette of blush. Sinead always wore make-up but went for a minimalist approach at work. Another epaulette shifted in the bottom of the bag. Blane lifted it out and ran his thumb over the numbers when he noticed the number three was missing. It must have grown loose. He grabbed the bag, turned it upside down and shook it. The silver number rattled on the table as it dropped out. Closely followed by another blaze of silver.

Blane moved the pin aside and gathered up the other item. A silver necklace with a Celtic-style heart. The delicate chain slipped around his fingers.

He lowered himself into a chair, eyes glued to the chain. Where had this come from? Because it sure as hell hadn't come from him.

CHAPTER 36

Helen checked the illuminated digits on her bedside clock. It was almost 6 a.m. She rolled over to face the space beside her. If she concentrated, she could still hear the distinctive bellow of her late husband's laugh, feel the bristles of his beard as they kissed. The memories unearthed a longing deep inside.

He'd never seen his boys grow and become the young men they were today: didn't know she'd joined the police force. They'd spent more years apart than they had together now, yet he still felt integral to her life. Oh, she'd had the odd fling since, away from her children. Until recently. Only one man had rivalled John's closeness and earned the right to be introduced to her family. And now he was dead too, killed on their last investigation.

Dean's dark features and athletic bearing couldn't have been more different to John's amusing face and wiry frame, but he'd dug deep and captured her heart the same.

A tear slipped down her cheek. She reached out a hand, stroked the creases out of the pillow beside her. She'd been looking forward to having the house to herself this week, to focus on settling back into work, although without her family here it felt empty.

Her boys were growing fast. Matthew would be gone in

a couple of years, Robert soon after. Leaving her mother and she in the house together.

In many ways, she was lucky. Her mother was her closest friend, her confidante. She made a point of not interfering and retreated to her adjoining flat to give them privacy. While Helen had been off work, she'd been careful to give her space. They trundled along, their lives revolving around the children. Helen knew she would never be able to do this job without her help. In return, Jane Lavery relished the time with her grandchildren. The arrangement suited them both.

Though, without the children, things would inevitably change and she was pretty sure sharing a home with their mother wasn't a prospect any other thirty-something woman dreamt of.

She wondered how different things would be if Dean hadn't died.

What if? Those two tiny words had been mulled over so many times this past eight weeks, it was exhausting. She couldn't go there again. She wouldn't.

With all her might, she forced the thoughts aside and stared at the ceiling, willing another few minutes of rest before the alarm signalled a new day. Her eyelids drooped, the warmth of sleep closing in when her mobile rang. She threw out a hand, patted the bedside table until she found the phone.

'Morning,' Pemberton said. 'Do you want the good news or the bad news?'

Helen blinked and checked the clock again. 6.06 a.m. Barely ten minutes had passed. 'You're up early.'

'That's the good news.'

'And the bad?'

'I've just had a call from Tappers, a mate on incident response. Yvette Edwards was found dead in her house by her husband last night.'

Helen recalled Sinead's neighbour's blonde hair. Her youthful complexion. 'What?'

'She drowned in the bath, a bag of coal over her head to

weigh her down. Looks like suicide. They've called in the IOPC.'

Helen thanked Pemberton and rang off. The Independent Office for Police Conduct, or IOPC, were alerted when a member of the public died after recent contact with the police and since she'd spoken with Yvette less than forty-eight hours earlier, they were obliged to examine the circumstances and decide whether or not an investigation was necessary. It was routine. They were there to check the police had acted appropriately and there was no intimidation or impropriety that contributed to the death. But it was also a pain in the arse, because if they decided to take on the case, they'd appoint their own SIO and getting information would prove problematic.

Helen pushed herself up and rested her head against the cold wood of the headboard. Yvette had recently fought cancer and was clearly besotted with her ten-year-old daughter. She might have been distressed by her friend's death, but she also appeared to have a strong marriage and support of friends and family nearby. Not the kind of circumstances in which a person would usually commit suicide.

Unless there was more to it.

She scrolled through her contacts and pressed dial. She needed more information but would have to tread carefully.

The call rang out several times before Dr Charles Burlington answered, and when he did, his voice was full of sleep.

'I'm sorry to bother you so early, Charles.'

'Helen. How can I help you?'

'Response were called to a sudden death last night. It was Yvette Edwards, Sinead O'Donnell's neighbour.'

'And you think it's connected to the O'Donnell murder?'

'I'm not sure. The attending officers are treating it as suicide.' She relayed her conversation with Pemberton. 'I can't be seen to be involved; if the case is investigated it'll be allocated a different SIO. I suspect Yvette will be on your list for this morning. I wondered if I could attend the post-mortem and hear your initial thoughts?'

A slight pause. A rustle in the background. She imagined him pulling back the bedclothes, gently slipping out of bed so as not to disturb his wife sleeping beside him.

'Sure. I'll be at the mortuary from 7.30. I'll examine her first.'

'Thanks.' Helen cleared her throat. 'Listen, can we keep this between ourselves for now? It's only supposition on my part.'

'No problem.'

***

The sudden death of Yvette Edwards plagued Helen as she drove across town. She replayed their conversation on Wednesday evening. Yvette had demanded to see a senior officer. At the time, it appeared to be a reassurance exercise, not unusual, but now her detective brain probed with niggling questions. Was Yvette involved in Sinead's murder and checking to see how much the police knew? She couldn't deny that the number of phone calls and texts she'd made to Sinead's phone suggested a closer relationship than Yvette admitted to.

Did she know what Sinead was involved in? Yvette's movements had been routinely checked. She'd claimed she'd stayed home on the day of the murder after dropping off her daughter for her school trip. Her phone was sited at their home, although she wouldn't be the first criminal to leave it behind, knowing it was traceable.

Charles was already stooped over a body when Helen arrived at the mortuary. She watched him while she gowned up in the anteroom. She could see the corpse he was working on was female, but he was standing in front of the head area, blocking her view. He didn't move while she pulled on her overshoes, donned the hair cover. It wasn't until she entered the examination area that he looked up for long enough for her to catch the blonde hair spread across the top of the gurney.

Yvette Edwards was virtually unrecognisable from the woman she'd seen only days earlier. Her face was blackened with mottled bruises. Her mouth gaped, the lips dry and crystallised. Partially closed eyes had rolled back to reveal white slits. Traces of coal dust across her naked body glittered under the bright lighting.

'I can only do the preliminaries, I'm afraid,' Charles said after greeting her. 'I need to wait for the technician before I open her up.'

'That's fine.' Helen managed a grateful smile. 'Thanks for doing this.'

He gave her a sideways glance. Warm, intuitive, and she couldn't help wondering how many times he'd done this for her late father during the time they'd worked together.

Dusky rain-cloud bruising covered Yvette's chest. He lifted her arms, one at a time, and peered closely at intermittent marks running along her forearms. Her legs revealed more dark patches.

'The bruising is concentrated on the backs of her limbs,' he said.

'Could it be defensive?'

'Unlikely. If it was, we'd expect it to be spread more widely. This looks more like the body's natural defence mechanism. I understand she weighted her head down with a bag of coal.'

'That's what I'm told.'

'When she pulled the bag onto her head, she would have panicked. It's an innate reaction. No matter how much she might have wanted this, her arms and legs would thrash about against the bath in protest when it couldn't be removed.'

'Are you saying, you think she did this to herself?'

Charles paused a moment. 'According to the notes, your colleagues found a packet of Sertraline, a known antidepressant, at the scene, prescribed to Yvette. I'll run toxicology tests to be sure. If she was being treated for depression —'

'She'd recently recovered from cancer. Are antidepressants prescribed to people in remission?'

'Sometimes, yes. But that coupled with the fact that she'd lost a close friend could have sent her over the edge.'

Helen's eyes dropped to Yvette's hands. They were grubby, blackened with the coal dust, and hadn't been bagged. 'Can you still do her fingernails for me?'

Charles shot her a perplexed look, and with good reason. If they hadn't been bagged at the scene, it was possible any fibres or particles she was hoping for could have dropped out. That's if they hadn't already been washed away by the bathwater.

'I'll cover the costs in my budget,' she said. 'I want to be sure.'

'Of course, if that's what you want. Though I think you're wasting your time. There is no evidence here to suggest involvement of a third party or foul play. It's up to the Coroner, of course, but my initial assessment would be suicide.'

CHAPTER 37

Connor stirred to the sound of a shuffle. He opened his eyes, just in time to catch a shadowy shape pass through his bedroom. He jolted forward.

'You're jumpy this morning,' his mother said, bending down to scoop up his dirty jeans.

He'd been awake for most of the night, listening out for someone trying the doors, the sound of broken glass. The man returning.

When he did sleep, his dreams were filled with the dead cop, punctuated by a man chasing him down an alley. A figure closing in on him. That menthol aroma. And when he looked over his shoulder, it was the cop in zombie form, limping towards him, both images morphing together like a scene from a horror movie.

'It's nearly nine o'clock,' his mother said. 'You can't sleep all day, there's loads to do.' She tugged open the curtains and immediately blinded Connor with the sun's morning rays. 'You can start by putting the ironing away. It's piled up on the kitchen table.' She bustled out of the room.

Connor lay back on his pillow, waiting for the thud of his heartbeat to slow. He didn't want to sleep. The dreams terrified him. But he didn't want to be awake either.

Usually, the thought of staying in all day with no phone,

no computer and no gaming would drive him mad. Today it felt like a lifeline, and one he held onto with all his might.

The man hadn't knocked on the door or tried to break in last night. And if he did try, he'd have to face Connor's mother and Connor didn't envy him there. Everyone they met joked about how scary Fiona Wilson was before they got to know her. If she worked in a call centre, they'd put her on complaints because she wouldn't take any crap. Someone probably had – she'd done so many jobs he'd lost track. No, she could handle herself all right. He'd be safe here.

But he couldn't stay here, could he? He needed to see Rhys.

Once again, he wished he'd trusted his instincts and stayed out of the factory on Wednesday evening. He wouldn't have seen the dead woman. Wouldn't have got mixed up in a murder case, with a killer on the loose. Wouldn't be the victim of a stalker.

If only he could turn the clock back.

His mother called him again. He climbed out of bed, pulled on some clean jeans, threw a hoodie over his head. The sun had disappeared behind the clouds. He glanced out of the window, relieved to find the street below empty.

The man who'd attacked him last night shared the same menthol aroma as the guy at the park. Was he the killer? He wanted to know what he'd seen at the factory, and if that was the case, he wouldn't only stalk Connor. He'd be after Rhys too.

Another shout from his mother. 'Are you coming, or what?' She wouldn't take no for an answer.

He needed to find a way to slip out, to warn Rhys. Before it was too late.

***

'I can't believe her husband went out and left her if she was vulnerable,' Helen said.

She'd arrived back at the incident room to find Pemberton stowed away in her office, writing up his notes.

She'd considered Charles's assessment of suicide on her drive to the station. Had they missed the signs of desperation, of hopelessness, when they'd visited Yvette? Should they have taken any more action to safeguard the woman? No. Depressive signals weren't always obvious, not even to those near and dear. She'd never forget attending the suicide of a teenager that had celebrated a birthday dinner with his family only hours before he'd flung himself off a bridge; the shocked faces of his parents when she'd delivered the news still haunted her to this day. He'd been on antidepressants for months and was improving. Back at work, doing better. In tragic cases like suicide, loved ones yearned for a clue, a trigger, and sadly there wasn't always a clean explanation.

'Her husband said she insisted on him going out,' Pemberton said. 'It was some kind of work corporate event. Yvette's sister had been around to visit. She only left an hour before he found her.'

'I don't buy it.'

Pemberton scratched his bald scalp. 'I know. I'm struggling with it myself. But with no suspicious circumstances—'

'What about the husband?'

'Devastated. Naturally. He gave an account to Tappers. Said he came back with a friend, planning to collect the car and give him a lift home. He wasn't alone. And there are bound to be witnesses at the golf club event he attended.'

Helen rubbed her forehead and looked out into the incident room, just as Jenkins entered the main door. 'Looks like the news is spreading fast,' she said.

Pemberton gave a sympathetic stare and made for the door. 'I'd better leave you to it,' he said, exchanging a brief nod with the superintendent before he closed the door behind him.

'I take it you've heard the news?' Jenkins said, undoing his jacket and settling himself on the chair Pemberton had left.

'I have. It's disturbing.'

'Disturbing? It's a downright pain in the arse. The sudden death of Sinead O'Donnell's neighbour, within forty-eight

185

hours of contact with the police. Sheesh! The press is going to have a field day.'

Helen inwardly recoiled. A woman had died. A family were in mourning.

'I've had a call from the IOPC.' His face twitched. 'They've started gathering evidence to assess whether or not they need to carry out a full investigation. They don't know yet it was a senior rank that visited.' He looked away, sucked his teeth. 'Christ, what were you even doing visiting her, Helen?'

'Spencer had delivered the news about her neighbour's death. The team were searching Sinead's house next door. Yvette was distressed and asked to speak to a senior officer.'

'Why you? Where was the response shift sergeant?'

'Attending an affray in the town centre. Multiple offenders. He'd got his hands full. We made the usual checks, there was no intelligence on her or her family. No reason to suggest any involvement on her part. I went in there and explained the situation, calmed her down.'

'Did you question her?'

'Only the usual. When she'd last seen Sinead, when they'd last spoken, that sort of thing. Sinead wasn't even cold, Yvette was her neighbour and friend.'

He huffed.

'We've done nothing wrong, sir.'

'That might be the case, but now we have the IOPC breathing down our neck. I hope you've covered all the bases here, Helen.'

She ignored his response. 'What I'm more concerned about is a potential link with Sinead's death.'

'What do you mean?'

She explained her reservations, carefully leaving out her attendance at the autopsy and the tests she'd requested. No sense in exacerbating the situation further, especially since the results might come back negative. If there was an ensuing investigation, she'd deal with it later. 'There's also the number of text messages she sent to Sinead on the days leading up to her murder. We'd made an appointment to go out and see her this morning, to check them out. It wasn't high priority yesterday when we were tracking Natalia Kowalski down. Now I'm not so sure.'

'What do we know about the husband?'

'We've done all the usual checks. He was working nights and claims he was at home asleep on the day Sinead was murdered.'

Jenkins looked past Helen and out of the window. 'Who actually visited Yvette on the night of Sinead's murder?' he asked eventually.

'Spencer, Dark and me.'

'Okay, we're going to have to play this carefully. We can't be seen to be investigating Yvette's death or treading on the toes of any potential IOPC investigation. But we do need to check on the messages and any possible link.' He looked through the blinds and out into the incident room beyond. 'Send DC Dark. Dress it up as a welfare visit. Make sure she's discreet and Mr Edwards knows we are not investigating Yvette's death. She can ask him about Yvette's relationship with Sinead and the messages on the day she died. Even ask for her phone if it hasn't already been seized. Take it gently.'

***

Helen stepped out of her office to find DC Dark at the filing cabinets, a ring of officers around her, broad smiles plastered on their faces. Pemberton was drooling over a large box of doughnuts on the table beside.

'Rosa got engaged,' Spencer said to Helen, helping himself to a doughnut. 'Are you going to eat one or just stare at them?' he asked Pemberton.

'There are no calories in looking.'

'There's no fun either,' Spencer said.

Helen smiled. 'Congratulations, Rosa.'

Dark beamed and lifted her left hand to reveal an emerald

set on a band of gold, the stone clustered by tiny pinprick diamonds.'

'That's unusual.'

'It was my grandmother's. I used to play with it as a kid.'

'It really suits you. Have you got a date for the wedding?'

'Not yet. It'll be next year sometime. Help yourself to a doughnut.'

Helen thanked her and chose a caramel number. The bodies around them dispersed. 'I have a job for you,' Helen said as they perched on the edge of a nearby desk and ate together. She passed on the details.

The mixture of good news and sugar seemed to disperse the tension in the room and perk everyone up.

Spencer, who was now back at his desk, shoved the last of his doughnut into his mouth, clicked at his keyboard with his clean hand and gave an excited grunt. They waited for him to finish his mouthful. 'DNA results are back on our syringe,' he said, licking his fingers. 'The labs have found a match. They're sending over the details now.'

CHAPTER 38

'Forty-eight-year-old Gordon William Turner. Convicted of the brutal murder of twenty-two-year-old Evelyn Ferguson in Leicester in 1996.' Spencer was standing at the front of the room now, reading from an A4 sheet.

'What happened?'

'Evelyn Ferguson worked as an admin clerk in the offices of a carpet company called Charlton's. Turner was one of their fitters. Her body was found on wasteland. She'd been beaten and her head wrapped in cling film until she suffocated. And get this... her hands were cuffed together and there were cigarette burns on the insides of one of her wrists.'

A low murmur passed around the room.

'There was no cling film or plastic wrap in our case,' Pemberton said.

'Maybe he's changed his methods, become more violent.'

'Let's not jump to any conclusions,' Helen said. 'How did they find Turner at the time?'

Spencer scanned his notes. 'The case went on for a while by the looks of things. The victim was walking from her home in Oadby to a friend's house only two streets away. Alarm was raised when she didn't arrive. It was a dark night. There were no witnesses. The police didn't release details of the cling film or burns to the press.' He was quiet a moment. 'A profiler was brought in and he suggested the plastic wrap and cuffs might be connected to someone playing out a sexual fantasy. Detectives spoke with local sex workers and one came forward to say she'd had a client who'd shackled her with cuffs and wanted to wrap her head in cling film and, when she refused, he tried to burn her with a cigarette. He fled when her friends heard her screams, but she was able to tell detectives he arrived in a Charlton's carpet van. Then it was a matter of elimination. There were only four fitters and two vans.

'Turner was out alone on the day the sex worker was attacked. He also took the van home on the night Evelyn was killed. When they raided his home, they found extreme sadism magazines. Under the floorboards in his bedroom, they found video tapes. He'd filmed the whole attack, sick bastard.

'He was given a life sentence,' Spencer continued. 'Apparently, he was a model prisoner, attended all the workshops, expressed remorse. He was granted release on licence from Bedford Prison last September.'

'How could that happen?' Pemberton asked.

'The doctors assessed him, marked him suitable for release.'

'That's madness.'

'That's the system.'

'If he was convicted of a sexually motivated murder then he'll be on the sexual offenders register,' Helen cut in. 'Surely he's been monitored by MOSOVO?' MOSOVO, or the Management of Sexual Offenders or Violent Offenders, were a team of police officers who worked in the community, monitoring the habits and behaviour of convicted criminals. They visited offenders after their release, checked their movements and online activity to ensure they were complying with the requirements of their licence. Which meant they'd have an address. 'So, we know where he is.'

'Not quite.'

'I don't understand.'

'His case officer turned up a month ago, on a routine visit, to find his flat cleaned out. All the usual checks were made to track him down, to no avail. He hasn't touched his bank account since and doesn't have a mobile registered to him.' A low-bellied groan sounded.

'That's not all,' Pemberton said. 'His case officer has only been dealing with him for six months, since he joined the team. Before that, his case officer was Blane O'Donnell.'

A heavy silence filled the room. Helen recalled Blane's sergeant saying he moved from the MOSOVO team to training six months earlier. If Gordon Turner had been released from prison last September, Blane would have monitored him for three months before he left.

'Looks like Turner singles out his victims,' Spencer said. 'Police found photos of Evelyn at his address, taken over a long spell of time. The sex worker said he talked about where she lived, the times she worked, even her clients. He creeped her out so much she moved home afterwards.'

'So, he stalks his victims and learns their habits before he acts.' Helen was quiet a moment. 'Are you suggesting he got to know Blane, researched his family and developed a fixation with Sinead?'

'It might explain her injuries. He seems to have a penchant for watching his victims suffer.'

'Okay,' she said, playing devil's advocate. 'How would he lure Sinead out to a disused factory?'

'People in his home community were shocked when he was arrested. Called him a polite boy, a gentle giant. He worked full-time, still lived at home and cared for his mother who suffered from MS. Of course, they didn't know what was found in his bedroom until after the trial. Sounds like he's pretty manipulative.'

'Have you spoken with his case officer?'

'Only briefly, he was on a visit when I called. He said Turner was struggling with life outside prison, couldn't get work. Otherwise, he seemed to be behaving and living within the terms of his licence. It came as a complete shock when he disappeared.'

'Wouldn't Sinead have known him if he was listed as wanted?' Pemberton said.

'His offences were committed across the border in Leicestershire. He was discharged to Hampton to keep him away from his victim's family. Our local bobbies wouldn't be familiar with him, there's no record of him reoffending since he left jail.'

'He'll have been circulated as wanted though.'

'Sinead might have seen his details in a pile of other wanted and missing persons. There are so many of them these days. Right or wrong, incident response officers tend to focus on those they know. If they spot them while they're out on shift, they bring them in.'

'Let's work this through,' Helen said. 'So, we're thinking he'd been watching Sinead for a while, planted the screw in her tyre that morning and then drove by, picking her up, under the pretence of a random stranger offering help. Has anyone checked his image against the ATM suspect?'

'Already done,' Spencer said. 'MOSOVO emailed us the photo from their files.' He crossed to his computer and brought up the ATM suspect up on the screen, then clicked a key and another face shot up alongside. Whereas the ATM suspect was skinny with a pointy nose and an angular face, Gordon Turner was thick-set with a flattish nose. They couldn't have been more different.

'Was his old address anywhere near the ATM?'

'No, he lived on the other side of Hampton before he disappeared. DVLA shows no vehicle registered to him, but he was inside for a long time. He's bound to have made contacts. Or maybe the car he used was stolen.'

She scratched the back of her neck. 'If he attacked Sinead, why would he leave his needle and syringe at the factory?'

'Maybe he shot up afterwards and forgot it. Or perhaps

he'd used it when he'd checked out the place and didn't realise it was still there.'

'Okay, what's the last known address we have for him?' Helen asked.

Spencer reeled it off.

'Let's get a team out there anyway. Check it over. Speak with the landlord, talk to his neighbours. I'm sure this was all done when he disappeared, but it won't hurt to go over it again. Get force intelligence to send their handlers out to the field, will you? See if any contacts in the community have seen or heard anything of Gordon Turner. The syringe indicates he's been using and maybe living rough, so check the soup kitchens and the hostels too. And contact Bedford Prison. See what associations, if any, he made on the inside.' She turned to Pemberton. 'What about family, close friends?'

'He has a brother. He lives in Worthington, on the edge of town. That was why he asked to be discharged to Hampton.'

'Right, you and I will get out there and see what he has to say.'

CHAPTER 39

Once a village, before the town of Hampton expanded and swallowed it up, Worthington still retained a quaint feel with its sandstone cottages and winding streets. They passed the church with its bell tower and sweeping graveyard and continued up the hill to a modern estate, filled with an array of semi-detached and detached houses with long front gardens.

'What do we know about the brother?' Helen asked Pemberton.

'Nigel Turner. Fifty-eight years old. Used to work as a welder until he injured his back in an accident four years ago and had to retire on health grounds. He's lived here in Chambers Close with his wife, Nancy, for eighteen years.'

'Any convictions?'

'No, he's not known to us.'

They rounded the lip of Chambers Close and rose up the hill to a row of bungalows. Number 43 was in the corner, separated from the road by a sloping driveway, a lawn to the side. Bees buzzed around the hanging baskets and tubs neatly arranged along the front.

Helen was aware of curtain twitches nearby as they climbed out of the car. The sun was high in the sky now, the heat radiating off the block paving. She could feel sweat on the back of her neck.

The door opened before Pemberton rang the bell. It seemed the neighbours weren't the only ones watching their arrival.

A thick-set man with thinning hair and a short beard appeared, his free hand resting on a wooden stick. 'Can I help you?' he asked.

Helen introduced them both. 'We're looking for Nigel Turner.'

'That's me.'

'We're here to talk to you about your brother, Gordon. May we come in?'

He shuffled aside and cast a cursory glance at the houses opposite before he closed the door. 'Go through to the front room.'

They followed his direction into a bright and airy sitting room. Soft pink walls co-ordinated with a thick-pile grey carpet that squished beneath Helen's boots.

Nigel lifted a blue Persian cat off the sofa and indicated for them to sit. 'Can I get you a tea or coffee?' he asked.

'We're fine, thank you,' Helen said, perching on the edge of the sofa in an effort not to spoil a display of cushions behind her. The cat brushed up against her ankles and purred. 'Do you have any idea where we might find your brother?'

'Why? What's he done now?'

Helen bypassed the question. 'We need to speak to him in connection with an investigation.'

Nigel levered himself into an armchair with a wince and balanced his stick beside him. 'I have no idea where he is. Haven't seen him for ages.'

'Has he been in contact? Phoned at all?'

'No. What's the investigation?'

'I'm afraid I can't share the details.'

The drone of bees sounded through the open bay windows.

'I can only tell you the same as I told the officer that came knocking when he disappeared. Last time I heard from Gordon was four weeks ago and that was only the second time I've spoken with him in the last year. We're not exactly close.'

'You did maintain some contact then?'

'Gordon called me when he was released from prison, told me he was living in Hampton and asked to meet up. I was shocked, to be honest. We hadn't been in touch for years.'

'How did he seem when you met him?'

'Okay, I suppose. We were like strangers really. Jenny, my wife, didn't want him anywhere near us, so I met him in secret.' He grimaced. 'I felt a bit bad really because he was living in a drab flat on East Grove. He kept going on about the mistakes he'd made, how sorry he was. Oh, I don't know. I had my family to think of. My kids are grown up and live nearby. I don't want him contacting them.' He glanced at the window and shifted in his seat.

Helen desperately wanted to ask him about their latest meeting, but he seemed on edge.

'Were you close when you were young?' she asked.

He surveyed her suspiciously. 'Not particularly. Gordon's ten years younger than me. I left home when he was eight.'

'I understand he cared for your mother.'

'Yes, sort of. She was diagnosed with MS and had to give up work in the end. We all rallied around. Gordon lived with her, so he took the lion's share. Until he was arrested, of course.' His face tightened. 'I don't see how this is relevant.'

'We're looking for contacts, Mr Turner. People that Gordon might be staying with. Maybe you have some mutual associations, or family?'

'There's only us. Our mother died years ago. We've no other family, not that we keep in contact with.'

'Why don't you tell me about the trial?'

His cheeks billowed as he exhaled. 'There's not much to say really. We all knew the case, it shocked everyone where we lived in Oadby. She was a local girl. It was even more of a shock when they arrested our Gordon. I mean, he's always been an odd fish. Spent a lot of time in his room. Never had a girlfriend. I used to tease him about being a mummy's boy. What they found in his bedroom... I was gobsmacked.'

'How did your mother react?'

'She didn't believe it. Not a word. Argued with the police. Accused them of fitting him up. Fought for his release. That's before we knew what they'd recovered from his room, mind you, the video, the magazines.' He paled. 'You think you know someone…'

'Did you attend the trial?'

He nodded. 'Mum wanted to go every day. Wanted to watch his face as everything uncovered. I think she was still hoping for a reprieve, some scrap of evidence to clear him. When we heard what he'd done to that poor girl,' his voice sank to a whisper, 'she collapsed in court. Three months later she was dead. I don't think she ever fully recovered.'

'I'm sorry.' Helen paused. 'Did you keep in touch with him afterwards?' she asked eventually.

'I couldn't bring myself to. We were still living on the same estate in Leicester. Close to the family of the dead girl. People spat at us, shouted things in the street. It nearly finished off my wife. After Mum died, we sold up and moved here, where people didn't know us. I changed jobs and we left it all behind us. Until that phone call last year. I was so angry he'd chosen to come to Hampton to live and tracked me down. I mean, how dare he? After everything he's put us through.'

'How was your brother when you last saw him?'

'A bit out of sorts actually. I wondered about talking to the police at the time, but I didn't want to get involved, and I didn't want Jenny to find out I'd seen him. She's been upset enough.'

'How do you mean, "out of sorts"?'

'He called me out the blue, said he needed to talk. I tried to turn him down, cut him off. He just kept calling. He seemed desperate. So, I agreed to meet him in town at Hayes Coffee House.'

'And?'

'He was already there when I arrived, sitting outside beneath the awning. He looked as if he hadn't changed his clothes in a week and they hung off him; he must have lost at least two stone. And he was uncomfortable, agitated. Kept picking at the skin around his fingernails. Looked like he was on something, you know?'

'Do you mean drugs?'

'Maybe. All I know is, he couldn't keep still.'

'Why did he want to see you?'

'He said he needed help. Someone was after him.'

'Who?'

'He didn't seem to know. Told me people were going into his flat when he wasn't there, moving stuff. He seemed paranoid. Kept looking about. Freaked me out a bit, to be honest.'

'What did you do?'

'I gave him thirty quid, to clean himself up, and told him to talk to the police. The next I heard was when your officer came to the door and told me he was missing. That was about four weeks ago.' He shot another furtive glance at the window.

Helen followed his gaze. The curtains danced in the soft breeze. 'Mr Turner. Is there something else you want to tell us?'

'Pardon?'

'Why do you keep looking towards the window?'

'It's my wife, Jenny. She doesn't know about any of this. Doesn't even know he's back in Hampton. And she's due home, any minute. If she finds you here, she'll be worried.'

Helen nodded and stood. The poor man seemed genuinely upset. 'Do you know who your brother has been spending time with since his release? What he's been doing? Anything will help.'

Nigel shook his head. 'As I said, I made it my business not to know.'

***

They were at the car, wrestling with their seat belts when Helen's phone rang. Rosa Dark's name flashed up on the screen.

Helen plugged her lead into the USB port. 'Hi Rosa. You're on speakerphone.'

'I've been out and spoken with Yvette's husband. He's in a pretty bad way. The grandparents are bringing their daughter home from holiday early. They should be back today.'

In all the excitement of tracing a potential suspect, Helen had almost forgotten she'd sent Dark to see Sinead's late neighbour's husband. 'Anything on Sinead?'

'He said they were friends. When I asked about the number of text messages they exchanged, he said his wife sent a lot of texts to all her friends, usually jokes she'd pulled off the internet. She gave up her job as a teaching assistant after the cancer scare, couldn't face going back. Had a lot of time on her hands at home and was always scouring the internet and sending things on.'

'What about her phone?'

'He can't find it.'

'What?'

'I know. It's a mystery. He's looked all over the house. He half wondered whether she'd seen something on there, on the internet, that had upset her and she'd disposed of it before she'd killed herself.'

With the DNA trace and a potential suspect in mind, Yvette's missing phone seemed low priority. But it bothered Helen, especially as they still hadn't located Sinead's phone.

She thanked Dark and updated her on the DNA results and their current priorities. 'Where are you now?'

'On my way back to the station.'

'Could you meet Gordon Turner's case officer on the management of serious offenders' team? I don't care if he has to cancel the rest of his appointments today, arrange to meet him and see what he can tell you about Mr Turner. I'd like to take a look at the file too.'

CHAPTER 40

Connor turned the corner into Rhys's street and immediately ducked behind a Nissan parked diagonally opposite. Rhys's sister was leaning against the pebble-dash frontage of their house, chatting to a man in baggy jeans and a white T-shirt. He peeped through the car window at them. They were standing sideways on, him only inches away from her protruding stomach, deep in conversation. She gave a giggle and glanced at the road. Connor ducked down again. He'd only been in Rhys's house a couple of times, but enough to know they didn't get along. She hissed swear words at her brother when they passed in the hallway and gave Connor odd looks. Rhys loathed Bronwen, said she was always getting him into trouble. There was no way Connor was going to get past her without a string of questions.

Connor cursed his mother again for taking his phone and darted across the road, keeping low. Within seconds, he was in the alley at the rear of the houses. Two high brick walls ran the length of the alley, facing each other, leaving a broken path between, just wide enough to get a small car down. The walls were mossy and pitted. Wooden gates painted a variety of colours marked the back entrances to the houses. It didn't take long to count down the gates to Rhys's. A graffitied picture of a hand sat beside a rickety white gate. He tried the gate, surprised to find it unlocked, and slipped inside.

Weeds and dandelions pushed through the cracks in a pathway that led to a back door. The handlebars of an old bike were visible beneath the overgrown grass; a punctured football lay beside the back door. Connor looked up. Rhys's bedroom was at the back. If he could get his attention...

A peal of laughter sounded. Bronwen. She was still talking out front. He didn't have long. Grass tickled his calves as he searched the garden and gathered up a couple of stones. He stood back, found his aim and threw. The first one bounced off the window ledge. He tried again, but the second missed altogether, pinging off the wall. He turned to search for another stone when the back window flew open.

'What are you doing?' It was Rhys.

'Shush!' Connor pointed at the house. 'Bronwen's out front,' he said in a low voice. 'We need to talk.'

'Are you kidding? My mum'll go nuts if she finds you here. You dobbed me in.'

'I didn't!'

'No? Who else sent the police to my door? I told you to tell no one.'

'I didn't. My mum recognised us from the camera footage, told the police. I never said a word about you. I swear.'

Rhys didn't answer. He turned suddenly, and disappeared, leaving the window hanging open.

'Rhys!' Connor hissed. He listened hard, eyes searching the window. Nothing. He was weighing up his options, thinking about trying the back door, when a shadow appeared behind the glass.

Rhys opened the back door and poked his head out. 'You need to go. If my family find you here—'

'Can't you come out for a few minutes?'

Rhys looked unsure. 'I'm supposed to be grounded.'

'So am I.'

A brief glance back. 'Mum's sleeping off a migraine.

They think I'm in my room. We'd better be quick, before they see us.'

He slipped his feet into some trainers beside the door and snuck out. They jogged up the back alley, onto the top street and headed towards the park. Connor checked over his shoulder a couple of times. When they reached the edge of the park, they were gasping. They headed for an old oak in the corner and slunk down, resting their backs against the gnarly trunk.

It was quiet in this corner. Apart from a woman walking her dog in the distance, they were alone.

'So, what happened?' Rhys asked when he'd got his breath back.

Connor explained how he arrived home the other day to find his mother staring at the CCTV footage. How she'd forced him to go to the station.

'Why didn't you call me?' Rhys said.

'She took my phone and my laptop. I couldn't contact anyone. Still can't.'

'What did you tell the filth?'

'Nothing. Said I was there on my own. When they said we were seen leaving together, I denied it. Even when my mum recognised you, I still denied it.'

'She's got a big mouth.'

Connor bristled. He didn't approve of his mum contacting the police, but he wasn't going to listen to anyone criticising her either. 'She didn't mean any harm.'

'Didn't mean any harm? My mum went crazy! I'll be lucky if I'm let out this side of the summer holidays.'

Connor felt his cheeks redden. He looked away. A crow circled the tree, cawing to its mate. 'What happened at the police station?' he asked eventually.

Rhys sniffed. 'Got asked a bunch of questions. Forced to admit I was there and saw the woman.'

'You told them you were there?'

'I didn't have a choice. They're testing the place for prints.'

They'd laundered their clothes and hadn't considered fingerprints. How could they miss that? Connor ground his teeth and pressed his back into the trunk. They'd done nothing wrong. Well, maybe a bit of trespassing. Not enough to warrant them getting tangled up in a murder investigation.

'What exactly did you tell them?' Rhys asked.

'That I was in the factory. I didn't say I'd seen the woman. I told them I didn't go upstairs.'

'What? You idiot. Now our accounts are different. I told them we both went upstairs and saw the woman.'

Connor's face reddened again. 'How was I supposed to know what you'd say? You said to tell no one.'

'Look, we didn't have anything to do with the murder,' Rhys said. 'We haven't been charged with anything, haven't even been arrested. It'll blow over.'

'There's more.' He shared the details of the man in the park yesterday, the attack outside his house last night.

Rhys didn't flinch. 'Probably just some nonce,' he said. 'There's loads of them around.' He broke off a handful of grass, opened his fingers and watched it drift to the ground.

'I've had enough,' Connor said. 'I wish I'd never gone into that factory.'

'The police think we know something, 'cos we were there. That's why that detective keeps coming to the house.'

Connor recalled the impish detective, the one who'd interviewed him in the station. She'd visited him again yesterday evening, asking for details of his movements over the past two weeks, wanting all the contacts in his phone, details of who he spent time with. So that was why she was asking all those strange questions. He looked across at Rhys. 'A detective came to you too?'

'Yup. She came yesterday and said she'd be back. Even questioned Bronwen. I'm really gonna pay for that one. If they thought we were involved, they'd have arrested us by now.'

***

Pemberton was pulling out of Nigel Turner's housing estate when Helen's phone buzzed again. It was Spencer.

'The flat is cleared out, only a few bits of furniture left,' he said. 'No clothes, toiletries, food in the cupboards. Turner's decision to leave was clearly planned.'

'No indication of where he moved on to?' Helen asked.

'Afraid not. He was careful to leave nothing of any consequence behind.'

'What about the neighbouring flats?'

'One side of him is empty, we're yet to trace the resident. The other side is an elderly gentleman who barely goes out. He passed Turner a couple of times in the hallway when he was here, they never really spoke.'

'What about the landlord?'

'He remembers him, of course. He was one of the few to know his background, admitted he was a bit reluctant to take him on, but he said he didn't give him any trouble. Apart from leaving without notice. He's advertising for a new tenant now.'

'Okay, thanks,' Helen said. 'Keep trying other flats in the block.'

CHAPTER 41

Time passed easily in their quiet corner of the park. A woman wandered along the nearby path with a pushchair, a sleeping toddler inside. A Labrador trotted over to check them out before its owner called it back. Slowly, the heat of the day was starting to kick in.

Connor's stomach growled. It was almost lunchtime. He needed to get back home before his mother noticed he was missing.

He looked across at Rhys, laid out beside him, staring up at the blue sky between the leafy branches of the ancient oak. 'We should make a move,' he said. One of his laces had come undone. He reached down to tie it and noticed a man in a baseball cap leaning against a nearby tree, fiddling with his phone.

He was tall. Well-built. Wearing a black T-shirt, dark jeans.

'Oh, shit.'

'What is it?' Rhys jerked forward.

'Over there, look!'

Rhys followed his direction. 'What? I don't get it?'

'That man. He's the one who was watching me here yesterday.'

The man caught his eye and stared.

Connor's mouth dried.

'I think I know him,' Rhys said. He squinted. 'Oh my God, it is. We've got to get out of here. Now.'

They jumped up and turned towards the road, walking at first, trying to appear normal, although there was no hiding the urgency in their step. They left the park and headed towards town. Traffic blasted along the main road. Connor glanced over his shoulder. He didn't want to. Didn't want to see the man following them. But the pull was unbearable.

'He's behind us.'

They both turned at the same time. The man quickened, drawn to them like a magnet.

'Run!' Rhys said.

They could hear footsteps behind them as they sped up. Pounding the pavement. Eyes darting in all directions. They needed to turn off the main drag, it would be easier to lose him in the side streets.

A short break in the traffic. They edged towards the road, attuned to each other's movements. Weaved their way through, narrowly missing a cyclist speeding towards town.

Connor didn't need to look over his shoulder to know the man was still there. The brakes of a driver howled in protest as he followed; the horn of a van blasted.

A side street presented itself ahead. Twenty metres away. Within seconds they were there. Connor steered Rhys into it. They turned, then took the first street on the left. Another quick glance. He was making ground, closing in on them.

They were in the old terraced streets that marked the edge of Weston now, an area also known as Hampton's red-light district. Sweat coursed down their backs, the blistering sun picking at every ounce of bare skin. Further down the road was Roxten and the Rabbit Warren with all its alleys and back entrances. If they could reach there, they had a better chance of losing him.

Another turn, another street. There seemed no let-up. Lungs were starting to burn, hearts pounding in their chests. They were running alongside a house when Rhys suddenly nudged Connor into the back entrance. A gate sat ajar. Connor guessed his thinking. They snuck inside, pushed the gate to.

Footsteps thudded the pavement. They listened intently. Wide eyes staring at one another. No sooner had the footfalls gone than they were back. Followed by heavy panting. He sounded close. Close enough to touch.

Connor imagined him looking around, contemplating where they'd disappeared to. In a house maybe? Down a side alley? He checked the gate. It looked closed, but the latch wasn't down. If he pushed it, they were finished. Their two lithe bodies were no match for the man's thickset muscular frame.

They weren't sure how long they stood there. Switching their gaze between the gate and the back of the flat where the curtains were tightly drawn. On the uneven paved yard, amongst the black bin bags and old boxes piled beside an overflowing wheelie bin. The smell in the heat of the day was acrid.

Minutes ticked by. They heard the bell of a cyclist in the distance. The thrum of an engine.

Connor pulled the gate open a crack, peered out. From his narrow view, the road appeared to be empty.

'I think he's gone,' Connor said.

Rhys slid to the floor. Connor bent over double and moved his tongue around his mouth. He needed a drink.

'What did you mean?' he said to Rhys.

'About what?'

'You said you knew him.'

Rhys stared at the ground. 'He's the dead woman's husband. Another cop.'

'What?'

'I saw him talking on the telly.'

'But…' Connor gathered his thoughts. The man chasing them wore a baseball cap obscuring his face. 'How can you be sure?'

'I told you, I saw him on the telly. And there's an overgrown mole on the side of his head. If he stands a certain way, like in the park, you can see it. It's gross.'

Connor worked this through in his mind. He hadn't noticed the mole. 'Why is he chasing us then?'

'We were at the factory. Maybe he thinks we saw something.'

Connor could barely process this. The man who'd been watching him, who attacked him last night, who'd chased him today, was connected to the victim.

An inquisitive face appeared at the window.

'We need to get out of here,' Rhys said.

They dashed out of the gate, looked both ways and headed down towards the corner, away from the house. Breaking into a jog. They couldn't afford to be chased by an angry resident thinking they were trying to break into their property. Or worse, be stopped by the police and questioned.

A couple more streets and they were in Roxten. When they were sure they weren't being followed, they slowed to a walk. A bell rang over the door of a shop on the corner.

'You got any cash?' Rhys said.

Connor placed his hand in his pocket. Drew out two twenty pence pieces, a couple of tens and a pound coin.

'Enough for a Coke,' Rhys said. 'I'm gagging.'

***

Helen was almost back in Hampton when her phone rang. It was Dark again.

'I'm with Chris Francis, Gordon Turner's MOSOVO case officer,' she said. 'He's not able to give us anything new in terms of Gordon's whereabouts, but he did say Gordon's been increasingly frustrated about not being able to get work. He was being treated for depression, kept complaining about money problems. Chris says he was visiting another ex-con who lives in the flats near Turner shortly before he disappeared and he spotted Turner with one of the Gladstone brothers. He wondered if he was touting for work, maybe as a minder or as one of their heavies. He's bigger than a lot of their other muscle and people here don't know his background.'

Helen thanked Dark and rang off, her mind whirling. The Gladstone family were those suspected of stepping into Chilli Franks's shoes and rebuilding his organised crime network. It seemed strange to think Gladstone himself might meet Turner personally; Chilli was always shrewd about meeting contacts in public, though Gladstone wasn't the cleverest. And if he was looking for some muscle, Turner, at 6 foot 4 inches with a bulky frame, would certainly fit the bill.

She made a quick call to DI Burns in the organised crime unit, passed on the details and asked him to look in to any association between Turner and the Gladstones. If Sinead had looked to borrow money, it may be Gladstone was the lender and Gordon Turner the enforcer. She was reminded of the bruising across Sinead's body. It might explain the violence. Perhaps the association went back even further.

'How did you get on with the inquiries into Blane's and Sinead's personal backgrounds?' she asked Pemberton.

'Pretty much exhausted. She only had a couple of long-term relationships before Blane. His last girlfriend lives in France. I've left her a few messages, she hasn't come back to me yet.'

'Okay, let's go and speak with Blane. See if he can shed any light on where Turner might be or any connections he had.'

CHAPTER 42

The shop assistant stood beside the till, watching them make their way past the crisps and chocolate bars to the fridges at the back.

Connor lifted a small bottle of cola down from the fridge and pressed it to his face. It was deliciously cold.

'Come on,' Rhys said. 'I'm gasping.'

Connor felt the heat of the assistant's gaze as they approached the counter. He stared back at her defiantly. Did she really think they were in there to shoplift?

She didn't speak as he handed over the cash and they left the shop. Outside, they walked around the corner and sat on a low stone wall, cracking open the cola and passing it between them. The bubbles fizzed in Connor's mouth. After they'd drained the bottle, he felt decidedly refreshed.

They watched a dog walker pass, and then a cyclist. Roxten was quiet on this sleepy Saturday afternoon.

'I ought to get back,' Connor said eventually. 'Are you coming?'

Rhys widened his eyes. 'I'm not going to your house. He knows where you live.'

'My mum's there,' Connor said. This man was blatantly following them in broad daylight, with only a baseball cap to shield his face. And he wasn't letting up. Now he knew who he was, that he'd lost his wife to a brutal murder and clearly thought they were involved in some way, Connor couldn't be sure what he'd be capable of. His mother hadn't asked for any of this. When he was satisfied she was safe, he'd decide what to do next. 'I'm going,' he said. 'You're either with me or you're not.'

Rhys looked uncertain. He followed him back towards the main road. They paused outside the shop on the corner, dropped the empty bottle in the bin and started. A man was hurrying down towards them, one hand holding a baseball cap, another pressing a phone to his ear.

It was him.

'Leg it!'

Connor didn't look back. He could feel his friend on his heels as he ran, past Lime Street and into Groves End. Oakwall Park loomed in the distance, the other side of the main road. A brief glance over his shoulder. The man was less than thirty metres away.

Horns blew as the boys ran into the traffic, weaving in and out of the cars. Connor narrowly avoided colliding with the nearside of a Volvo. They could see him on the other side of the road now. He was almost on them. But the traffic was too thick, he couldn't cross.

They reached the cricket pavilion. Beyond that was the river and then the modern housing estates at the edge of Hampton. If they could get behind the pavilion, they'd be out of sight and could double-back, cross the main road at the top and head towards home.

The man was jogging beside the cars, eyes darting about, looking for an opportunity to cross.

'Up here,' Connor said and they both jumped off the path. The grass was softer under their feet.

The man was still on the other side of the road, his face strained. He was losing them.

Along the side of the pavilion, they ran, hard and fast. Rhys was struggling to keep up. They were almost there, the end in sight, when Rhys glanced over his shoulder and grabbed Connor.

Connor slowed and turned to see the man jogging across the main road, zigzagging through vehicles steering in all directions to avoid him. A chorus of horns mingled with motorists shouting expletives out of their open windows. Pedestrians pausing to watch.

He was across, toes touching the kerb, when he crashed into a cyclist. It happened quickly, the boys catching it in snapshots, through quick checks over their shoulders, like an old movie flickering in the background. The brakes of the bike screeched in protest. The cyclist was thrown into the man. Both men thumped to the ground.

The boys reached the end of the pavilion wall and turned to watch, clutching each other. Miraculously, the cyclist stretched out and appeared to be unhurt. The man rolled from side to side on the grass verge, holding his leg. Cars pulled over, motorists got out and huddled around them.

One more glance back, and the boys scarpered. Connor's heart hammered in his chest. When they rounded the pavilion and crossed the road at the top, heading back into Weston, they could see a small crowd had gathered on the verge.

'What if he's hurt?' Connor panted.

'Well, if he is, he won't come after us.' They crossed the road and didn't slow their step, didn't dare to walk, until they entered Connor's road.

Connor's lungs were bone dry, his chest ached and his legs were seizing up. They didn't notice the car parked outside in the row of others, the officer climbing out and approaching his front door. Barely spoke as they slipped down the aperture between the houses and around the back of Connor's house.

They rushed inside the back door, the key rattling in the lock as Connor secured it, and turned to find Detective Dark and Connor's mother standing in the kitchen, arms folded.

'Hello, boys,' Rosa said. 'I think you'd better tell me what's going on.'

CHAPTER 43

A dishevelled Blane O'Donnell answered the door that afternoon. His usually manicured beard looked ruffled, his hair bedraggled. Mud was smeared up the thigh of the tracksuit bottoms he wore.

'Everything all right?' Pemberton asked, noticing a slight limp as he led them down the hallway.

'Tripped playing with the kids in the garden,' Blane said.

Helen looked through the kitchen window at the empty lawn outside.

'Where are the children now?' Pemberton asked.

'Mum's taken them over the park.'

'Do you know a man named Gordon Turner?' Helen said, getting straight to the point.

Blane placed his hands on his hips and scrunched his eyes. 'Yeah, I was his case officer when I worked on the MOSOVO team. Why?'

Helen chose her words carefully. Blane might be police, but he was also the victim's husband. The syringe found in the factory hadn't been released outside the investigation team and she wanted to keep it that way. For now. 'His name has cropped up in the investigation,' she said. 'When was the last time you saw him?'

'Well, it would be...' he lifted his chin for a second, 'six months ago now, maybe longer. You'll be able to find the exact date from his file.'

'You haven't seen him since you moved to training?'

'No. Why would I? He's not the sort of guy you'd hang around with.'

'Not even passing in the street, in the shopping centre maybe? This is a small town, Blane.'

'No.' His face was deadpan.

'What about Sinead?'

'What about her?'

'Has she ever dealt with Turner?'

'I don't understand. What do you mean his name has cropped up? What's happened?'

Helen sidestepped his question. 'His name has been mentioned. We need to locate him.'

'Then speak with his case officer. Look at his file. I don't see what this has to do with me.'

'He went AWOL about a month ago.'

Blane's face darkened. 'You're not suggesting he had anything to do with Sinead's death?'

Helen gestured at the chairs around the table. 'May we?'

He checked his watch, nodded. 'Okay, just for a few minutes. I need to have a shower before the kids get back.'

The chair squeaked as Helen sat down. She waited until Pemberton and Blane were settled before she continued. 'Why don't you start by telling us what you know about Gordon Turner?'

Blane gaped at her for several seconds, then scraped a hand down the front of his face.

Helen let the silence in the room linger.

'Well, he was one of the most serious offenders I looked after on the team, I guess you'll know that from his file. Others were deemed more dangerous, like some of the paedophiles, but somehow Gordon... I don't know, he was different, manipulative. I was warned not to let him chat, to stick to the brief. Vowed not to let him get under my skin. But he was clever. Would answer every one of my questions with another question, constantly trying to change the subject, deflect the attention from himself. I wasn't sorry to leave his file behind when I left, I can tell you.'

'Did Sinead ever meet him?'

'She knew about him. I mentioned him to her several times. Mainly to get things off my chest. We didn't like to talk shop, especially at home, but there were some exceptions and he was one of them. As far as I'm aware she didn't meet him. She never mentioned it if she did.'

'Did he ever talk about her?'

Blane's eyes widened. 'He talked about everything rather than himself. Wanted to know all about me, my family. When I didn't answer, he remarked on my wedding ring. I remember taking a phone call there once and Sinead was the screen saver on my phone. He made great play of telling me I was punching above my weight. After that he asked after her every time I visited. Said things about her.'

'What kind of things?'

'Oh, the usual crap. "Tell her the dark underwear suits her better." "She should wear her hair up more often." Mostly general. There was one line he said towards the end of my time on the team that really got to me. "Tell her not to wear the red coat when she collects the kids from school. Too sexy."'

Helen raised a brow. 'Did Sinead own a red coat?'

Blane nodded. 'Her mother bought her one years ago. She rarely wore it though. That wasn't what bothered me. It was more he knew, or guessed, we'd got kids. I'd never mentioned them.' Blane tapped at his temple. 'As I say, manipulative. I felt sorry for the poor lad who took over when I left.'

The shrill ring of a mobile filled the room. 'I need to take this,' Pemberton said.

Blane watched him wander out into the garden. 'What's going on?' he said to Helen as soon as the door closed. 'Is Gordon Turner a suspect?'

Helen held his gaze a moment. Everything Blane said

supported the theory that Turner had developed a fixation with Sinead. A fixation that culminated in her murder. They needed to track him down fast.

'He is someone we need to question. Is there anywhere you think he might be? Any friends or associations he mentioned when you worked with him?'

Blane shook his head. 'Turner was a bit of a loner. Oh, he had contacts, plenty of them from prison. He'd talk about them from time to time and meet up. There's no law against associations and Turner wasn't one to miss out on an opportunity. But he generally kept himself to himself. Satisfied the conditions of his licence, kept his nose clean. Everything he mentioned to me, I recorded on his file.'

The door swung open, interrupting their conversation. Pemberton's face was stern. 'Where were you earlier this afternoon?' he said, looking directly at Blane.

Helen passed a confused gaze between them. Pemberton was rarely ruffled.

'I went out for a walk to get some air.'

'Where did you walk exactly?' Pemberton's eyes hardened.

What the hell had happened?

'Around here.'

'You were spotted in Weston.'

Blane swallowed. 'I can explain...'

Pemberton glanced at the mud down the leg of his trousers. 'Did you, or did you not, follow Rhys Evans and Connor Wilson?'

'What's going on?' Helen said. This was moving way too fast.

For once in his life, Pemberton ignored his boss. 'Chase them, in fact?'

Blane gulped. 'I just wanted to ask them some questions.'

'They're twelve years old!'

'Those kids were at the factory on Wednesday, when Sinead—' His voice cut.

'We know, we've already questioned them. How the hell did you find out who they were?'

Blane looked away.

'And where were you last night?'

He didn't answer.

'You were at the Wilsons' house, weren't you? Connor claims you grabbed him. He's a minor! You can't take the investigation into your own hands. Christ, you should know that better than anyone!'

Blane's face pained. He looked at Helen imploringly. 'I didn't mean to hurt him, honestly. I just wanted answers. For Sinead.'

Helen dropped her head into her hands. This was all she needed.

***

Helen stared at Blane O'Donnell via the CCTV monitor. He struck a sorry state, the palms of his hands resting on the table, his head hung low. For the past hour, he'd been questioned regarding harassment allegations made by Connor and Rhys. He'd admitted to every single one, from watching Connor in the park to grabbing him in his back garden, and later chasing the boys through town. He was looking at charges for assault and harassment of witnesses. Facing a suspension from duties. If convicted, his career was on the line. Who would put themselves and their family at risk of losing their livelihood, their home, everything? But one look at Blane answered that question outright. Desperation seeped out of him. Desperation to get answers, for Sinead, had overridden every rational thought.

There was still one burning question plaguing her. 'How the hell did he get hold of the boys' identities and their home addresses?' she said to Pemberton, standing beside her.

He shook his head. 'No idea. He's refused to say. The boys' details hadn't been released to the press.'

Which meant the leak had to come from within the team.

Helen baulked. After everything she'd said and done, the appeal, the locks on the incident room door. She ran through her team in her mind, stopping at each name, desperately searching for any reason why they'd disobey a clear command. And came up with nothing. No, she trusted them. Each and every one of them. Didn't she? They all knew how important this inquiry was and the need for confidentiality.

'Call technical support. I want to know the names of every user that has accessed the homicide network system in the past four days.'

CHAPTER 44

Helen opened her front door to the rhythmic thud of Matthew's music. Her family were home. She heeled the door closed and dropped her bag beside the array of shoes and trainers in the hallway.

Yvette Edwards's face looked up at her from the local newspaper on the mat; the photo was taken in the sunshine, her blonde hair glistening. Helen reached down, opened it out and scanned the headline: *Murder Victim's Neighbour Found Dead*. She flicked through the short article while shedding her jacket, a couple of paragraphs about where Yvette was found and when, a short quote from her husband expressing the family's sadness and a line to say police weren't treating her death as suspicious. The story was continued at the bottom of page three where they talked about Sinead's ongoing investigation and shared a grainy photo of Gordon Turner, with a note appealing for any sightings and calling him a person of interest. It was about a quarter of the size of Yvette's. Helen's stomach pitted. They could really have done with his photo on the front page, gracing news stands. Perhaps Turner's photo would be more prominent online. She hoped so.

Suddenly, she was knocked sideways by Robert, who'd rushed out of the front room and wrapped his arms around her.

'That's a nice welcome,' she said, hugging him tight. 'Good time?'

'It was amazing!'

'I can't wait to hear all about it.' She slipped the newspaper on top of the pile of magazines underneath the hall table. Her mother still insisted on having a physical copy delivered, even though it had dropped from a daily to a weekly newspaper, but the news article on the front, and the headline relating to their inquiry, was the last thing Helen needed her to see this evening.

Matthew appeared at the bottom of the stairs, surprising her by stepping in with a hug after his brother.

Helen grinned. 'I am popular tonight. It's good to see you guys.'

She lifted a carrier bag and followed them through to the kitchen.

Her mother was standing beside the kettle. 'Hello, darling,' she said. 'Tea?'

'Wouldn't say no. I hear you had a good week?'

'Lovely, thank you.' She poured the tea and passed over a mug. 'Now, what would the worker like for dinner?'

'I'm cooking,' Helen said. The boys, who'd followed her into the kitchen, gawped at her. 'Well,' she raised the bag, still in her hand, 'courtesy of M&S. We're having Chinese.'

They roared their approval.

'Should be ready in about twenty minutes,' she said, lifting the cartons out of the bag.

Dinner was an animated affair, full of chatter and laughter. Robert talked about learning to windsurf and teased Matthew for his fear of swimming in open water. Matthew claimed to be the family archery champion. Helen's heart warmed as she sipped her wine and listened to their stories and anecdotes from the week. It was lovely to have them back, their excitement and enthusiasm filled every corner of the house, restoring it to a home once again.

When they finished, Matthew scraped a carton, eating the

last remnants of rice, and everyone looked happily full. Robert disappeared into the front room to watch television. Matthew drifted upstairs. Within seconds, the gentle thud of his music resonated above and for once Helen resisted the temptation to ask him to turn it down.

Jane eased back in her chair and surveyed the plates and cartons on the table.

'Thanks for taking the boys away,' Helen said.

'They're such fun.' Her mother tipped her glass back and finished the last drops of wine. 'What about you?' Her face turned grave. 'How's the case going?'

'Oh, you know, the usual,' Helen said, brushing it aside. 'Waiting on forensics.' She didn't want to have that conversation now.

Her mother opened her mouth to speak, then closed it again. The silence in the room was broken by Helen gathering up the cartons, placing them in the bin. Whether she was reminded of how much her daughter had lost, the hours she put in to make the job work and still find time for her family, or how much she tried to do the right thing by her boys, Helen wasn't sure. When she looked up, a switch flicked behind her mother's eyes and she pulled back. The conversation stored away for another day.

'You look beat,' Helen said eventually.

As if her cue, her mother yawned. 'Yes. I won't be late to bed tonight. There was a crash on the M6 coming back, took us an hour to navigate around it.'

'Ouch! Never mind, Matthew will be driving next year. He'll be able to share.'

'Lord, don't remind me.' She chuckled. The plates chinked together as she started to gather them up.

'Leave those, Mum. I'll sort them out. Won't take a minute.'

'Well, if you're sure.' She stood with a slight wobble and giggled. 'I think the wine has gone to my head.'

Helen laughed and gave her a hug. 'Thanks again.'

'You off early in the morning?'

'Afraid so.'

'Okay, don't disturb us, will you? I'm looking forward to a lie-in.'

Helen watched her mother totter off through the door at the side of the kitchen, up to her flat, and continued clearing the table.

It was nearly 9.30 p.m. when she finished loading the dishwasher. She reached into her bag for her laptop, opened it up and waited for the screen to light, her mind switching back to the case.

They'd identified a target. The public appeal had gone out to the newspapers, the online sites, and his name would be mentioned on the radio as a person of interest. If Gordon was their offender, then he'd been in Hampton within the last few days. Somebody must have seen him.

As she started writing her daily report, she was reminded of Jenkins's absence earlier. He rarely read her updates, although he moaned like hell if they weren't on his desk first thing in the morning, preferring to be informed of developments personally. When they'd brought Blane in, she'd tried to call him, left several voicemails. In fact, when she thought about it, he seemed to have disappeared after their chat about Yvette Edwards that morning.

It was hard to believe, with the rumour mill as it was in the police, he wouldn't have heard about Blane, and he certainly didn't know about the DNA results and their pursuance of Gordon Turner. His absence left her with a sense of foreboding. He'd been more intense than usual on this case. The stakes were high, the pressure coming from all directions: the press, the family, senior officers, not to mention the public and, of course, colleagues in the police. Surely, he wasn't looking to sideline her. He'd tried it before, bringing in a senior officer 'to assist' when the results didn't come fast enough for his liking on her first case last year. Thankfully, they'd wrapped it up before additional help was needed, but it didn't mean he wouldn't try again. His lack of faith in her was irritating.

She tapped away at her report, reflecting back on the change of direction. Gordon Turner was a man that liked to watch his victims suffer; the syringe connected him to the factory. Blane commented on Gordon's interest in Sinead, an interest that appeared to have developed into a fixation. But she couldn't understand why, after such careful planning, he'd be shoddy enough to leave Sinead there, and why he didn't remove the syringe. Had he planned to come back later and clean up? It seemed a risk.

And, as if that wasn't enough, she'd had to contend with Blane's own efforts at investigating his wife's death. They'd had to drive him to a station in neighbouring Leicester to be interviewed, to ensure the custody staff didn't know him, and when they'd read out his bail conditions earlier, reiterating he wasn't to go within two hundred yards of Connor's and Rhys's addresses he'd leant across, touched her forearm and asked her to apologise to the boys and their families. 'I never intended to frighten them,' he'd said, his face full of remorse.

What was left of the afternoon was spent in damage limitation, desperately trying to placate the boys' mothers and assure them of their safety. Rhys's mother was stern but accepting. Connor's mother had taken a lot more persuading.

Helen typed the last words, clicked send and massaged her lower back.

Tomorrow, she not only had to track down a killer, she also had to investigate how Blane obtained the boys' personal details and face the prospect of a leak in her team, the very idea of which left a sour taste in her mouth.

***

Blane O'Donnell watched the patrol car pull out of his driveway, closed the door and leant up against the cold plastic. The last twenty-four hours had been a whirlwind, an aberration. How had it come to this?

The house was quiet and still; his family tucked up in their beds, sleeping.

All he wanted, all he had ever wanted, was to protect his family. Raise his children in a loving and supportive home. A modest dream, now shattered.

A few days ago, they were a family of four, working through their problems with their elderly relatives, pulling together, a bright future in front of them. Today, he'd been suspended from his job and charged with common assault and harassment. He'd become obsessed, allowing his need for information surrounding Sinead to take over. Now, he'd not only lost his wife, but his livelihood was also threatened. And it was all his fault.

Bedsprings creaked above. He pulled himself forward, the bruises on his calf screaming in protest as he shuffled into the kitchen. Tears sprang from his eyes. Wretched, thick tears. He rested his elbows on the table, dropping his head to his hands. Time passed slowly. Eventually, as his tears eased, he lifted his head and caught sight of the silver necklace, still sitting on the edge of the window ledge. He hadn't mentioned the necklace to the police. He needed to deal with it. Tomorrow.

CHAPTER 45

Helen traipsed up the back stairs of the station the following morning. All night, the possibility of a mole in her camp had played on her mind. Everyone was aware of the umbrella of confidentiality in this case, it was baffling to think someone would jeopardise their position on the team by sharing details with the victim's husband, even if he was a fellow cop. On the other hand, she couldn't see how Blane had managed to access such sensitive information without help.

In the incident room, she was surprised to find Pemberton hunched over his computer, Dark sat beside him, Spencer on the next desk, all tapping away. It wasn't yet 7 a.m.

'Morning, ma'am.' Pemberton shut down his laptop as she approached. 'Coffee?' he offered.

Helen declined. 'Has anyone seen the super?'

Heads shook. She moved into her office, dropped her bag behind her desk and looked out warily at her team, then closed the blind, shutting off her view into the incident room. Was this how it was going to be now, looking at every member of her staff, questioning their loyalty? It couldn't be Pemberton, he'd saved her life on the last case, gone out on a limb. No, she was pretty sure she could trust him. And Dark and Spencer were her best investigators. But the others? What would they have to gain? She placed her head in her hands. These were people she worked closely with, day in, day out. She spent more time with them than her family.

The sour taste in her mouth spread across her tongue. Jenkins's continued absence irritated her. She was thinking about heading up to his office when a single knock at the door was followed by Spencer entering. He looked excited.

'What is it, Steve?'

'One of the incident response officers from core shift three has just phoned. Reckons he knows our ATM guy.'

'And he's only just realised?'

'His shift only returned from their rest days this morning. He took his wife away to Bruges for their anniversary, hadn't seen the news coverage. Apparently, he picked up a Sean Marshall on Wednesday morning for trying to pinch batteries from the Co-op. To coin the officer's description, Marshall was as "high as a kite". He had to let him sleep it off in the cell before the doctor cleared him for questioning. He remembers it specifically because he only managed to charge him before his shift finished at 6 p.m. and he wanted to leave on time because he had an early flight the next morning.'

'So, the offender was banged up all day?'

'Yup.'

She sat back in her chair. If he was in police custody, he couldn't be their killer. 'Are you sure he's got the right guy?'

'He reckons so. Says he's always hanging around in that same Adidas hoody. He's bringing him in now.'

***

Helen stared into sable eyes of Sean Marshall. The response officer wasn't wrong about the clothing. He wore a black Adidas top today with the same white lines running down the sleeves and, from the pungent smell in the room, she suspected it was the same one he'd worn at the ATM on Wednesday, when he'd withdrawn money using Sinead's card. They'd arrested him for using a stolen bank card and spent another half an hour at the station, waiting for the duty solicitor to arrive. By the time they were ready, she'd lost all patience and decided she was interviewing herself. It felt disloyal to her team, but if there was a mole out there somewhere, feeding information back, then she'd make sure she was at the heart of the investigation from now on.

She ignored his solicitor when she marched into the room and worked through the formalities quickly. Marshall hadn't come forward, despite the public appeals, and he'd been identified with Sinead's bank card. When she asked him about his movements on Wednesday evening, after he left the police station, he shrugged and said he couldn't remember. And the way he slouched with his head to one side, arm over the back of his chair, did nothing to curb her annoyance.

Helen opened a buff file and laid out the still of Marshall at the ATM. The date and time were clearly marked at the bottom.

Marshall looked at his solicitor and shrugged again.

'Do you know where this was taken?' Helen asked.

He made great play of examining the photo. 'Looks like I'm withdrawing money. I guess it would be a cashpoint.'

'Which one?'

'Don't know.'

'It's the cashpoint on Weston High Street,' Helen said.

'So, I live around the corner. That don't mean a thing.'

'Whose account were you withdrawing money from?' she asked.

'No idea.'

'What do you mean, no idea?'

'Well, a fella stopped me like, and asked if I could get him two hundred and fifty quid out with the card.'

'Why do you think he asked you, instead of doing it himself?'

'I dunno. Suppose he didn't want to be on your camera.' He widened his eyes.

His attitude was starting to rankle. 'This is serious, Mr Marshall. Do you know who this card belonged to?'

He shook his head.

'You don't remember the name on the card?'

'No.'

'This card was owned by Sinead O'Donnell. She was brutally murdered on Wednesday.'

'The dead cop.' He looked genuinely surprised. 'I don't know nothing 'bout that. Look, I was helping out a mate. He offered to pay me twenty quid.'

Pemberton looked up from his notes beside him. 'And the rest.'

'What your mate's name?' Helen said.

'Don't know. Haven't seen him before.'

'I thought you said he was a mate.'

'We're all mates on the street. Help each other out. Not that you guys'd know.'

Helen clenched her teeth. The constable that brought him in said Marshall was registered at an address in Weston, but could often be found sleeping off a trip under the railway bridge in town. 'What did he look like?' she asked.

'Who?'

'The guy who asked you to withdraw the cash.'

'I dunno. Errm. Tall, stocky.'

'Is that it?'

'He had a hood pulled right down over his face, I remember now.'

'Oh, come on, Sean. You must have seen more than that. What was he wearing?'

'I dunno. I'd not long since shot up. Wasn't paying attention.'

'So, you make a habit of withdrawing cash from strangers using stolen cards, do you?'

'I didn't know it was stolen.'

'Are you telling me you didn't look at the name on the card?'

'No, I didn't. Like I said, I was helping out a mate.'

Helen retrieved a photo of Gordon Turner from the file. 'Is this the man who approached you?'

Marshall stared at the photo for several seconds, then met her gaze. 'No idea.'

Helen cussed inwardly. The ATM linked Marshall with Sinead's card, but he was nowhere near the scene of the murder in the daytime because he was in a police cell. He couldn't have a better alibi. She was about to call for a break, rethink, when he tapped the edge of the photo with a grubby finger. 'I do know where this guy's been staying though.'

Helen stilled. 'You know him?'

'I wouldn't say I know him. He's hooked onto the hard stuff.'

'Not like you?' Pemberton said.

'Nah. I'm a social user.'

'So, where does he live?' She pushed the photo further towards him.

Marshall sat back in his chair and eyed her a moment. 'What am I getting out of this?'

'A cup of tea and a lift home, if you're lucky. Now what's his address?'

CHAPTER 46

Helen spotted the squat as soon as they turned off Birch Road into Groves End, a road of Victorian terraces with front doors that led directly onto the pavement. The Sytex screens covering the windows and doors of their target, number 72a, glistened in the afternoon sunshine.

At the rear of the terrace was a single lane leading to narrow back yards and it was here that Marshall said the squatters were entering the flat and where Helen now stood, surrounded by a tactical support team. White paint flaked off an ill-fitting wooden gate, warped with years of rain.

'Handy place for a den,' Pemberton whispered beside her. And he was right. It was within walking distance from the shops, cafés and banks on Weston High Street. It was also near Lilian Cooper's home, where Sinead's bag had been dumped, and less than five minutes from the ATM where her card was used.

After deploying two officers to watch the front, she signalled for the others to creep across the paved yard and watched the officer in front check the Sytex around the back door. His colleague stood beside him, the battering ram in his hand, in case they needed to force entry. The sheet wobbled as he touched it. He slid it aside to expose a missing bottom windowpane beside the back door – the squatters' access point – and called out, announcing their arrival, followed by, 'Anyone home?'

When there was no answer on his second call, he turned. Helen gave him the nod and he climbed through the gap. Colleagues crawled in behind him.

Within seconds, they were teeming out again.

'Well?' Helen asked. She was in the yard now, her coverall itching against her skin. 'Is he not there?'

'Oh, he's there all right. Well, what's left of him.'

***

A thick smell of singed cloth and must filled the air as Helen climbed into the squat. She entered a small galley-style kitchen with a scuffed floor and cheap laminated cupboards. Empty milk cartons and egg boxes were discarded across surfaces marked with coffee stains that had yellowed with age. A lone kettle stood on the side, beside a sink full of dirty mugs and plates. Flies buzzed around an overflowing black bin liner in the corner.

The hallway was a small passage. A grubby toilet, seat up, was visible through an open door to the right, the main living area to the left. The end was blocked off. Access from the front door, it seemed, led to the flat upstairs.

Helen wandered into the sitting room, an open space that ran the length of the house. She pulled out her torch and illuminated the area in a tunnel of light. A blackened piece of foil crunched under her feet on the bare concrete flooring.

There were no sofas or settees, no table and chairs. Instead, three single mattresses were laid on the floor, one against each wall. Used needles littered the floor. In the middle, the concrete was singed and blackened where it looked like someone had lit a fire. More empty milk cartons, egg boxes and chocolate bar wrappers piled in the corner.

Spoons, pieces of foil and candles were strewn about the floor.

Every time Helen entered a drugs den it saddened her. Heroin was such a cruel drug. So much so that the body craved it at the expense of every other routine habit and the addict's whole being, whole focus, concentrated on how to get their next fix. They existed on cheap food, like milk and eggs, and sold anything and everything to fund their habit. It was a pitiful existence.

At the end of the room, beneath the window, a body lay on a dirty mattress. His bare torso was partially covered by a grubby orange blanket. His right arm was exposed, a needle still injected into the vein. With his eyes closed, head turned to the side, Gordon Turner could have been mistaken for being heavily under the influence, or sleeping, if it wasn't for the grey tinge to his skin, the bluish lips.

Helen instinctively bent down and checked the pulse on his neck. His skin was stone cold through her rubber gloves.

'I doubt we'll be seeing any of his housemates anytime soon,' Pemberton said, eyeing the empty mattresses.

Helen glanced at an upturned blue bottle on the window ledge. Coincidences rarely happened in law enforcement, especially on a homicide case, yet over the past few days they'd lost Sinead's neighbour, a possible witness, to suicide and now they were looking at the corpse of their prime suspect.

'It seems a bit convenient, don't you think?' Helen said to Pemberton.

'Has all the markings of an overdose.' Pemberton crouched down, ran his torch over the dead man's arm. 'No obvious defensive bruising. Doesn't look like there's been a struggle.' He pulled back the blanket. 'Well, what do you know,' he said, fishing something out of Turner's pocket. 'We've got a phone, at least.'

'Bag it up,' Helen said. 'We'll take it back with us, get it examined.'

CHAPTER 47

Helen combed her hair back from her face with her fingers. Pemberton and she were in her office, scrolling through endless names and times on the internal audit sheet, which listed all those who'd accessed the homicide systems, looking for something unusual. She should delegate this task, there wasn't time to look now. But the burning desire to crush the question hanging over a potential leak in her team was all-encompassing. Teamwork existed on trust and the very idea that one of her people had betrayed that trust was like a fishbone lodged in the back of her throat. So, with her team co-ordinating the search of Gordon Turner's home and the station techies retrieving the details off his phone, she'd spent the past hour wading through names.

She was about to suggest coffee when Pemberton looked up. 'Who's Stephen Rotherham?' he said, his face grim.

Helen paused. 'Well, unless I'm mistaken, there's a PC Rotherham on the core training team. Why?'

'I think we have our culprit.'

'What?'

'Stephen Rotherham. Accessed our systems at 2.20 p.m. on Friday.' He pushed out a long sigh. 'We'll need to get it checked, of course, but it's a breach. Especially since Blane worked in training and was in the office on Friday afternoon.'

Helen slumped in her chair. Everyone who accessed the homicide network had their own unique entry codes. 'How the hell did Rotherham manage to get access to *our* system?'

'I'm not sure. We need to refer this to Professional Standards for investigation.'

She rubbed her forehead, the idea of coffee no longer palatable. 'Blane called into the office on Friday. Can you remember what time it was?'

'Early afternoon.'

'So, the timing could fit.'

'These aren't his login details. Perhaps he used Stephen's,' Pemberton suggested. 'We'd have to assume Stephen was in on it, everybody is supposed to log out of the computer when they leave their desk.'

Helen closed her eyes. When she'd worked in CID, a fellow detective, Louise Fleming, had been accused of looking up a new boyfriend on the PNC. She'd been dismissed and the day the allegation broke she was accompanied out of the office and suspended until a full investigation into her actions had been completed. Helen never saw her again, but she'd never forget Louise's flaming cheeks, her shameful face. The idea of putting a fellow colleague through that, especially when she didn't know whether or not they were guilty, sent a chill down her spine. But they couldn't afford to ignore it either. If Rotherham was their leak, he could be feeding back information right now.

'At least it doesn't look like it's someone on our team,' Pemberton said.

Helen nodded, her relief coloured by the grim reality of what the situation presented.

She gave a sigh, reached over and grabbed the phone. Shopping a colleague, whatever the intention, was never pleasant.

***

While Helen reported the security breach, Pemberton chased up Gordon Turner's phone with the station techies and he'd now returned with a bunch of photos, which he laid out across his desk.

'These were all taken at various times over the past four months,' he said.

'That was quick,' Helen said. 'The phone wasn't locked or coded?'

'Apparently not.'

'Odd. You'd think he'd want to protect these from prying eyes, especially when he was high.'

'He lived in a squat with nowhere to hide. Anything precious, he'd keep with him.'

Helen ran her gaze over the photos. Sinead at the supermarket, with Ava sitting in the trolley; her standing outside the school gates, coat buttoned up to her chin, waiting for her children; at the park, pushing Thomas on the swing; climbing out of a police car in uniform. There were a mixture of distance shots and close-ups, although some of the close-ups held the blur of a hurried zoom lens. In every one Sinead was occupied elsewhere or looking away. She clearly had no idea she was being photographed.

'It looks like he's been watching her for a while,' Helen said. 'Do we have the exact dates each of these were taken?'

'Not at the moment, I asked them to print them out urgently. It wouldn't be difficult to check back on the phone and find out the specifics. And that's not all.' Pemberton grabbed his laptop and indicated for her to follow him into her office, where he inserted a memory stick and clicked a key. The screen turned black.

Within seconds, the screen crackled and cleared. The lens was focused on something green and rough. As it panned out, she could see it was corded carpet. It caught the arm of a chair, the edge of a desk, blurring slightly as it moved around.

It was the offices in Billings factory.

The lens halted on a woman leaning her back against a radiator.

A cloth was tied around her mouth, her hair hung limp, the

curls jiggling on her shoulders as she shook her head, short sharp jerks.

'Oh my God!' Helen's throat constricted as the camera zoomed in on Sinead's terrified face. 'He filmed her?' The muted sound only added to the sinister backdrop.

'The whole bloody thing.' Pemberton gave a sombre nod.

Helen had seen many gruesome sights during her career in the police, but this was probably the most harrowing. She flinched as a gloved hand burnt the insides of Sinead's arms, one after another. Flinched again as Sinead jumped. Moments later, the camera focused in on her severed fingers across the floor. It was brutal. When the footage ended, she felt both nauseous and angry in equal measures.

Pemberton closed the laptop to a heavy silence.

'Any evidence he made contact with her before the attack?' Helen asked eventually, trying to supress the anger burning within her. It was barbaric to think someone could do this.

'That's the strange part,' Pemberton replied. 'There are no contacts on his phone, no evidence of calls made, or texts to anyone. No downloaded apps or links to social media.'

'Are you saying he kept this phone as a camera?'

'It looks that way. There's a couple of early shots on there, of his old flat. The High Street. Nothing much. It's mostly Sinead.'

'This isn't the number the landlord gave us, is it?'

'No. We've already got billing on that number. He hasn't used it in a month or so. Maybe he threw it away, his brother did say he'd grown paranoid and thought someone was after him.'

'If these photos were taken over the past four months, his call records for the old phone showed he was using that to make calls over the same period. I don't understand. Why keep a separate phone for photos and film?'

'Maybe the camera wasn't working on the other one. Or maybe he wanted to keep them separate.'

'Hmm. What about Sinead's phone?'

'No sign of it at his address.'

When Helen spoke, her tone was low, almost as if she was speaking to herself. 'If he fixated on Sinead, stalked her and killed her, as this evidence might suggest, why would he record this on a phone, and keep that phone on his person?'

'As a keepsake maybe? It's well known some killers keep trophies. And we know he filmed his other victim while she suffered.'

CHAPTER 48

Helen sat at her desk and looked out into the incident room, her gaze falling on the photo of Sinead before she died. The vital young woman, the capable cop.

It seemed unbelievable she'd be taken in by a man of Gordon Turner's calibre, a heroin addict, no matter what stories he constructed or how manipulative he was. Even if he had cleaned up, surely she'd be suspicious? Which meant if he did pick her up in the country lane, he'd probably hit her over the head and dazed her. But there was no blood at the scene, no sign of an altercation.

She clicked her pen on and off, on and off.

They still had to establish how Gordon Turner died, and why. But there was something else bothering her.

She pulled a blank sheet of A4 from the side of her desk and wrote down six words: *who, what, how, when, where, why* – the key questions for a senior investigating officer to answer in order to solve a homicide case. Usually, these were the questions asked at the beginning of a case and when these components were unravelled, the motive came to light. And it was the motive for Sinead's murder she couldn't decode.

Sinead ultimately died from a severed carotid artery at Billings factory on Wednesday afternoon; the pathologist confirmed she died on site. Her handbag was found dumped close to Turner's flat. On his phone was a file of photos and footage of Sinead, clearly taken over a prolonged period, some as long as four months ago. Blane had been his case officer and intimated that Turner had shown an interest in Sinead. An interest he'd shrugged off as manipulation by an ex-offender.

They were aware Turner stalked his victims before he struck.

The bag with Sinead's finger stubs was dumped close to his squat. The ATM used to withdraw cash on her card was nearby too and the close proximity bothered Helen. If he had taken the trouble to kill Sinead, play out his fantasy, surely he'd be more likely to dump her possessions on the other side of town, away from where he was staying. And who was the man who ordered Sean Marshall to withdraw money from Sinead's card at the ATM?

What really bothered her was the change in MO. Turner's previous attacks were sexually motivated. He wound cling film around the face of his last victim and filmed her suffocating. He'd tried the same with the sex worker. He'd filmed the attack on Sinead and this time he was recording gratuitous violence. There was no plastic wrap at the scene, no evidence of sexual assault.

***

Pemberton walked up Nigel Turner's drive towards his car. Delivering news of a death was never easy and this one was particularly tricky.

Until they knew more, they'd treat Gordon Turner's death as 'unexplained'. There was nothing to suggest it was suspicious, but nothing to suggest it was intentional either. On face value, it appeared to be an overdose and in view of Gordon's recent medical history and his addiction to heroin, it was possible he'd administered it himself, either purposely or by accident. In view of the other circumstances surrounding the case and Sinead's murder, they couldn't be sure. He'd ordered Spencer to stay with the body until the pathologist had done his initial assessment and it was removed to the mortuary, and then arranged for an officer to guard the premises until the CSIs finished their sweep. Uniform had started house-to-house nearby. They now had to dig further into Gordon Turner's background, to establish exactly what had happened.

He was climbing into his car when his mobile rang. The caller ID was unknown.

'Acting DI Pemberton.'

'Hi. My name's Angela Ingram. You left some messages for me.'

Pemberton thought hard. It was the ex-girlfriend of Blane O'Donnell who hadn't responded to his messages. With the recent discovery, it didn't seem quite so important now. 'Thanks for coming back to me,' he said. 'I understand you were in a relationship with Blane O'Donnell. I'm working through details for a case and wanted to check some dates with you.'

'Okay. I don't want to talk on the phone. Are you free to meet?'

The woman's chipped tone threw Pemberton. She sounded hurried. 'I can be. I thought you lived in France?'

'I do. I'm in Hampton at the moment. I arrived this morning. Can you meet me?'

'You're welcome to come to the station,' he said. 'I'm sure I could find us a room.'

'I can't do that. Do you know Hayes, the coffee house on High Street?'

'Yes.'

'Okay, I'll meet you outside there in half an hour. I'll be wearing a denim jacket and sunglasses. Please come on your own. If I see anyone else, I'll leave.'

She called off, leaving Pemberton staring at the phone, nonplussed. He'd left three messages over the past few days, which she'd seemingly ignored. Now she was in Hampton, she wanted to meet urgently. And why alone?

He inserted his key and turned over the engine. It wouldn't be much of a detour to stop off at Hayes on the way back to the station.

CHAPTER 49

Jenkins was winding up a telephone call when Helen entered his office. He waved her in and gestured for her to sit as he placed the receiver in its cradle.

The way his jacket was tossed to the side of the desk was incongruous with the fastidiously neat piles of paperwork.

'How are you?' he asked.

Helen eyed him warily. 'I'm fine. Did you get my email?'

'Yes.' He squared his hands on the desk. 'That's bad news about Blane. Won't do the force PR any good at all. How are the young boys holding up?'

He'd not only received her report, he'd read it. Yet he hadn't returned any of her calls. 'They're doing all right. I've spoken to the parents, explained the bail conditions.'

'Good. I've talked to Professional Standards. They've suspended PC Rotherham pending an investigation.' He looked down at his hands a split second and when he raised his gaze, his face was grave. 'Helen, are you sure there are no other leaks within the team? Only, after the initial problems, the chief constable is jumpy.'

Helen took a breath. The people on her team were like family, it was bad enough that she'd questioned their integrity in the past twenty-four hours. 'I'm sure.'

'Good. Well, we'll see how the investigation pans out. The

IOPC have been in touch too. They have your statement and will be looking at the evidence this week to decide whether or not an inquiry is warranted.'

Helen thanked him. 'We found Gordon Turner's body this afternoon. On the face of it, it looks like an overdose, but I do have concerns. I tried to call—'

He held up a hand. 'Yes, I'm sorry about that, I've been detained. Why don't you fill me in first?'

The lack of explanation for his absence made her uneasy. What was going on? She gave him an update of the investigation since yesterday lunchtime. He listened carefully to the details about Gordon Turner.

'I've written up my initial report and emailed a copy to the chief constable,' Helen said. 'But—' She was interrupted by his phone ringing.

'I'll just get this.'

She watched him grab the receiver, his eyes darting about as he answered the questions with one-word answers. She couldn't determine who he was talking to, or what the conversation was about. It seemed to go on forever.

'Okay, please continue,' Jenkins said, before he'd had chance to replace the receiver in its cradle. The fact that he didn't mention who he was talking to was disconcerting.

Helen talked him through the issues with Gordon Turner. 'It seems odd he would leave evidence on his own doorstep,' she said. 'He left a syringe behind in the factory too. Surely, he'd realise we'd trace his DNA.'

'Perhaps he was high when he left the syringe behind.'

'And why torture her to such lengths?' she continued. 'He clearly has a penchant for cling film, his previous attacks were about a warped sense of control. Sinead was beaten.'

'He'd twisted the facts in his mind. His prison governor said he had a major dislike of police. When he discovered Sinead was a cop, perhaps he decided to make her pay for his treatment.'

'I'm not sure, sir. The man who withdrew cash using Sinead's card didn't recognise Turner.'

'By his own admission, he himself was high. He'd be an unreliable witness if he did recognise someone.' He raised his tone a notch. 'Come on, Helen, photos and footage were found on Turner's phone. He burnt Sinead in the same place as his last victim. The syringe puts him at the factory.'

'I still think there might be more to this. It all seems too... convenient. And Turner was last seen by his case officer talking to one of the Gladstone brothers, who we suspect are rebuilding Chilli Franks's network. We know Sinead had money problems. It's possible he was working with them, collecting debts. Or perhaps they set him up.'

'It's possible,' Jenkins repeated. 'I take it you don't have any evidence to back this up?'

Helen sighed inwardly. 'I've contacted Inspector Burns in organised crime. He's looking into any association between the Gladstones and Turner.'

'Okay, let's see what he comes up with. In the meantime, we run with what we have.'

'But—'

You're questioning the evidence, Helen,' he cut in. 'It's one of the things that makes you such a good detective. Don't overthink it.'

His words knocked her off balance, such was the rarity of praise from Jenkins, and she couldn't help wondering what effected this sudden change in his mood.

'We've plenty of time to establish the answers to these questions, if indeed there are any. In the meantime, we need to allay the fears of the public and the press. And let Blane know we've tracked Turner down.'

Helen tucked a stray strand of hair behind her ear. 'Okay, I'll go out and speak with Blane.'

'I'm afraid you can't. That was the chief on the phone. The press office is organising a conference for the major news channels in less than an hour. You're to be there as the senior investigating officer in the case. Chief constable's orders. He wants a united approach.'

'Someone needs to alert the family before the media. Blane's police. He'd usually be told by a senior officer.'

'He should have thought of that before he harassed a couple of kids. You need to delegate this one, Helen. Send Dark. She doesn't know him personally and she's a trained liaison officer. She can look after any welfare issues, point him in the direction of counselling and support.' He didn't wait for her agreement. 'Right, while you're here, there's something else I'd like you to take a look at.'

He moved his jacket, rootled through a pile of papers on the side of his desk, pulled out a sheet of A4 and handed it over.

'What's this?' she said, taking it.

'It's the last performance report for Ivan Newton.'

The new inspector. With the events of the past few days, she'd put his imminent arrival out of her mind. She ran her eyes over the sheet and started. 'He's a trained Senior Investigating Officer?'

'Yes.'

'Is it wise to have two SIOs on the same team?' she asked, astounded. An SIO usually ran an investigation. They kept their own policy log, theorising on different approaches, explaining every judgement they made, and deployed their team accordingly. It was a bit like employing two head chefs in a restaurant.

'He's keen, enthusiastic and fiercely ambitious. All he needs now is a mentor.'

'You want me to mentor him? I haven't even been with homicide a year myself.'

'Yes, and during that time you've had good results. Now it's time to take a step back and pass on some of the knowledge and insight you've learned.'

Helen felt a flare of anger. This wasn't about finding the right fit for her team. It was about keeping her off the streets, in the office. It was about Jenkins appeasing his own guilt for not supporting her decisions on the last case.

Suddenly she realised why she recognised the name. Ivan Newton and she had been on the same course last year. 'Human Exploitation and Modern Day Slavery', a three-day residential course in Derbyshire. And now she pictured him: a stocky Lancashire man in his early thirties, with a bushy beard and a bellowing voice, who saw himself as the joker of the pack. Nothing wrong with that in essence, until he stretched the bounds of humour when he froze another delegate's car keys in a block of ice on the last day of the course. What he didn't anticipate was the panic when the delegate was called home because his pregnant wife had gone into early labour and he couldn't find his car keys. And when he did finally find them, he couldn't use them, the water had messed up the mechanism.

Ivan had been sorry afterwards, but him taking such steps 'for a laugh' sat uncomfortably with the whole course. Shame really, because he'd also shown moments of real vision. Though the two together were a recipe for disaster.

'I'm not sure about this,' she said, relaying the story.

'An unfortunate judgement call,' Jenkins said dismissively. 'I've seen worse.'

Helen levelled Jenkins's gaze. The last thing she needed was someone with poor judgement on her management, especially if she was to mentor them. 'He needs more time to mature.'

'The decision's made, Helen. He's joining you on Wednesday, I hope you'll make him welcome.'

She stared at him, working hard to prevent her jaw from hitting the floor, about to protest further when he spoke up again.

'There's something else.' His face tightened. 'My partner, David, has testicular cancer.'

Helen baulked. She wasn't even aware he was in a

relationship, let alone with a man called David. 'I'm so sorry.' She cringed at the banality of her words.

Jenkins gave a brief nod of acknowledgement and turned to the window.

Suddenly it was her that felt awkward. 'What's the prognosis?' she asked quietly.

'We don't know. That's why I've been absent, yesterday and today. I wanted to tell you, I'm applying for a career break for three months to look after him. I need to ask you to cover my position.'

'Me?' From what she'd seen, the superintendent role was full of politics, budgetary constraints and strategy meetings. She couldn't be more unsuitable for the role. 'I'm not sure I'm the right person.'

He lifted a hand to silence her. 'You know what this place is like. Plenty of people waiting in the wings to take over. I need someone I can trust. With so much uncertainty hanging over us, I need to know I've got this role to come back to.' A sharp intake of breath. 'Think about it. That's all I'm asking. If you decide to take it, another trained SIO will alleviate the strain.'

***

Helen's eyes grew watery as she left Jenkins's office and traipsed downstairs. This was the most emotion he'd ever displayed, the most insight she'd ever had into his personal life, and it was heart-wrenching.

She'd questioned his absence in the office, his focus on the potential organised crime link, his lacklustre interest in the investigation over the past twenty-four hours, and now she knew why. She'd been so convinced he was struggling to work with her since her return from injury leave and searching for the opportunity to sideline her, that she'd single-mindedly failed to consider alternative explanations. And for that she felt wretched.

What was it she was constantly saying to her staff? Assume nothing. Believe Nobody. Challenge Everything. It was the basis of detection, their mantra. Well, it was about time she took a dose of her own medicine.

***

DC Dark was at the filing cabinets reading a sheet of A4 when Helen entered the incident room. 'Where's Pemberton?' she asked.

'Out delivering the news to Gordon Turner's family.'

'And Spencer?'

'Finishing up at the crime scene, I believe.'

'Okay.' Helen talked her through going out to see Blane. She was finishing up when she was reminded of her first encounter with him at the factory, the bruising on her shoulder still aching. He'd been contrite yesterday evening, but he certainly had a quick temper and the suspension from duty would do nothing to lift his mood. 'I'll give Spencer a ring, get him to meet you there,' she added. 'You can go in together.'

CHAPTER 50

Apart from a couple of parked cars and a family wandering out of the nearby pizza restaurant, Hampton High Street was empty for a Sunday afternoon, the warm weather encouraging locals away from the town centre to BBQs and picnics in the country. Hayes's cheery pink awning stretched out onto the pavement, tables and chairs set neatly beneath it. In the far corner, a woman sat with her head buried in a magazine. A messy ponytail hung out of the back of her baseball cap. She wore sunglasses; a denim jacket draped over her shoulders.

The woman didn't look up as Pemberton strode across. 'Angela Ingram?' he asked.

She slid her glasses down her nose, peered over them and nodded.

'Acting Detective Inspector Sean Pemberton,' he said.

She ignored his proffered hand. 'Do you have ID?'

Taken aback, Pemberton nodded and reached into his pocket.

She examined his badge, then checked the street before she removed the sunglasses to reveal an angular face framed by a wavy fringe. A few curls had escaped her ponytail and nestled at her cheeks.

Pemberton noted the empty latte glass in front of her. 'Can I get you a drink?'

'I'll have another latte, thank you.'

He moved into the café and ordered coffees, all the time keeping half an eye on the woman outside. They got lots of time-wasters on murder investigations. Crank calls, people giving differing accounts. He desperately hoped this wasn't another, especially with the wealth of paperwork he had to work through in connection with the Turner case. But something about the woman's demeanour bothered him. The way she kept looking around her, checking the street. If he wasn't mistaken, this was one very frightened woman.

'What did you want to see me about, Ms Ingram?' Pemberton said after he'd carried out the coffees. He settled himself into a shaded area in the corner.

'You're investigating the murder of Sinead O'Donnell, aren't you?' She paused, awaiting his acknowledgement before she continued. 'That's why you contacted me.'

'I contacted you to check dates with regards to your relationship with Blane O'Donnell. It's quite routine.'

'I have some information. I need to be assured whatever I say will be treated in confidence.'

'You sound like you are in some kind of trouble.'

'Not really. Well… I could be. Oh, God.' She rubbed the back of her neck.

The new information on Gordon Turner and the connection to Sinead hadn't yet been released to the press, the powers that be were working on a press conference as they spoke. He was aware there were a lot of unanswered questions and they still needed to find Turner's killer, if there was one. Perhaps if he could settle her nerves, she could help.

He gave a brief nod. 'I'll do what I can.'

'I don't know where to start,' she said.

Pemberton sat back in his chair. 'Why don't you tell me why you felt the need to come here today?'

She took a sip of her coffee. 'Blane and I lived in Dorset before he moved here. We were together for just over two years, shared a home for about eighteen months. After we separated, I went to live in France; he moved up here to be closer to his mother and transferred to Hampton police.'

Pemberton gave a brief nod, resisting the temptation to shift in his seat. This wasn't how he'd seen the talk unfolding.

'Blane was a very attentive partner. Interested in everything I did, liked to know where I was, who I was with. He was also kind, gentle, patient. I was flattered, to be honest. My previous partner had worked away and travelled a lot and when he was home, he was lazy. Blane was always around. We spent more and more time together until moving in seemed the only option. We'd only been together eight months or so, but it felt right. He was what I'd been looking for all my life, or so I thought.'

'What changed?'

'It's hard to pinpoint. Difficult to say an exact time. It's almost like you become a possession and he won't let you go. When I look back, I can see now he was controlling. He knew every aspect of my life, every movement I made. At the time, I mistook it for attentiveness.'

A car passed, the heavy beat of music momentarily filling the air, and then all was quiet.

'I think it must have been when I changed my job. I was a buyer for a clothes company and the new job required more time on the road. He was forever phoning and texting, asking where I was. It was stifling. Anyway, I asked for a break, said I needed some space. He wasn't keen on the idea. It took a while for him to agree. Eventually, he moved out and stayed in a hotel nearby. We were separated about a month, although we still met up for drinks and he called in to see me. During our time apart, I realised our relationship was oppressive and decided to end it. So I asked him to come around and we talked. I told him how I felt. It all seemed to go okay, he was shocked, sad, but... he listened. Until I said we should give up the house. I don't know what it was, but at that comment he turned. One moment, I was sitting on the sofa talking about places to live, the next he'd thrust a hand at my throat and

251

lifted me from the seat. He slammed me against the wall. I thought he was going to kill me.'

Pemberton sat forward. 'What happened?'

'Somebody knocked the door. One of our neighbours. They'd heard the noise. He let go. Got rid of the neighbour. When he came back, I was in the kitchen, trying to get out of the back door. It was locked and I couldn't find the key. I could never understand why he always kept the doors locked when he was in the house, front and back. He was sorry, remorseful. Said he didn't know what had come over him.'

'What did you do?'

'Asked him to leave. I was terrified.'

'Did you call anyone, report the incident to the police?'

She closed her eyes. It was a moment before she opened them. 'What, and tell my account to Blane's colleagues? They'd never believe me. He was popular around the station, he'd received a commendation the month before for using the... What do you call it?' She waved her hand in the air. 'The Heimlich manoeuvre, to save a baby from choking.

'Blane pleaded with me to keep it quiet. He'd lose his job if it came out. He said if I told anyone, he'd find me, finish what he'd started and hide my body. He'd always said criminals were stupid, if they were clever our jails would be empty. Used to joke about committing the perfect crime. I should have realised.'

'Had he ever been violent or aggressive to you before?'

'Not violent, no. Blane doesn't like confrontation. He's fine with it in the police, not in a personal setting; not with family. We barely exchanged cross words when we were together. If I had a moan, he listened, apologised. When I said I needed a break, he was upset and said he loved me, would do whatever it took to make it work. But this... this was something else.

'When he left the house, I was terrified. The man I'd known for two years wasn't who I thought he was and I couldn't tell anyone. My neck was covered in bruises. I was mindful of his caution, worried he'd come back. So, I left. That night, I packed my things, took a night flight and went to my sister's in France. He wouldn't be protected by his police cronies there. And I haven't been back.'

'Did you speak with him afterwards?'

She shook her head. 'His mother turned up at my sister's a week after I left. I was petrified. I told her exactly what happened and she apologised, pleaded with me not to report it to the police. Blane was an only child and could never please his father when he was young. When he was eight, his father left and his mother moved them both in with her parents. They didn't hear from him for years. Blane tried to trace his dad in his late teens. His dad refused to have anything to do with him. His mother said Blane suffered from a fear of rejection and he was dealing with it, getting help. All he wanted, all he ever wanted, was a family of his own. She convinced me he'd never been aggressive before, even offered me money, although I didn't want her cash.'

'Why contact us now?'

She tugged at her collar. 'I wanted to call. I did. Several times. I felt guilty for not reporting the incident in case it happened to someone else. But I kept losing my nerve. I was worried I would be talking to one of Blane's mates. Then, when I saw an article online about his wife's murder, I couldn't stop thinking about what happened to me. What if she asked for a break, or wanted to end the relationship? Perhaps this time he was more controlled. He'd rather kill her than lose face.'

CHAPTER 51

DC Rosa Dark checked the clock on the dashboard again. Where the hell was Spencer? He'd been in the town centre when the DCI called and asked him to join her at Blane's mother's house. Only minutes away. He should have arrived before her.

The street outside Blane's mother's house was empty that afternoon, the press interest in the family waning. She watched a couple of pigeons wander up and down the nearby telegraph pole. It was probably a good job Blane's charge and suspension hadn't yet been released to the media. It was late when he was released on bail last night and, after the discovery at Gordon Turner's that morning, the line was to deliver an upbeat press conference, reiterate the positive result. The DCI had somehow placated the boys' families. Blane's charge and suspension would be pushed out later no doubt, under the cover of the result. Played down as a distressed husband taking the law into his own hands, his actions coloured by grief.

A glance in her rear-view mirror. Nothing. The pigeons left the telegraph pole and flew above the housetops. Dark checked her phone. Spencer hadn't responded to her texts. She opened the door and climbed out of the car. There was no point in waiting around. She might as well make a start.

It was a welfare visit, after all. She was here to deliver good news to the family. News that Sinead's killer had been found. Blane had been calm when they'd taken him in for interview yesterday. Remorseful. He'd taken his own investigation too far, but this had been the essence of his actions, to seek justice. She'd deliver the decision, check on the family and get back to the station to assist with processing the evidence recovered from Gordon Turner's squat. They were snowed under. Plenty of time later to chew off Spencer's ears.

Dark rang the doorbell. When there was no answer, she tried it again, stepped back and checked the front room window. Hopefully they weren't out. The press conference would be starting shortly, she wanted to pass on the message before they heard the news elsewhere. She was mulling this over when a door slammed inside.

Seconds later, the front door opened a fraction, Blane O'Donnell's stocky frame filling the gap. Gone was the coiffed shiny hair, the manicured beard. Not surprising after what he'd been through the past few days. But there was an uneasiness to him. Nothing to do with the straggly hair that looked in dire need of a wash, the shadows beneath his eyes. It was his twisted, contorted face that unsettled her.

He stared at her.

'I need to talk to you, Blane,' she said.

He didn't answer. Didn't move.

'There's been a development. May I come in?'

He seemed to hesitate for the shortest of seconds, then moved aside. 'You'll have to be quick. I've got an appointment.'

This was going to be more difficult than she'd anticipated. Dark glanced back as the door closed behind her.

She stepped over the toys strewn across the sitting room floor. 'How are the children doing?' she said, glancing around. He seemed to be alone.

'My mother's taken them into town shopping. Thomas needs new socks for school.'

'Ah.' She gave a brief smile. A Ford Focus drew up outside.

255

She looked out hopefully, expecting to see Spencer's spindly frame when a man in a T-shirt and jeans climbed out and crossed to a house on the other side of the road.

'Shall we sit down?'

Blane remained standing. 'As I said, I need to go out.'

'It won't take long.'

Reluctantly, he edged towards the sofa.

Dark moved a teddy bear on the armchair beside the window and sat. If she turned sideways on, she could still keep half an eye on the window.

She folded her hands into her lap and passed on the information about Gordon Turner in as much detail as she was able. As she spoke, Blane's shoulders relaxed, and when she mentioned the press conference, he looked visibly calmer.

'I can't believe it,' he said. 'I mean it was always possible, but... I don't know. I had hoped Turner would piece his life back together. He'd even reached out to his brother.'

Dark pressed her lips together empathetically.

'At least it explains the syringe found in the factory.'

'Why don't I get us both a drink?' she said. 'I've given you some tough news. Take a moment to let it sink in.' He shifted in his seat. 'Unless you're in a hurry for your appointment?'

'No, no, it's fine. I'm meeting Mum and the kids in McDonald's in town. I can manage a few more minutes.'

She made to stand.

He was up before she could do so. 'I'll do it.'

While he was in the kitchen, she checked the road outside. Over half an hour had passed since she'd arrived. It was odd that Spencer wasn't there. He hadn't messaged her either. She was wondering how the team were getting on with the retrieval of evidence at Turner's squat when a thought struck her.

The discovery of the syringe at the factory hadn't been released. The DCI was quite insistent. How did Blane know? Did he find out when he accessed their files? Christ, Blane was a cop. And one thing Dark hated more than anything else was cop's abusing the systems for their own ends, whatever their intentions.

Her temper bubbled. Before she knew it, she'd followed him into the kitchen.

'Blane.'

He jolted around like a naughty schoolboy caught pinching food. 'You made me jump!' he said.

She noticed a packet of Benson and Hedges on the window ledge. 'I didn't know you smoked.'

'Oh, they're my mother's.'

She was reminded of the cigarette burns on the victim's wrists. She'd never seen his mother smoke either. In fact, very few people did these days.

A muffled sound rang out.

'What's that?'

'Nothing.' Milk sloshed over the sides of the mugs as he finished up the tea. 'Let's go back into—'

'How did you know about the syringe in the factory?' Dark said, unmoved.

'What?'

He didn't look up, too busy mopping up the sloshed coffee with a dishcloth.

'The syringe found at the factory. It wasn't released.'

'You must have told me.'

'I didn't.'

'I must have seen it in the paperwork. It hardly matters now.' His voice was strained.

There it was again. A muffled squeak. No, more of a squeal. A person's squeal. Somebody was outside.

Their eyes met. He looked afraid.

Dark reached for the back door and made to pull it open when she felt the blow to the back of her head. The room spun. She was aware of his voice in the background but couldn't decipher the words. As if in slow motion, her legs buckled. And the floor came up to meet her.

Rosa Dark felt someone pulling her. A tug at her wrists. She flinched, flexed her hands. Made to move and faltered. Her wrists were tied together. She opened her eyes. To find Blane O'Donnell fastening cable ties around her ankles.

'No!' she bellowed. She struggled and winced. The cable was secure. Every time she moved, the plastic dug into her the skin. 'Don't do this!' she pleaded.

Blane worked like a robot, oblivious to her words. He checked the ties again.

'Blane, no!'

He stopped. She'd caught his attention.

'We can talk about this—'

Before she could finish, he'd grabbed a tea towel off the side and shoved it into her mouth.

Dark choked as the material pushed in deeper, wedging her jaw open.

Blane leapt to his feet, bent down and lifted her over his shoulder.

Her stomach wrenched. She tried to wriggle, to kick, but her resistance was no match for his strength.

Out of the door, she bounced on his shoulder, every movement winding her. Down the garden. As they approached the car, the boot flicked open. Dark could see something inside. It looked like...

Her screams were muffled by the tea towel. She had to think fast. Spencer hadn't arrived to relieve her. The DCI was in a press conference. It could be hours before anyone noticed she was missing.

Dark worked her hands. Blane didn't notice her engagement ring slip off her finger. Didn't hear it nestle into the grass. Her body clattered into the boot with a thud. And the door came down, immersing her in darkness.

CHAPTER 52

A dull ache pulsed Helen's temple as she left the press conference. She'd stood beside Jenkins in his Armani suit, her hair freshly combed, with Chief Constable Adams in full regalia on the wing. It was a PR exercise, with Adams valiantly announcing the capture of Sinead O'Donnell's killer. Jenkins thanking his staff for working around the clock to track down a dangerous criminal; any suggestion of organised crime involvement now dropped from his agenda as he expressed his gratitude to the press and the public for their support on what had been 'a difficult investigation'.

Even when the men and women of the press had countered with questions about Gordon Turner's background, his previous convictions and speculated about whether or not he should have been released from prison, they were undeterred. 'That's out of our remit,' Adams had said. 'I'm sure there will be an inquiry and those questions will be raised.'

Helen hadn't uttered a word. Wheeled out as the SIO heading the case, to show a united front. A PR exercise of the worst kind. She'd never been more relieved to leave Jenkins and Adams behind and return to the paperwork on her desk and a fresh investigation into how Gordon Turner died, though even without those pressing needs, somehow this didn't feel like a result to be celebrated.

She snuck outside for some fresh air, surprised to find Vicki Gardener standing outside the back door, cigarette in hand.

'Well done,' Vicki said.

Helen gave her a thin smile. 'Didn't know you smoked.'

'Guilty pleasure.' She took a last drag and stubbed it beneath her foot.

'Don't suppose you can spare one?'

Vicki flicked open the box and offered them across.

Helen thanked her and took one. An occasional smoker, she'd given up when Matthew was suspended for smoking at school last year. She'd always indulged away from the house and usually only at work, keeping the habit away from her family, but she was aware her boys were growing up, experimenting. And the secrecy of her actions wasn't setting much of an example. But there were times, like now, when she really missed its calming effect.

'I'll see you inside,' Vicki said and wandered back in.

It was a warm day, a low-level breeze whistling across the car park. Helen relished the long drag she took, holding it several seconds before she exhaled. A crow cawed overhead. She took another drag, and another, feeling the tension ease out of her shoulders. Her mobile buzzed against her thigh. She stubbed out the cigarette and clicked to answer.

Pemberton didn't bother with preamble. 'Spencer's been involved in a car accident.'

Helen froze. 'Is he okay?' A car engine ignited nearby. She placed a hand on her free ear to block out the noise.

'Think so. Some idiot jumped the lights at Cross Keys, crashed into the side of his car. He's conscious. The paramedics have taken him to hospital on a board. I'm told it's only precautionary though. Chris Tappers from incident response is with him.'

'Where are you now?'

'The incident room.'

'I'm on my way.'

A cacophony of noise was seeping out of the incident room as Helen approached, animated voices all talking at the same time. She opened the door to find officers firing messages at a shocked Pemberton beside the door.

'What happened?' Helen asked.

The voices immediately quietened. 'Incident occurred at 3.05 p.m. at Cross Keys roundabout,' Pemberton said. 'Car looks like it's going to be a write-off. Steve's being checked out by the docs now.'

'We need to get down to Hampton General.'

He touched her elbow as she turned to go. 'Wait.' The urgency in his tone caught her attention. The room stayed silent while he relayed his conversation with Angela Ingram, pinching the skin on his throat as he finished. 'It seems our Blane O'Donnell isn't quite the upstanding individual he claims to be.'

Helen's mind raced. Spencer would have been on his way to see Blane when the car crash stopped him in his tracks. Which meant Dark went unaccompanied. She searched the room for DC Rosa Dark's spiky hair. 'Where's Rosa now?'

'Don't know. I've tried her mobile twice since I left the café. Goes straight to voicemail.'

'Has anyone tried Blane?'

'He's not picking up.'

'What?'

'There's more.'

'Natalia Kowalski's brother called twenty minutes ago. Claims she's disappeared.'

'Disappeared?'

'She stayed with him on Friday evening, after she left the station. He took her home the next morning, helped her unpack. When he messaged her last night, to check on her, he got no response.'

'Has anyone been to her flat?'

'He has a spare key and went around this morning. No sign. He'd given her a spare phone, since we have hers, and it was on the kitchen table.'

Helen stiffened. 'Get proof-of-life checks done on Natalia, find out when she last used her credit card and accessed her bank account,' Helen called out to the room.

Blane had broken into the homicide systems, stalked the young witnesses, tenacious in his attempts to investigate his wife's death. What if he'd read about the private phone Sinead kept to speak with Natalia and confronted her? If Angela Ingram's account was to be believed, he was jealous, controlling.

She turned to Pemberton. 'We need to get to Blane O'Donnell's mother's now.' She was out of the door before she'd finished the sentence.

CHAPTER 53

The car rattled as Pemberton screamed through the traffic, overtaking vehicles, waving crossing pedestrians aside. Inside the car it was stifling. They wound down the windows, the background hum of the traffic becoming white noise as they focused on the task in hand. Helen phoned for backup and arranged for a patrol car to stop by the O'Donnells' house to check for any presence. Even though Blane hadn't moved home since Sinead's murder, there was every chance he could have retreated there and she wanted to cover all bases. When they'd tried the landlines of both properties, they were unanswered, but that didn't necessarily mean the houses were empty.

Her mobile erupted. Charles was calling. She pinched her lips together, answered.

Helen didn't have time for greetings. 'Charles, I'm rather tied up—'

'Sorry to bother you,' he cut in. 'I've had the tests back on Yvette Edwards's fingernails – the labs are on overtime to clear their backlog – you'll be interested in the results.' A car horn beeped as Pemberton overtook another vehicle.

'Okay, you'll need to be quick.'

'You were right. Small skin particles were found underneath

her nails. They ran them through the database and found a match with Blane O'Donnell.'

'What?'

'He must have surprised her, she lashed out when he placed the bag of coal over her head and she caught him. Anyway, it's a definite match.'

Helen thanked him and ended the call. She recapped the conversation to Pemberton.

'So, he was there when the neighbour died,' Pemberton said. 'That's interesting.'

'The question is why, Sean? Why would he murder his own neighbour?'

'Sinead and Yvette were close. Perhaps he thought she knew something…' His words tailed off as he steered around a corner.

'Blane was on the duty stats for the whole day when Sinead was killed,' Helen said. 'We did double-check, didn't we?'

'Yup. And we've a statement from another member of staff, saying she was with him.'

His ensuing silence put her on edge. 'What is it?'

'Doesn't mean he didn't have help.'

Helen grabbed her phone and dialled Jenkins, relaying the pathologist's findings and urgently requesting a check on Blane's movements last Wednesday. They were pretty sure he'd already accessed the homicide computer systems using a colleague's login. Had someone helped him to commit murder?

Every tick of the clock scratched at her. Right now, finding Rosa Dark and Natalia Kowalski was her priority. Jenkins would have to deal with the rest. She'd witnessed Blane's temper first-hand. At the time, she'd put it down to the anxious frustrations of a grieving man. He was a decorated police officer, a man of purported respectability and integrity. But he wouldn't be the first officer to hide corrupt or controlling behaviour behind a police badge.

Pemberton's interview with Angela Ingram rolled around

her mind, along with reminders of her conversations with Blane. He'd said Sinead had a lot of friends and was always messaging someone, yet when they'd checked her phone records, most of the calls were to the nursing home, him and her neighbour, who was now also dead. It seemed Sinead actually had little family and few close friends. And she'd kept her friendship with Natalia private.

Was he monitoring his wife? If so, if he suspected her of having an affair, it might give him a motive for murder.

She tried Blane again, every ring grating at her, then ordered an urgent trace on his phone.

As soon as they rounded the next corner, they spotted the silver Focus outside Blane's mother's house. The police pool car. Rosa hadn't left.

The brakes screeched across the asphalt as Pemberton parked.

Blane's mother was at the door before they reached the step. 'Can I help you?' she asked, looking at their car blocking the driveway.

The high-pitched sound of a child's laugh was heard from inside.

'Is Blane here?' Helen asked.

'No. I've just got back from the shops with the children. His car is missing from the car port, he must have gone out.'

'An officer visited here earlier. DC Rosa Dark. Have you seen her?'

She shook her head. 'What's all this about?'

'May we have a look around? The officer's car is still parked outside. She can't be far away.'

Small faces peered up at them as they entered the front room. Helen managed a small smile and retreated, nodding for Pemberton to check upstairs. She looked in the dining room, the playroom, the kitchen. By the time Blane's mother joined her, she was trying the back door.

'Do you know where Blane's gone?' Helen asked her.

'No. I noticed his car was gone when I came back with the children a few minutes ago. What's happened?'

'How was Blane when you saw him earlier?'

'Okay,' she said warily. She looked afraid.

Pemberton was back down the stairs now. He gave a quick headshake.

They raced outside, down the pathway at the side of the lawn and to the car port. Her station wagon was there, alone.

'I'm trying Blane again,' Pemberton said. 'He can't be far away.'

Helen placed her hands on her hips, eyes sweeping the ground when she noticed something sparkle.

She moved closer and crouched down, holding it up for Pemberton to see. 'It's Rosa's engagement ring.'

Pemberton ended the call and dialled another number. She could hear his voice in the background, chasing the trace on their phones, checking up on the patrol car dispatched to the O'Donnells' family home, putting out an urgent trace for Blane O'Donnell's car.

She imagined Dark arriving. Checking her watch. Sitting in the car, waiting for Spencer. Trying his phone when he didn't arrive and, when he didn't answer, deciding to continue solo. She was a trained liaison officer, accustomed to dealing with families in distress. And she was here to deliver news to alleviate Blane's stress, to tell him they'd apprehended his wife's killer. He'd be pleased. No reason why she couldn't make a start.

She looked back at the house. What happened in there? And how did Blane lure her out here?

Pemberton ended his call. 'We've got a trace on O'Donnell's phone. He's at Keys Trading Estate.'

Helen's heart thumped her chest as they darted back into the house, past Blane's bewildered mother and out into the street.

Within seconds, they were in the car heading towards town. Cross Keys was only five minutes away. Every pedestrian, every traffic light, every vehicle in front plagued them.

'I don't understand,' Helen said. 'If Blane's evading us, why would he leave his phone on?'

'He's playing a game. Drawing us in.'

The derelict factories looked eerie in the late-afternoon light, the road and surrounding car parks empty. Pemberton drove down the road and stopped outside Billings. There was no sign of Blane's Peugeot. Helen tensed. Cell-site traces on phones could only pinpoint the location of a device to within a couple of hundred yards. Which meant he could be anywhere on this side of the estate.

Billings was quiet. The CSIs had finished their examination of the factory yesterday and there was no longer a guard standing outside. If ever they needed one, Helen thought, it was now.

It seemed unlikely Blane would bring Dark to Billings, the scene of Sinead's murder, but they knew he'd visited there before and they had to start somewhere.

Sunshine bounced off the windows as Pemberton left the car, approached the door and looked through the glass panel. Helen followed him. They moved around to the rear. The back door with the faulty lock had been boarded up. The Bracken Way in the distance was empty.

They walked the perimeter of the building and found nothing to indicate a presence.

Back at the front, Pemberton called a number, put his finger to his mouth and held out his phone. The faint sound of a phone ringing came from inside. His eyes glistened.

Helen looked back over her shoulder. Where was their backup?

They couldn't wait. Preserve life was an officer's first priority. If Blane was inside, there was a chance he had Dark with him and there was no knowing what state either of them were in.

Pemberton motioned for Helen to move away, then swung his elbow back and thrust it into the long window beside the door. He looked away as it shattered, then pushed the loose glass aside and climbed through the gap.

The entrance was empty and eerily quiet. The CSI boards now disappeared, it was another derelict unit. They rushed up the stairs to the first floor. Helen resisted the temptation to switch on her torch. While the broken window would alert Blane to their presence, he wouldn't know when they were inside. Which still gave them the element of surprise. They entered the offices tentatively, checking beneath each desk.

They ran out into the factory, feet clanking the stairs. Sweat was coursing down Helen's back now. 'He's not here,' she said.

Pemberton rang the number again. They followed the ring tone back to the office, checking the surfaces, the floor. The sound drew them to the side window. On the ledge was a phone merrily ringing out.

CHAPTER 54

'What's he playing at?' Pemberton said.

'He wants to delay us finding him.' She recalled Sinead's injuries: the marks on her arms, the blows to her head. The severed fingers. The longer it took to find Blane, the longer he had to inflict pain on Rosa and Natalia.

Back down the stairs, they ran out the front of the building. Blane had been there, planted the phone and left it as a decoy. Which meant he had a key to access. He knew they were tracking him and in his twisted mind he was playing a game. This couldn't end well.

It troubled her why he'd taken the girls to the trading estate. Why not a more desolate location, like Henderson's trail on the edge of Hampton, a single track down to Pitsford Water? But there were no hiding places there for cars, no hidden areas. And with Dark on board, he'd been held up. He knew they'd be looking for him, which is why he'd planted his phone in Billings. Maybe he was hoping he could dispose of both women and make off before they reached him.

Helen wracked her brains. There were over twenty empty units on this side of the estate, many of them much larger than Billings. This could take all afternoon. She remembered their conversation about Sinead and him visiting the estate. A factory with a conference room that seemed suitable. Which one was it?

They were out the front now. Feet pounding the tarmac to the next factory. 'There it is,' she cried, pointing at purple signage in the distance. It was plusher than the others, newer. And much further down the road.

'What?' Pemberton said, gasping.

'Blane said Sinead and he viewed these factories for somewhere to run a self-defence class. He almost chose the conference room in Wilton's shoe factory.' They'd fallen into a jog now. 'It has to be worth a try.'

Wilton's layout mirrored the front of Billings, with a reception area at one end, a factory at the other. The small car park out front was empty. They ran past the goods-in entrance and around to the rear, where there was another, larger car park.

Helen's heart plummeted. He wasn't there. She placed her hands on her hips, turned on her heel, 180 degrees, and stared back at the building, desperately searching for any sign of life. The sun glinted off the empty windows, glaring back at her. A flat roof extension had been added at the far end, behind the old offices.

Pemberton reached for his phone and gave a quick update of their position. Sirens rang out in the distance.

She ran to the other end of the building, and back up the side towards the reception at the front, with a view to trying the unit next door, and stopped. Parked up beside a fire exit, and out of view of the main road out front, was a shiny blue Peugeot, the driver door hanging open, keys still in the ignition.

'Here!' she called.

Pemberton joined her. The side entrance door to the unit was also open. Another key he appeared to have.

They rushed inside. Which way would he go? A left turn would take them to the front of the building. Right, to the rear. Reception areas were usually at the front of buildings with lifts and stairs to the floors above. It seemed a good place to start.

They ran down a corridor, through a fire door and into a wide foyer. A door on the left had a stairs symbol above it.

Helen rushed across, taking to the stairs, two at a time to level one. How many levels were there? The sirens were louder; lights flashed outside. Backup was arriving.

She glanced into a few of the rooms on the first floor. They looked like empty offices, all arranged in a square, with lifts in the middle of the building. No sign of anyone.

On the next floor there were more offices. Helen was starting to lose heart, wondering if this was another one of Blane's false starts, when she heard a scraping noise. Something was being dragged across a floor. Pemberton rushed into her as she froze. She placed a hand out to steady herself against the wall and shushed him.

The crash that followed shook the entire building. They both ducked. It sounded like glass breaking, as if something had driven into the back of the building. Helen didn't move for several seconds, fearing the worst, when she heard Blane's voice in the distance. Raspy. Coming from the back of the building.

He was on this floor. They made their way slowly around the quadrangle of offices. The side entrance was far away from up here and, without the alarm working, it was possible he hadn't heard them enter. But he wouldn't have missed the sirens outside.

At the back of the building was a room with two doors, one at either end. It would be a vast space. Perfect for a self-defence class.

More scraping. He was inside.

Helen paused outside the door for a split second. All was quiet. 'I'm going in,' she whispered.

'Armed officers have arrived outside,' Pemberton said, phone pressed to his ear. 'They're just surrounding the building.'

She motioned for him to move to the other door, further down the corridor.

When he was in place, she pushed her door open.

A blast of fresh air hit Helen as she entered a room that overlooked the flat roof and the car park below. A long table sat at one end, a stack of chairs beside it, left behind by the former occupier. Her eyes were instantly drawn to the source of the crash: Blane had thrown one of the chairs through the window. It lay on its side on the flat roof outside.

Beside it, Blane stood with Dark.

Helen's breath caught. Dark's hands were bound, her ankles tied together. Blane was holding her in front of him, a knife to her throat.

Helen stepped outside to join them. 'Don't come any closer,' Blane said.

They were precariously close to the edge of the roof. The car park loomed below.

Helen halted. 'Blane, please. We can talk about this.'

'Stay where you are.'

She held up her hands, froze. 'You don't want to do this.'

Blane's eyes hooked hers. They were eerily dark, the pupils dilated. 'You have no idea.'

'About what? Talk to me. I can help.'

'Talk. You sent out this one to talk and look where she's ended up.'

Rosa squeaked as the edge of the knife nicked her neck. A thin line of blood trickled down.

'That wound needs attention,' Helen said, fighting to keep her voice calm. She made to take a step forward.

'Stop!' Helen froze. 'If you come any closer, I'll slit her throat. I swear.'

In her peripheral vision, Helen could see Pemberton had entered the room through the other door and was now peering around the edge of the broken window, phone still pressed to his ear. He'd be liaising with backup, pointing out Blane's location, requesting a hostage negotiator. She needed to calm Blane, keep him talking.

'Think of your children,' Helen said slowly.

'That's all I've ever done. Think of my children. Think of my family. And look what I got in return. Sinead, planning to go off with someone else.' Spittle flew out of his mouth.

He tightened his grip on Dark. The armed response team would be in place now. Blane would be aware of that. He'd also be aware they needed a clear aim. And he kept Rosa close, his head near hers, an arm around her front, shielding his body with hers. Preventing a clear line of fire on him.

Rosa whimpered again.

Helen dug deep. She recalled talking a suicidal male down from jumping off a shopping centre car park in her early years. What was it they were taught? Appeal to their humanity. Find their Achilles heel. Something they could hold on to, something they would engage with. And keep them talking.

What was Blane's Achilles heel? Family.

'Rosa got engaged this week, Blane,' Helen said, the triviality of the words clawing at her. 'She's planning to get married later this year and start a family of her own.'

Blane said nothing.

'Your Ava will be like that in twenty years,' Helen continued. 'Starting out, her life in front of her.'

She felt the heat of his gaze, silent and unwavering.

'She'd be wanting you to support her, help her.' His eyes softened, for a nanosecond his mind taken elsewhere. 'Let Rosa go, Blane. She has no place here. She was doing her job. Following orders. Like you or I. Like Thomas or Ava might one day. Don't deny her the chance of happiness.'

For a second, he was still, as if he was considering her words.

A voice shouted from below.

And suddenly his face contorted. He pulled Rosa back. They teetered on the brink of the roof, only millimetres between them and the edge. One false move...

Helen raised a hand. 'Don't do this, you've got children. Please, Blane. Let Rosa go and we can talk. You and me.'

Footsteps. Helen was aware of officers spilling into the office behind them. So was Blane. He pulled Rosa back, off the floor, her feet dangling in mid-air, over the edge of the building.

Dark's eyes widened.

He adjusted his grip. She slipped slightly.

'No, Blane. Don't do this!'

Then, at the last minute, he tossed her aside.

Arms and legs still bound, Helen could hear her muffled scream as Dark dropped to the floor like a rag doll, juddering as she lay, head and shoulders over the side of the roof. She tried to wriggle back, wobbled. With no limbs free, she couldn't save herself. Helen and Pemberton rushed forward. Helen grabbed her arms, Pemberton her legs, pulling her away from the edge.

Footsteps pounded the roof, instructions called out as armed officers closed in. They were almost on Blane when he raised the knife and sliced it across his throat.

'No!' With Rosa safely away from the edge, Helen ran towards him. Blood spurted out, spraying across her, the roof, the broken glass at their feet. Blane dropped to his knees before he fell face down on the roof. The whole building shook like thunder under his weight.

A paramedic rushed to his side, checked for a pulse. Helen's heart dipped as she looked up and shook her head. Helen moved back to Dark.

Pemberton was tugging the gag out of her mouth. She doubled over, coughed. Tried to speak, but the words disappeared in a wheeze. Pemberton retrieved a Leatherman from his pocket and worked on the cable ties.

'The car,' she squawked.

Another paramedic knelt by her side. 'Try not to speak,' he said.

Dark grabbed Helen's sleeve and pointed towards the window. 'The car!'

'She's trying to tell us something,' Helen said.

Dark wheezed, spitting out a thread. 'She's in the car.'

Pemberton pushed past the other paramedic leaning over Blane and checked his pockets. The car keys jingled as he removed them.

The stairs seemed to go on for ever. One flight after another. They darted past more officers, a bewildered Jenkins, who'd heard about the fracas and come out to support.

The Peugeot was still parked beside the fire door. They searched the seats, clambered around to the boot and flipped the lid.

The sight inside wrenched at Helen. Natalia Kowalski's bruised and battered body lay coiled in a foetal position. She reached for her neck. 'There's a pulse. Get a paramedic here now!'

CHAPTER 55

Helen dragged her feet down the polished flooring of the hospital corridor; she'd spent far too much time here over the past few months.

Pemberton and she had raced here from the scene, only leaving the rear-view of the ambulances for a brief stop-off at the station to change her bloody shirt.

The sorry body of Natalia Kowalski was already hooked up to IVs on the floor above when they arrived. She'd suffered mild concussion, the doctors had said, where Blane had knocked her out, and heat exhaustion from being confined in the boot of his car, and was deeply traumatised, but they were hopeful she would make a good recovery.

It could have been so much worse.

The phone he'd planted as a decoy rang persistently in her mind. He'd tried to delay them. Thankfully, she'd remembered the other factory he'd mentioned and they were too quick for him; he'd only managed to carry one of the women upstairs when they arrived.

It was a wonder Natalia hadn't choked on the necklace he'd stuffed into her mouth behind the gag. A necklace they later discovered the woman had bought for Sinead only weeks earlier, a sweet gesture from a close friend to encourage Sinead to be kinder to herself. The same necklace that was innocently returned with the personal contents of Sinead's locker. Helen could imagine Blane's anger when he found it. An anger that warped, supporting his theory that Sinead was having an affair. An anger that would have no doubt built when he'd broken into the homicide systems, read the case material and discovered Sinead's secret friendship with Natalia.

Helen paused outside the door of the room housing DC Rosa Dark and stole herself. Dark was still in assessment when they arrived. Having confirmed she was out of danger, they'd rushed through to check on a surprised Spencer, only to find his injuries were superficial, and she'd left Pemberton with him to arrange discharge while she checked on Natalia. Such a wave of destruction, it was difficult to comprehend.

Helen knocked the door, then peered around the door frame. 'Is it a good time?' she asked.

Rosa looked across from her bed and smiled. She was sitting up, her left hand tucked between her partner, Tim's, who sat in the chair beside her. 'Of course. Come on in.'

The enthusiasm with which Rosa introduced Helen to her partner brought a tear to Helen's eye. He nodded, his face impassive. It wasn't an enthusiasm he shared and Helen didn't blame him. She'd deployed the detective to speak with Blane O'Donnell, and although she couldn't have known the ramifications of that decision, she was still the reason his fiancée was here, sitting in a hospital bed with a bruise the shape of Australia above her left brow and a bandage covering her neck.

'How are you doing?' Helen asked.

'All right, thanks, especially as I've just been told it's cottage pie for dinner.' Dark gave a brief husky chuckle and coughed.

Her fiancé excused himself to get them coffee.

Helen watched him go, waiting for the door to close before she spoke. Suddenly she was overcome with emotion, seeing the young woman's tiny frame in the hospital bed. The same frame that had been trussed up, teetering on the edge of a flat roof with a knife to her throat, only a couple of hours earlier. 'Are you sure you're okay, Rosa?' she said. 'You've been through a terrible ordeal.'

'I'll be fine, really. What happened to Spencer?'

'Some idiot drove into the side of his Focus at Cross Keys roundabout. He had to be cut out. Luckily, he escaped with a few cuts and bruises. His phone took the biggest hit, it was flung out of the windscreen. We only found out when uniform attended.'

'That'll please the super,' Dark said, a smile tickling her lips.

Her ability for humour in such circumstances warmed Helen's heart. 'It'll certainly strain his budget.'

They both laughed.

Helen glanced down and caught a spatter of blood on her trousers. Blane's blood. She covered it with the corner of her jacket. 'What happened back there?' she asked.

Dark described how Blane had been tense when she arrived. His reticence to allow her near the kitchen. How his mention of the syringe found at the factory touched a nerve and she'd followed him anyway, only to hear Natalia Kowalski's cries from his car outside. The scuffle that followed, culminating in her being thrown into the boot of his Peugeot with a semi-conscious Natalia. 'The next thing I knew I was being lifted out of the car at Keys Trading Estate,' she said.

He'd bound the wrists and ankles of both women, gagged them, but hadn't bothered to cover their eyes because he didn't expect them to stay alive to tell their tale. Helen suspected he'd arranged to kidnap and kill Natalia when Dark became a by-product of his plan. A plan that had gone askew as he lost all sense of reality.

Silence fell upon them. A bird landed on the windowsill and chirped, it's voice crystal clear, and after everything they'd been through that afternoon, the two women found themselves listening and smiling at the simple gesture.

'I have something for you,' Helen said. She placed her hand in her pocket and pulled out Dark's engagement ring.

'Oh, thank you!' Tears glittered Dark's lashes. 'I wondered if it would be found.' As she slipped it onto her finger, the door opened and her fiancé returned with two cups of coffee. 'Look!' Dark said, holding up the ring. He smiled back at her.

Helen made her excuses and left. They needed some time alone together.

As she made her way back along the corridor, a wave of fatigue flew over her. She needed to check on Pemberton and Spencer, count everyone in, before she could consider rest. She was almost at the lifts when a familiar voice called from behind. It was Jenkins.

'Hello, sir. I wasn't expecting to see you here.'

'I heard about the incident at the factory.' He looked her up and down. 'Are you okay?'

She nodded. He asked about the others and she updated him in the lift on the way down.

'Join me for a tea,' he said, when the lift doors finally opened on the ground floor.

He directed her along the corridor to the café and motioned to a table in the corner, although he needn't have worried. Apart from a rather bored volunteer behind the counter, the room was empty.

The smell of sugar filled the air when he returned with steaming mugs. Helen took a sip of her tea and did her best not to wince at the sweetness. Over the years, she'd made endless cups of tea for traumatised members of the public, heaping sugar into the mix to alleviate the shock, and it was a touching gesture.

'We spoke with the support worker who was helping Blane on Wednesday,' Jenkins said when he'd settled himself into a chair opposite.

'And?'

Jenkins huffed. 'She wasn't there between ten thirty and three thirty.'

'What?'

'Left to watch her son's cricket tournament. Apparently,

she's received several warnings for lateness and absence and didn't like to formally apply. So, Blane and her kept it between themselves. It had been arranged for weeks.'

'And she gave a statement, covering him?'

'She's mortified. Said he was charming, fun, supportive to work with. A real family man. She thought he was doing her a great favour.'

Helen shook her head, incredulous. 'That doesn't explain how he got to the factory. His car didn't ping on the cameras.'

'He wasn't in his car.'

'I don't understand. We'd have known if he used a pool car, they're tracked.'

'He wasn't in a pool car either. The same support worker had hired a car for one of the other trainers to attend a conference in Nottingham. The other trainer went sick. The car was sitting there, in the car park. And the keys were in her unlocked drawer.'

Helen swiped a hand down the front of her face. 'I don't believe I'm hearing this.'

'It's true. We'll have to check the cameras, of course. My guess is he used the hire car to pick up Sinead and transport her to the factory.'

Helen swallowed, recalling Blane's phone inside the locked-up Billings factory earlier. How easily he accessed Wilton's. He must have copied the keys when he'd viewed the factories last year, which meant he'd been planning this for some time. She wrestled with the notion. 'Whoever killed Sinead would have been covered in blood. Surely his colleague noticed he'd changed when she got back to work.'

'They were in civvies. He always wore a black T-shirt and jeans when he wasn't in uniform. Probably wouldn't have been obvious if he'd changed.'

'Tell me we've still got the car.'

'That's the one piece of positive news I do have. It was due to go back yesterday and the hire company didn't collect it. At least we can seize it and check it forensically.'

Helen sat back in her chair and exhaled a long breath. 'Any news on the compromise to our computer systems?' she asked.

'Professional Standards are handling it. Off the record, PC Stephen Rotherham, whose login was used, was in a meeting when the system was accessed on Thursday afternoon with the whole training department. They were in the conference room. He'll still be disciplined, of course, for leaving his login vulnerable. The time corresponds with when Blane visited. It's possible he saw the empty office and the computer, logged in and took his chance.'

Helen thought about Blane's previous experience as a digital media officer. His sergeant's remarks about what a whizz he was with a computer. Without that login, he wouldn't have got hold of the boys' home addresses. 'Christ, he worked them over good and proper,' she said.

Jenkins scraped his chair back and stood. 'Right, I'm off to visit the injured parties. I suggest you go home, get some rest. There'll be a mound of paperwork to sort out when this hits the fan tomorrow morning.'

She watched him go, took another gulp of tea and flinched again at the sweetness. What if Gordon Turner's death wasn't accidental? It wouldn't have been difficult for someone to plant the phone in the squat. Remove a used syringe. Especially for someone who knew him. His brother said he'd been acting strangely and was convinced someone was going into his flat and moving things. Perhaps Blane had been hanging around, watching his movements, planning out the murder.

Blane had been clever. He'd suspected Sinead was having an affair for a while, felt their relationship slipping through his fingers. And, as with Angela, his last girlfriend, it seemed he couldn't face the prospect of rejection. If he killed Sinead, he kept up the pretence of a perfect relationship because she was taken from him.

He'd hidden behind his police badge, meticulously planned everything: the retreat, the screw in Sinead's tyre, the hire car and break from work. Used enough of Turner's former torture tactics to frame him, and planted the needle and syringe, knowing the DNA would link back. And with Turner's previous connection in MOSOVO and the photos on the phone it pointed the blame in one direction.

But he'd become paranoid. A paranoia that had eaten away at him. He hadn't banked on the kids discovering the body and then he'd worried they'd seen something. She could imagine the guilt picking away at him, morning, noon and night, forcing him to stalk them, to find out what they knew.

When he'd broken into the homicide systems, he'd have seen the concerns over the number of messages Sinead exchanged with her neighbour and the arrangements to visit her again, suggesting a close relationship. He'd also have seen the details regarding Sinead's secret phone and be aware she was using it to contact Natalia. Perhaps he found the phone in her bag and accessed it. Once he'd pieced it all together in his mind, the jealousy and paranoia had taken over.

He certainly hadn't reckoned on Angela resurfacing to tell her story.

Blane had done what he'd always done. Played the part – this time of the grief-stricken husband. Like before when he'd played the role of the perfect husband, in the perfect marriage with the perfect family.

He'd tried to commit the perfect murder. Only the perfect murder didn't exist.

EPILOGUE

The van parked up outside as Connor kicked the football in the air, bounced it off his knee and kicked it again. A man emerged and gave him a backwards nod of acknowledgement. Connor kicked the ball up again, caught it, then stopped and watched in silence. The man pulled a 'property to let' sign out and hammered it into the ground beside their front gate, unspeaking.

It didn't matter that the killer had been apprehended, the officer who'd chased him was dead and the detective chief inspector had visited them, to assure them of their safety. His mother was doing what she always did with her problems: running away from them.

This time it wasn't a boyfriend. It was Rhys Evans. The 'bad influence' on her son that she wanted to leave behind.

'We're going back to Sheffield,' she'd said, 'to stay with my sister. It's safer there. Might even be able to get your place back on your old footie team.'

In a few weeks, he'd be introduced to a new home, another school. Have to renew friendships.

The man checked the sign was stable and then bade his farewell. He climbed back into the van and shot off down the road, whipping up a cloud of dust in his wake.

Another goodbye.

***

Helen moved away from her colleagues and ordered another vodka at the bar. It was a balmy evening, the June sun reaching in through the open door of The Royal Oak. They'd waited a week to celebrate closing the case to ensure everyone was fit enough to attend and it was good to see her team relaxing and enjoying themselves.

DC Dark looked her usual animated self as she chattered to Spencer in the corner. She wasn't back at work yet, although she'd visited the station several times over the past week; the bruises on her forehead were yellowing and the bandage, or neck scarf as she'd come to call it, had now been reduced to a plaster. It was heart-warming to see her there, happy and smiling.

It had been an exhausting week, the media focusing on the guilt of a fellow cop, speculating on whether he'd abused his position to commit a murder, and the press office playing it down as a domestic incident. The only saving grace was her family, who soon lost interest in the politics and seemed to put the case behind them. Even her mother hadn't raised the subject of work, tiptoeing around the issue when they discussed their days, Helen's plight largely assisted by the fact that Dark's ordeal wasn't reported in the news. Had their minds been put to rest? Helen doubted it, but she was grateful for the brief respite.

Helen thanked the bartender and swirled her vodka in the glass. There were always more casualties than the dead in a murder investigation. Blane O'Donnell had left his children to be raised by their paternal grandmother, one day to discover their own father had killed their mother in brutal circumstances and murdered their neighbour. What would that knowledge do to the developing mind of a child?

Blane's mother's mouse-like face skipped into her mind. She'd paled when they'd delivered the news of his death and the events surrounding it. When Helen considered it, apart from the initial statement they'd taken, Blane's mother had barely spoken to the police, or even appeared, when they visited the house throughout the investigation. She crept around meekly in the background, caring for her grandchildren, part of the wallpaper of their family life. But behind the scenes she'd fought for Blane, fought for his dream of the 'perfect family' and silenced Angela all those years ago.

An examination of the hire car showed tiny particles, hair samples and spots of blood on the wheel brace, indicating that was the weapon Blane used to beat Sinead with. Hair samples and fibres from Sinead's clothing were in the boot. His bloody clothing, the murder weapon and neither of her mobile phones had been found, although samples of Blane's hair had also been recovered from Gordon Turner's squat. Had he killed him too? They were awaiting more details from forensics, but it would make sense to take out the last link in the chain. A dead man couldn't defend himself.

At least, with the evidence against Blane, the IOPC had closed the file on Yvette Edwards's death. Dodging an internal investigation was certainly a small mercy to be thankful for.

Laughter bellowed from the corner. Ivan Newton. He was doing squats, up and down, a full pint of beer balanced precariously on his head. He'd joined them on Wednesday, then promptly left for a training course on their computer system. They'd only crossed paths briefly and his instant need to show off to an audience gave her a deep sense of foreboding. Would he be able to knuckle down, do what was needed during the fast-moving hours of a major investigation? Time would tell.

She held up her glass to the bartender for another refill. Leaning her elbow on the bar as he filled the glass and resting her chin on her hand, she swirled the drink in the glass again when he handed it back.

'How's the new super doing?'

Helen looked up at Pemberton and gave a disgruntled smile.

'Well, you don't look very pleased about the promotion,' he said with a sarcastic laugh.

'It's temporary.'

'I'll drink to that.'

They clinked their glasses together. She'd accepted Jenkins's offer to step into his shoes; in view of the circumstances, she hadn't been able to think of an acceptable reason to turn him down. Another bellow from the corner. It was going to be a long three months.

The stool beside her creaked as Pemberton shifted his weight onto it. 'Penny for them,' he said and signalled to the bartender for another beer.

Helen turned to face him. 'What? Oh, I don't know. I was thinking about Chilli Franks. What do you think he's doing right now?'

'Preparing his defence, if he's got half a brain.'

Helen gave a hollow laugh. The question mark over the involvement of organised crime groups and specifically Chilli Franks had haunted her this past week, the use of handcuffs to restrain Sinead initially raising the question of a personal vendetta. Inspector Burns hadn't been able to find any link between Sinead and Blane and the organised crime community, and the relief she felt at receiving the news was palpable. Chilli's trial was scheduled to be heard late summer and the CPS were confident of a conviction. It was about time she shelved his ghost and moved forward.

They supped their drinks in silence. A song played out in the background, a cover by Ed Sheeran that Helen didn't recognise. The vodka warmed her insides.

'A few of us are talking about getting a curry,' Pemberton said eventually.

'Won't do the diet any good.'

'I won't tell Mrs P if you don't.'

Helen laughed.

'You coming?'

'Why not?'

She finished the last few drops of her drink and followed him out of the bar.

ACKNOWLEDGEMENTS

I find writing acknowledgements a challenge because I always worry I'll forget someone. So, if you helped in any way with this novel and aren't mentioned here, please know that I'm heartily grateful. I didn't mean to omit your name, I just have a terrible memory!

First, I'd like to thank Sam at Kettering Motorist Centre for finding time in his busy schedule to talk me through how tyres and punctures work. As usual, any errors or inconsistencies are my own.

Also, my paramedic sister-in-law, for advice on injuries to the head and neck and the placement of arteries.

Gratitude to Lauren, Lucy, Tom and all the team at Legend Press for their continuing support and belief in my work. It's lovely working with you guys. Also, a huge thanks goes to the cover artist who designed this wonderful cover.

The crime writing community is incredibly friendly and through it I've made some wonderful lifelong friends. I'd like to thank all the authors who've supported me, and send special thanks to Ian Patrick and Rebecca Bradley who are my early readers and always there at the end of the phone or email, with a generous helping of support. It's much appreciated.

Also, to all the wonderful book bloggers who shout from the rooftops when they enjoy a story. Far too many to mention individually, but all of whom are truly the unsung heroes of the book world. And the book clubs online that provide such great support: Anne Cater and all at Book Connectors; Shell Baker and Llainy Swanson at Crime Book Club; Susan Hunter at Crime Fiction Addict; Tracy Fenton, Helen Boyce, Teresa Nikolic and all at The Book Club (TBC); Wendy and all at The Fiction Café Book Club; and David Gilchrist at UK Crime Book Club.

So many friends have listened to early storylines, helped with cover art, proofread, talked through characters and generally offered a shoulder to lean on, most notably Colin Williams, Emma Thompson, Stephanie Daniels, and Abi and Philip Bouch.

As always, heartfelt thanks to my dear family, for sharing their days with my characters. Especially my husband, David, who tirelessly helps with research and always reads my first drafts, even when they aren't very good! And my daughter, Ella, who cooks me super meals when my head is stuck in edits. I couldn't do this without either of you.

Finally, to you, the amazing readers. Without readers there would be no writers and no stories, and what a dull world that would be. Please know that I'm incredibly appreciative of your ongoing support.